Rock the Shores

A CINNAMON BAY ROMANCE

WHITLEY COX

Whitley Cox

For my friend and fellow author Shannyn Leah.
Thank you for welcoming me into the Cinnamon Bay world so warmly and just being a wonderful friend.
I'm so lucky to have "met" you. Hopefully one day we can meet in person.
xoxo

Contents

Chapter One

J uliet Clarkson stumbled in her flats as she scrambled to catch up with
her friend Stella. It was a warm April evening on the North Carolina
coast, and even though the lights from the parking lot helped make the
dark night not so treacherous to navigate, her new contact lenses were
messing with her vision.

"Come on. Shake a leg," Stella called after her with a giggle. "I can
already hear the opening band."

Juliet rolled her eyes. "I'm coming." She caught up with Stella, and her
friend took pity on her and looped an arm through Juliet's.

"Here, boss, I'll lead your blind ass into the stadium. Do I need to
describe everything I see?? Are your senses heightened now? What do
you smell?"

Juliet shot her friend a glare. "I'm not blind. I just came from the eye
doctor, and against his suggestions, I decided to put in my contacts."

"On your heavily dilated pupils, you mean."

"Yeah."

"Why?"

Despite Stella "guiding" her, Juliet narrowly missed bumping into a
concrete trash can. "Because I don't want to wear my glasses tonight."

"Why?"

"Because I don't."

"But *why?*" Stella probed in that singsong, annoying, I'm-not-going-to-let-up-until-you-spill voice of hers.

"Because *he's* here, and I don't want him to see me in my glasses. Okay? Are you satisfied?" Juliet growled just as they approached the line to get into the concert.

"Very," Stella said smugly. "I knew you weren't wearing your glasses for a greater reason than just *because.* And not that *my* opinion matters, because I'm only your best friend, best employee and, well, the best thing that's ever happened to you, but I happen to think you look hot as hell in your glasses. You've got the whole sexy librarian thing down pat. Just put your hair back up with a broken pencil like you do and then pull it out, wave your dark locks around and—" She bit her lip, squinted her eyes and went, "Mmm ... mmm ... mmm. You are one hot lady."

Juliet rolled her eyes again at her friend. "Well, when I wore glasses back in high school, he looked right through me. So maybe without them, he won't. If that's not the case tonight, then I'll take out my contacts and put the glasses back on tomorrow."

"He didn't notice you back in high school because he's Oblivious Evan. Not because you wore glasses. If you weren't sitting in his lap and the shape of a guitar you didn't exist," Stella replied.

"I was practically in his lap. He is my brother's best friend and was at my house every day for five years."

"Yeah, but unless you were literally in his lap ..."

Juliet pouted. "If only. I would have killed to sit in Evan's lap back then."

Stella snickered. "Don't I know it."

They handed their tickets to the guys at the door, then with still linked arms, entered the stadium in Summerfield to the upbeat rock music of the opening band.

She'd never heard the band that played right now, but she knew every word to every song that Evan Spencer and The October Coyotes played.

Every. Single. Word.

Did that make her a stalker?

Absolutely not.

It did, however, make her a die-hard fan.

And there was nothing wrong with being a die-hard fan, right?

2

She knew loads of people who as teenagers had various bands and singers' posters dressing their bedroom walls.

But you're not a teenager anymore.

And his poster isn't on my bedroom wall!

But you've loved him since you were eleven.

I've also loved Justin Timberlake since I was eleven. What's your point?

My point is, well, your *point is, because I'm you, is that Justin Timberlake isn't your brother's best friend and he wasn't over at your house every day for five years. And also, you loved Justin Timberlake, but you were IN LOVE with Evan Spencer. Big difference.*

"What's with the face?" Stella's voice broke Juliet out of her internal conversation, and she was grateful for it. Sometimes, her brain got on a bit of a self-flagellation tangent she struggled to get out of.

Juliet blinked and shook her head. "Just trying to help my eyes adapt to the lighting is all."

Liar.

They entered the venue hall through the side doors closest to the front of the stage. She'd splurged and bought them both floor seats, which actually just meant that they would be standing the entire time practically glued to the gate that separated the front of the stage from the mosh pit.

She'd never been a big one for crowds, but she'd float like a piece of driftwood in a sea of a million people if it meant watching Evan Spencer.

Notice she didn't say, *Evan Spencer PERFORM.*

Yeah, she knew she had it bad.

Time had not changed a damn thing for Juliet's heart.

Even after all this time, and a few boyfriends, school, and moving halfway across the country for grad school, Juliet Clarkson was still madly in love with her brother's best friend.

Stella grabbed Juliet's hand and pulled her through the swaying and dancing people who were staring up enthusiastically at the stage.

It was an all-woman band that played—Renegade Rosanna or something like that—and they were really good.

The lead singer had some serious range to her voice, and the guitar solo that happened after the second chorus was magical.

3

But even so, Juliet was champing at the bit for these ladies to play their final set, wave, thank everyone and vacate the stage.

She wanted to get to the main event.

To the reason she spent more than she could afford on these tickets.

"Good thing we got here early," Stella yelled at her, turning around and tugging Juliet past a few oblivious people who had been mentally swept away by the music.

Juliet came to stand next to her friend. "Yeah, good thing."

"By the time the Coyotes get on stage, this place is going to be a madhouse. You want something to drink?" Stella, Korean-American, always managed to look so edgy and put together. And she didn't give a shit what anybody thought of her. Juliet was often in awe of her best friend and how flawlessly she did her makeup and picked out her clothes.

Juliet couldn't execute a smoky eye if her life depended on it.

It made her scream inside on more than one occasion. *How can you not apply makeup? You're a freaking artist!*

Like, she had a master's degree in fine art, she was that much of an artist. Painting and sculpting were her jam.

And yet when it came to her own makeup, she constantly came away looking like she'd just smeared marmalade or something on her face.

Okay, well, maybe not *that* bad. But she could never pull off the perfect cat's eye that Stella was currently sporting.

And those chunky hot purple streaks in Stella's poker-straight black bob—forget about it! The woman was hot. And she completed the look with skin-tight black pleather leggings and an off-the-shoulder white sweater that had a completely lace back.

"Drink?" Stella asked again, sticking her thumb and pinky out from her fist and tipping it up toward her mouth like a drink.

Juliet nodded. "I'll come with."

Stella shook her head. "Keep our spot. I'll be right back." Stella squeezed Juliet's hand and took off back through the mob toward the bar, leaving Juliet all by herself in the drifting tide of music-loving people.

The opening band played two more songs before they bade their farewell and exited the stage. That was just about the time that Stella returned with two ciders and bumped shoulders with Juliet. "You ready to see him?"

Of course, Stella knew *alllll* about Juliet's borderline-stalker crush on Evan.

The two women shared everything with each other.

Stella knew the moment Juliet's crush began, back when they were ten, almost eleven, and Evan (who was thirteen, almost fourteen at the time) and his family moved from Fox Point to Cinnamon Bay. He was in the same grade as Eric, and the two—along with Tony Drake—became fast and inseparable best friends.

What Juliet didn't like, however, was that Stella was constantly ragging on her for pining over Evan.

"Do something about it," she had said on more than one occasion during high school.

But back then, Evan barely knew that Juliet existed. She was Eric's little sister, who always had an apron on since she was always painting or sculpting or something, and her hair was more often than not caked in clay and held up with a pencil.

Add in the glasses, the braces and Juliet's shyness, and she highly doubted Evan would recognize her today.

Not that she thought she'd changed too much over the last fifteen-ish years, but at least she'd grown into her teeth and knew to wash the clay out of her hair every night before bed.

"Jules," Stella said, turning Juliet to face her with a gentle hand on her shoulder. "He's here. In Summerfield. Now's your chance. We don't know how long he's going to be gone this time and when he'll be back in Cinnamon Bay. You only just got back, and neither of you have been here at the same time in the last fifteen years. If you want him to notice you, tonight is your night." Her dark brown eyes drifted down Juliet's body. "I mean, look at you, girl. I don't think I've ever seen you look so hot. White skinny jeans, tight black crop top and a retro jean jacket. Mama, you're looking so fine!"

Juliet's cheeks grew warm as she bit her lip and glanced away at her friend.

She'd gone and bought a new outfit for tonight. She saw the entire ensemble, right down to the flats and the tiered necklaces, on a mannequin at a store in Cinnamon Bay, and she'd walked right in and said, "I'll take all of that."

Again, she'd dropped more money than she should have, especially since her business was still in its fledgling phase and she had a loan to pay back to the bank and employees who needed paychecks that didn't bounce. But eating ramen for a week to look as good as she felt tonight was worth it.

"Can I just make *one* tiny little suggestion, though?" Stella asked, just as the announcer started to get everyone psyched up for the band over the loudspeaker.

Juliet hummed and lifted her brow. "What?"

Her friend reached behind Juliet and pulled out her ponytail. "Ditch the updo."

Juliet's smile was lopsided, but she thanked Stella.

And it was at that moment that Evan Spencer and the October Coyotes walked out on stage.

Juliet's heart rate picked up, her palms grew sweaty, and her gaze—thank God—became laser-focused on the lead singer with the guitar, who made his way to the front of the stage.

"Good evening, Summerfield!" Evan hollered into the microphone, smiling out at the crowd and waving. "It's so good to be back!"

The crowd roared and whooped with excitement, and Juliet got jostled a bit as the mosh pit they were in grew denser and more tumultuous from the increase in bodies. They'd been at the front gate but had been shoved deeper into the middle.

"I'm from Cinnamon Bay, and I cannot tell you all how good it feels to be home. To be back on the eastern seaboard and playing for so many of my *friends*. Because y'all are my friends and came out to see me when I was just starting out. Your support all those years ago has meant so much to me. So I'd like to dedicate tonight's concert to all of YOU. You are the reason I'm up here tonight. You are the reason that I was able to fulfill my dream. So let's do this, Summerfield! Let's party!"

The band started to play. Evan swung his guitar around to his front and joined in, leaning forward to press his mouth to the microphone, and begin singing.

Juliet's insides liquefied.

He looked just as good—nay, even better than he did fifteen years ago.

And yes, she'd followed his success closely over the years and knew that he'd let his hair grow out a little longer—particularly at the front—and that his face had become more chiseled and angular over the years, but seeing it all in person was a thrill she would have given anything not to miss.

A well-groomed light brown dusting of scruff covered his jaw, upper lip and chin, and she found herself wondering how those whiskers would feel against her own cheeks as she closed her eyes and listened to his gorgeous voice.

Stella nudged her. "Don't close your eyes, girl! We're here because of your mad crush. Stare at the man. Catch his eye. I bet you he'll remember you."

Juliet opened her eyes and smirked at her friend.

She mouthed the words to "Endless Summer Sun" perfectly in time with when Evan sung them. It was as if their lips were the same lips.

Oh, what a thought indeed.

With her attention focused on stage, she barely acknowledged the group of men who shuffled in behind them.

She only half-noticed them because there were several of them, all much taller than her and Stella, and they all smelled of beer.

One in particular stood a touch too close to her back, so she swung her purse off her butt and held it in front of her while also taking a step forward.

Stella joined her, though Juliet's friend seemed completely oblivious to the men behind them and had her hand in the air as she sang along to the song and bobbed her head enthusiastically.

Juliet needed to take a page from her friend's book and stop worrying about everything.

She was at an Evan Spencer and The October Coyotes concert, for Pete's sake. She needed to chill out and enjoy herself.

With a quick glance at Stella, who looked at her, they both grinned like idiots, clinked their cider cans and raised their arms in the air toward the stage, bobbing their heads in time with the music.

They were four songs in, and Juliet's face hurt from smiling, her feet hurt from standing, and her arm was devoid of nearly all its blood from still being in the air.

But she was happy.

Boy oh boy, was she happy.

Watching Evan do what he loved, do what he'd always dreamt of doing was a dream come true for her.

She was living her best life, doing what she wanted to do, which was run her own paint and pottery studio—Kiln or be Kilned—and he was a famous rock star in a band that had his name in the title. Could he get much bigger than that? They'd made music videos. Videos she'd watched dozens of times. Played in huge venues all over the states. Sold out arenas and opened for even bigger bands.

How many people out there could say that they'd done exactly what they said they were going to, what they said they wanted to be when they were a kid?

Certainly, her brother wasn't what he wanted to be when he was a kid. Eric wanted to be a wildlife photographer and travel the world, sitting like a statue for hours to get the perfect shot of some never-before-seen butterfly or whatever. And even though Eric was still very much into photography, he'd gone to trade school and was now an entrepreneur and ticketed electrician for his own electrical company, Zappy's in Cinnamon Bay.

Evan's sister wasn't the horse trainer she wanted to be either. She ran a daycare out of her home in Cinnamon Bay and made a very good living doing it.

But Juliet and Evan were literally living their dreams.

That had to mean something, right? That they'd both achieved their goals.

That they were meant to be?

She'd earned a partial scholarship to an art school in Virginia, where she earned a bachelor's in fine arts in ceramics. Then she was awarded a full scholarship to the University of New Mexico's master of fine arts program, where she studied under some of the most revered American sculptors and painters of the modern era, including the award-winning Native American painter Phillip Tall Tree. It was there that she branched out a bit more into painting as well, taking several classes, including watercolor and acrylic.

But at the end of the day, she knew she always wanted to return home to Cinnamon Bay and open up an art studio. She wanted to make what she wanted to make, sell it—or not—but also help others discover their own love of art and where their skills lay.

What she made on the wheel was sold on commission in about ten different stores all up and down the eastern seaboard—as well as The Hand Made Tale in Cinnamon Bay—along with a few of her paintings. She earned decent money off those commissions and made sure to carve out at least six to eight hours a week to do that kind of work in order to keep the stores flush with her products and the customers happy.

She was known for her beautiful ramekins, where a set of four cost over eighty dollars, as well as her big wave or petal-edged salad bowls, which usually sold for between two hundred and four hundred dollars each. But what had put her on the map, what people knew "Juliet Clarkson Pottery" for, was her one-of-a-kind vases. Each vase was unique, with hand-painted flowers and a clear glaze.

Once in a while, she got a call about a specific commission. It was usually from someone who saw her salad bowl or a vase in a shop somewhere, hesitated buying it, then when they went back to get it, it was gone, so they wanted to know if she had any more in stock or could make another one. She rarely said *no*; she just made sure the price was worth her while. She knew her worth, what her skill, education and time were worth, and she knew that her ideal customers were out there. So if someone tried to dicker down the price, she politely declined and suggested they try IKEA.

It was comforting to know that if she dedicated more time to her own pottery, she could easily make a decent living doing just that, but her dream had always been to open up an art studio. She wanted to help others find their artistic calling, help them hone their skills, and discover a productive and beautiful way to express themselves.

Juliet bobbed her head along to one of her favorite songs—"Take My Hand"—when something brushed past behind her and then cupped her butt.

She waited for a moment to see if it was just somebody passing behind her and it was an accident. But the hand did not move.

It squeezed.

Red flags went up inside her.

She stepped away and glanced over her shoulder, giving the group of guys and the one guy with a truckload of audacity a glare she hoped conveyed her disgust.

But Handsy Harold merely grinned at her, then glanced at his "bros," and they all started to laugh.

"Hands to yourself," Juliet yelled over the music.

Handsy Harold lifted his chin. "Come on, baby, we're just having fun."

Had he not been a complete douchebag, she actually would have found him not bad-looking. He would have even been passable for hot.

Tall, broad shoulders, chiseled arms. But this ballcap-wearing bastard just went from a solid eight and a half to a negative one when he grabbed her butt, and he was sinking into even chillier temperatures as he continued to eye her up like a piece of meat.

Juliet scoffed and showed them her back. She looped her arm through Stella's and tugged them closer to the stage. Stella was still oblivious to what was going on, so she merely gave Juliet a curious look, shrugged and followed.

They were only in their new spot five minutes before a hand, the same hand as before, was back on her butt and an arm was being wrapped around her waist.

The man was strong.

This time, Stella noticed, and her confusion quickly morphed into anger.

Juliet had been hauled backward against the guy's chest, his hand still on her butt, while his other one held her against him—against his erection—around her waist.

She struggled to get free, to pry his arms off her.

But the man had muscles.

A lot of them.

More than she could fight off.

"Come on, baby. Don't play hard to get. You're not safe here by yourself. Need a big, strong man to keep you safe." He thrust up against her butt and laughed in her ear, egged on by his chortling friends behind him.

Stella was screaming at them all now, but one of Handsy Harold's friends had maneuvered himself between Stella and Juliet and was slowly backing her up into the oblivious crowd. Separating Juliet from her friend. From the one person she knew in a stadium of five thousand strangers.

If she lost Stella, what was going to happen to her?

Barely aware of the music now, for the shrieking of her friend and the terror in her brain that tuned out the rest of the world, Juliet was drawn out of her state of vision-narrowing fear when everything in the stadium came to a stop.

Including the music.

The lights came on, and a booming voice—Evan's voice—yelling, "HEY, ASSHOLE!" caused them all to stop and freeze.

Juliet glanced up to find Evan Spencer of Evan Spencer and The October Coyotes standing on the edge of the stage staring at them.

"Get the hell off her now," Evan said, his voice hard and his gaze deadly.

Handsy Harold chuckled behind her, but his grip loosened just a touch. "We're just having some fun, man. She's into it. It's all good."

Evan's gaze slid to Juliet, and it softened. "Are you *having some fun?*"

Juliet's face was hotter than the surface of the sun. She held Evan's eye contact and shook her head. "No, I'm not."

Evan glanced to the side of the stage. "Get 'em out of here. All of them. And when the concert's over, please escort the ladies back to their cars."

Within seconds, big behemoth men—six in total—made their way through the crowd. They didn't have much trouble, though. People parted for them like the Red Sea. Even Juliet and Stella backed away, leaving Handsy Harold and his posse all alone in a circle, gawking like drunken idiots, not understanding why *they* were getting kicked out of a concert.

The security guards didn't have to say anything. They just waited for the idiots to walk single file through the parting crowd, then they followed them toward the side doors and outside.

Who knew what happened to them after that?

Juliet didn't care.

"You okay?" Evan asked her, concern in his eyes but absolutely no recognition.

With an achy heart and her body still on edge from what had just happened, Juliet could do no more than nod.

"Thanks, Evan," Stella said, wrapping a protective arm around Juliet.

Evan nodded, smiled, then stepped away from the edge.

A few seconds later, the lights were off, the music picked up, and the people closed back in around them.

It was like it had never happened.

Juliet remained glued to Stella's side for the rest of the night. So much so, she was sure her friend would be asking for some space and maybe even a day or two off work just to get some breathing room. But whatever she needed, Juliet would give it to her.

As hard as she tried, she wasn't able to enjoy the rest of the concert.

Not even when Evan played her favorite song of his—"The Only One For Me."

Not only had she been assaulted and humiliated, but Evan had stared right at her. Right into her eyes. He'd spoken to her.

And yet he didn't see her.

Didn't see who she was.

It was the exact same way he'd looked at her over fifteen years ago. Which was right through her.

She was nobody important.

Nobody special.

She was Eric's annoying little sister.

And even though she was all grown up, had ditched the glasses, let her hair down and put on makeup, Evan still couldn't see her.

And now more than ever, she knew that he never would.

Chapter Two

*O*ne month later ...

"*With eyes of emerald and hair of silk ... where has my mystery girl run to?*" Evan Spencer sang and strummed his guitar a few chords before slamming his hand against the strings and growling. "Garbage," he muttered. "Fucking garbage."

He'd been home all of one day.

Well, not *home* home. But he was home in Cinnamon Bay.

However, since his moms sold their family home and bought something a little smaller after Evan and Kate grew up and moved out, he decided not to cramp their style, and instead he rented a house on the beach.

His cottage was small, only two bedrooms, but the crash of the ocean woke him up this morning, so if he started to complain, he'd have to go take a jump off the pier to knock some much-needed sense into himself.

It'd been nearly a year since he'd written anything new.

Or should he say, *anything good*.

Sure, he'd tried to write, but nothing but trash had come out of his brain.

A brain that was most likely fried and needing this summer of respite.

They'd just finished up their yearlong tour of the U.S. Two hundred and fifty-five cities in three hundred days.

The entire band was wiped.

Evan had given up his apartment in Nashville because he was never there. There was no point paying rent for a place he hadn't slept in in months.

Now, all his stuff was currently sitting in storage.

All his stuff besides a duffle bag of clothes and his guitar, that is.

Maybe a break from gigs this summer was what his mind needed to recharge, to find inspiration for new material, because the stuff he'd been trying to write while on tour had made him want to gag. He hadn't even bothered to show it to his bandmates since he knew they'd all tell him the truth he already knew—that it was awful.

So there he sat, on a grassy dune, his cottage behind him, the horizon before him, with a sea of glittering diamonds carpeting the way to the edge of the Earth and a balmy breeze ruffling his hair. If he couldn't draw worthwhile inspiration from all of this, he wasn't fit to be a musician anymore.

With a sigh, he stared down at the guitar that rested on his thighs and drew his thumb down across the string. *"You had your eyes on the stage. I had my eyes on you ... No other woman in the crowd could hold a candle to you."* He hummed as he found a tune that worked for what he was trying to figure out. A slow start, minimal instrument, only to pick up tempo at the eighth bar.

He hummed some more, bobbed his head.

"My eyes on you ... I couldn't take my eyes off you ... The girl with the sad smile." He turned his body and jotted down the lyrics in his notebook, along with the chords he'd played. Just as he turned back toward the beach, something out of the corner of his eye drew him, and he lifted his head.

A woman jogging up the beach in a black sports bra and dark gray cropped running leggings loped forward. She wore a white ballcap and had wireless earbuds in.

A dark ponytail swooshed behind her, and her hands were in tight little fists that pumped up and down in front of her chest.

He was about to put his head back down when something—he couldn't put his finger on *what*—made him continue watching her.

Her pace slowed down as she spotted him. Recognition dawned in her eyes before he felt his own.

The girl from the concert.

The one who was getting assaulted.

His mystery girl.

Her steps in the sand faltered a little, and he thought she was going to trip as she ran past him, but she caught herself.

"Hey!" Evan stood up before he knew what he was doing.

Now she really did trip and then did a weird little hop, hop, skip in the sand before regaining her balance and stopping.

Leaving his guitar in the grass, Evan ate up the distance between them on the sand in seconds. She removed one of her earbuds and held it in her palm.

"Are you ..." He squinted for a moment, hoping that he wasn't wrong and that it really was her. She looked a lot different than the woman at the concert. No makeup. Hair up. Hat.

But when she lifted her head and pinned those green eyes on him, he knew he wasn't wrong.

It was her.

"You're the woman from my concert in Summerfield, aren't you?" he asked, feeling good about himself for recognizing her.

She nibbled on her lip for a moment but then nodded. "I am." She was already flushed in the cheeks from her run, but more color infused them now. "I'm also—"

"How are you after all of that?" He reached out and cupped her elbow as a gesture of kindness and concern. Because he was concerned. Never had anything like that happened at one of his concerts.

It absolutely has. It's just never happened where you could see it. Guaranteed.

Yeah, he was probably right.

They needed to up their security at their next concerts. Women—people—should feel safe when they go to enjoy music. They shouldn't constantly have to worry about being assaulted or attacked.

"I'm okay," she said softly. "I'll have to stick closer to the security guards by the doors next time I go to a concert."

"Shouldn't have to, though," he said almost angrily. "What that guy did wasn't right."

"Well, thank you for helping. When his friend started to push my friend away, that's when I really started to panic." Her lips pressed together, and her eyes darted around the beach as if itching to get away from him.

Was he making her uncomfortable?

That's when he realized he was still holding on to her elbow.

He immediately let go of it.

He held out his hand. "I'm Evan. I mean, I know you *know* who I am since you were at my concert. But I figure we could properly introduce ourselves, no?"

Her green eyes narrowed. "You really don't recognize me, do you?"

Huh?

"Yeah, I do. You're the girl from the concert. The one who—"

Holy shit!

Holy crap!

No freaking way!

"Juliet!" he yelled. Yes, yelled. "Is that you?"

Even more color entered her cheeks, along with a disappointed look in her eyes. "It's me."

"Oh my God. I ... you look so ... I had no idea. Eric's little sister. I ... Jules ..." Ignoring the fact that she hadn't taken his offered hand from earlier, because why would she when they were long-lost friends, he lunged forward and took her in his arms, hugging her as he would anyone he'd seen nearly every day of his life for over five years. "I can't believe it's you. This is wild."

She hugged him back, and he could have sworn he heard her sigh before her body went stiff in his.

He pulled away. "How are you? What are you doing back in Cinnamon Bay?"

She took a half step back. "I moved back just before Christmas last year. Opened up an art studio. Pottery, paint your own canvases. I do

and I teach." She hooked a thumb behind her. "Three roads up from
The Boardwalk. Kiln or be Kilned."

"That's incredible," he said, unable to shake the awe that this was Eric's
little sister. That Eric's little sister was the woman from the concert. The
woman he was trying to write a song about.

His brain was close to short-circuiting. This was not the Juliet
Clarkson he remembered. Not at all.

The Juliet he remembered was shy and always covered in paint or clay.
She had big glasses, braces, and a pencil holding up her frizzy hair.

The woman at the concert, the woman in front of him was ... nothing
short of spectacular.

She glanced down the beach again and rocked back and forth in her
runners. "I uh, I gotta get in another couple miles before I head to work."

"To the studio?" He wanted to smack himself in the face with his palm.
She just said she owns a pottery studio, dum-dum.

Juliet nodded. "Yeah, Stella opened for me today, but I need to be there
for noon."

An awkward silence fell between them, only to be punctuated by the
harsh, shrill screech of a gull overhead.

They both looked up.

Even though everyone knew better than to look up.

It was something you learned early on as a kid, almost before you
learned to walk.

Never look up, otherwise the chances of getting bird crap in your eye
went up like fifty percent.

Neither of them was obviously thinking straight, though. And thank
God the bird was more out over the water than their heads.

He was still getting over the shock that the woman from the concert
was the same person standing in front of him and that person was his
best friend's baby sister.

A best friend he actually had plans to catch up with after Eric was off
work for the day. They were meeting at Shenanigans for a drink at five.

He was already compiling a list of questions for Eric about Juliet that
he planned on asking.

Question number one: Was she single?
Ask her that yourself, dummy.

17

"I really should get going," she said, pointing down the beach. "But it was nice seeing you. Thanks again for your help at the concert. You played a great set."

Evan nodded like an idiot and waved like an even bigger idiot. "Yeah, no problem. Wish it hadn't happened to you at all, but I'm glad I could help. I hope it didn't ruin the rest of the show for you."

Her smile was grim, and he could tell that when she said, "Not at all," that she was lying through her teeth.

Now he felt even worse.

Juliet put her earbud back in her ear and headed off down the beach, offering him a halfhearted wave over her shoulder before turning away from him and continuing on her run.

Evan stared after her for a while.

For a while longer than was probably appropriate.

He was just struck dumb.

What in the Cinnamon Bay serendipity was the likelihood that the woman he hadn't been able to stop thinking about would have run right up to him on the beach, just as he was writing about her, struggling to make sense of his inspiration.

And like bird poop on his head, the inspiration, the lyrics, the tune, everything hit him in the head, and he ran back to the dune, grabbed his guitar and his notebook and started to compose.

***

"Good to see you," Evan said, taking Eric's dark hand in his and shaking it before pulling his best friend in the entire world in for a hug. "Been too freaking long."

"That's because you only come back to The Bay every couple of years," Eric said on a laugh, slapping Evan on the back. "Maybe if you came around more often ..."

"Yeah, yeah," Evan said, laughing as they came apart, both of them smiling. Evan had grabbed them a booth seat and been waiting only five minutes before Eric rolled up in his company van with the big Zappy's logo on the side.

Eric slid into one side of the booth while Evan slid into the other side. A waitress approached.

"What can I get you, gentlemen?" she asked.

"Whatever ale is on special," Eric said. "Thanks, Morgan."

"I'll have the same," Evan added. "And some of the mozzarella sticks, too."

Morgan lifted a sandy-colored brow. "You doing the contest?"

Evan glanced at Eric. "Contest?"

"Twenty pounds of sticks, a pitcher of beer, two people, twenty minutes. Free meal and your name and picture on the wall," Morgan said, pointing to a wall that housed dozens of Polaroids of very bloated-looking people.

"Naw, can't do that much dairy anymore," Eric said, leaning back in his seat and patting his flat stomach. "Wife won't let me live down the hell I caused in our house last time."

Morgan chuckled.

"I think we're good with just the pints and a *regular* basket," Evan said, thanking Morgan before she wandered off. He turned to Eric. "So, dude, what's new?"

Eric sighed wearily. "Dadding, working, husbanding, you know ... *life.*"

Evan chuckled. "Besides the working bit, I don't know. You're happy though? Kids are good? Isla good?"

Eric nodded. "Yeah, we're all good. Ruby and Dia are of course nutty and wonderful. And Isla's landscaping business has taken off. She's particularly popular among the elderly. They love it when she comes to their houses, putters in their yard and they can just sit out beside her under a big umbrella and talk her ear off. Most of the time she gets lemonade or cookies out of it, so she's not complaining. And they all pay her by the hour, so she's raking it in." Eric chuckled and thanked Morgan when she set their beers down in front of them.

"And your parents?" He needed to make it seem like he wasn't just diving straight in to ask about Juliet. He needed to ask about *all* of the Clarkson-Daigle crew so it didn't make Eric suspicious.

"Dad's good. Loving retirement. He's tutoring kids from the high school, since he can't just *give up knowing all there is to know about math,* or at least that's how he puts it." He chuckled and sipped his beer. "Been helping out with the girls a lot more, too. He takes them to swimming lessons for us every Tuesday and Thursday after school."

"That's great. I always knew that Ron Clarkson was going to make an awesome grandpa. He acted like a grandpa even when he was just a dad. Socks pulled up to nearly his knees, runners too tight, shirt tucked in."

"Early bedtime," Eric added, continuing to laugh. "Yeah, he's all those things and more."

"And your mom?"

Eric and Juliet were actually stepsiblings. Both of their parents had been widowed when their kids were small, and then Rob and Sandy married when Eric was ten and Juliet was seven. So even though Ron wasn't Eric's biological father, Eric called him Dad anyway, and Juliet called Sandy Mom.

"Mom's doing great," Eric said. "She's getting ready to retire from the hospital at the end of the year, so then both grandparents will be able to help out with the kids." Eric's fingers drummed against the weeping glass of the pint, and he glanced out the window before turning back to Evan. "Hear you're staying in The Bay for the summer."

Evan nodded. "Did your mom talk to my mom?"

Eric nodded. "Yeah. Small town. News travels fast."

"And Juliet?" Evan finally asked, his palms suddenly so sweaty he had to wipe them on the front of his shorts.

Could Eric tell what Evan was thinking? Did he know Evan had been thinking about his little sister for over a month? Only Evan didn't know that she was Eric's little sister.

"Jules is back in town. Moved back late last year. She's renting a big corner space a couple of blocks up and has turned it into one heck of a successful DIY studio. Isla takes the girls there at least once a week to paint or sculpt or whatever. She did these great little footprint and handprint ornaments at Christmastime. Parents from as far away as Bank's Ferry and Carringsville came to push their baby or kid's hand or foot in some clay, then Jules and her team hand-painted every single one into either a snowman, angel, reindeer or elf. By December twentieth, she had over a thousand orders. She was up until four in the morning painting for days."

Evan's eyes widened. "Holy crap."

Eric's head bobbed. "Made her a butt-load of money though. And put her on the map as the place to go. She had every single order ready for pickup by December twenty-third."

Morgan was back with their mozzarella fries. She slid them into the middle of the table, then gave them each a plate and some napkins. "Enjoy, guys."

Evan thanked her but then turned back to Eric. He didn't want them to get off the topic of Juliet. He wanted to know more. He wanted to know everything.

"She, uh ... she seeing anybody?" he asked, hoping that his mannerisms and tone were casual and didn't set off any red flags for Eric. He reached forward and grabbed a mozzarella stick, dunking an end of it in the dip.

Eric shook his head. "No. She hired Stella Yang as her right hand at the studio, though. You remember Stella?"

Evan shook his head. Was that the woman who was at the concert with Juliet?

The name sounded familiar.

Eric tossed his head back and laughed, showing off insanely bright white teeth. They were only made all the whiter when up against his dark complexion. "You always did have a bit of a blind spot for people who weren't fawning all over you or your friends."

Evan scrunched his nose at his friend. "What?"

Eric shrugged and reached for a mozza stick. "Stella was Juliet's best friend all through school. They were basically as inseparable as you and I were."

Evan's mouth dipped into a frown, and he shook his head. "I don't remember her."

Eric rolled his eyes. "Juliet had the absolute most massive crush on you in high school. I'm talking enormous. Like borderline *Fatal Attraction*. She never told me. Still hasn't, but it was obvious. Like golf-ball-size pimple on your nose obvious. The fact that you *didn't* see it just goes to show that you didn't think about much besides yourself, your music, the handful of groupies who purred when you played, and your friends. And by friends, I mean me and Tony."

Evan opened his mouth, but nothing came out.

He closed it and stared at the table for a moment. "Did I really have my head that far up my ass?"

"Surprised you're not still getting whiffs of shit, bro," Eric said with a chortle.

"I mean, I *remember* your sister. Smock, paint, clay, glasses, braces, frizzy hair. It's not like I went about my life thinking you were an only child or something. I *knew* you had a stepsister. A sister."

"Yeah, but Juliet wasn't always that awkward teenager. And the way she looked at you ..." Eric sucked in a breath before pursing his lips. "Bro, ain't nobody ever been that smitten. At least I've never seen it. And I'm madly in love with my wife. But I can guarantee you I've never even looked at Isla the way Juliet used to look at you."

How could he have missed her looking at him like the way Eric was describing?

Surely, he would have noticed a lovestruck teenager giving him the come-hither eyes. Particularly if his ego was as large as Eric was saying it was.

"Would you have given me your blessing to date your sister?" he asked, sipping his beer. He needed to lubricate his dry throat.

Eric shrugged. "Not my blessing to give. Jules is her own person. If there's anything having kids—having *daughters* has taught me, it's that the whole 'protective big brother' or 'overprotective dad' schtick is just placing another form of ownership on a woman. It's not up to us. It's up to them. So yeah, maybe back then I would have taken you behind the shed at my parents', shown you the shovel and the spot in the garden where I'd make you dig your own damn hole if you hurt her, but I'm a changed man. Isla's changed me. I'm a feminist now. My girls can date who they want, and if they want their father to come in and lay down the law with a man, I sure as hell will, but otherwise, I'm going to trust their judgment and pray to the lord almighty that I gave them the tools to pick a decent partner. One who *isn't* a tool." He reached for a mozza stick and dipped it.

Eric's brow lifted as he chewed, his dark brown eyes saying a thousand words that Evan heard loud and clear.

Eric was no idiot.

Far from it.

The man had run academic circles around Evan back in high school. Eric and their other best friend Tony both had. Of the three of them, Evan knew he was the least smart.

He wasn't stupid, but he had to work a hell of a lot harder in school to pull the *A's* that seemed to come as easy as breathing to Eric and Tony.

Eric knew why Evan was asking about Juliet. He read between all the lines.

"Heard from a little bird you ran into Jules this morning on the beach," Eric said, reaching for another mozza stick.

Evan's gaze narrowed on his friend. "What *little bird?* All I saw on that entire stretch of beach was a gull that nearly shat on my head and your sister, who was out for a run."

Eric's grin widened, but he didn't show any teeth. "Been a while since you've been in The Bay, friend. You seem to forget that news travels fast, there's always someone watching, and we've got a lot of busybodies cruising around. Particularly three old birds in a golf cart. Be careful and wear a disguise if you don't want your business known."

Evan smacked his hand to his head. "Right! Birdie, Hattie and Trixie. Those three are still alive and kicking?"

Eric chuckled. "Seems like the older they get, the more trouble they stir up. I've heard that can be the way of the aging. They stop giving a shit and just do what they want to do, say what they want to say."

"Oh, to have such freedoms."

"Have you heard from Tony recently?" Eric asked, changing the subject, which Evan was both grateful for but also frustrated with. He wanted to grill Eric for more info about Juliet, but he also didn't want this to turn into a Q&A session about Eric's sister. This was supposed to be two friends catching up, and if the shoe was on the other foot and someone spent an entire evening asking questions about Evan's sister, he'd get pretty annoyed.

Eric nodded. "Yeah, he and Jacqui are doing well. He's loving the new job, and it seems like they were made to be parents. Little Hope is adorable. Does he send you pictures?"

Evan smiled. "He does. But sometimes that's all I get. Takes the guy forever to answer his texts."

Tony, the third and final piece of their high school "bro menage," as Evan's sister Kate irritatingly called it, was a mechanical engineer.

He and his wife, Jacqui, had just moved three hours away after Tony got a new job with another company. Jacqui was a piano and voice teacher, and the two met several years ago at a grief support group in Carringsville—which was where Jacqui was from—for people with "dead parents." Tony's parents had died when he was seventeen, and Tony ended up living with Evan and his family for the remainder of his senior year, while Jacqui's parents died when she was thirteen, and she lived with her aunt—who was now also dead.

Both were only children, and so after they met, they knew they wanted to have a huge family and fill their home with love. Hope was born a year after they were married—which was the last time Evan had been in Cinnamon Bay—and the baby was now ten months old and the light of her parents' life.

"We should plan a boys' weekend while you're here this summer. Drive down and see him, go golfing, grab a hotel somewhere on the beach, get out fishing," Eric said.

"That's a great idea," Evan said, grabbing his phone out of his pocket. "I'm going to text him right now so that in a week, he can text me back and we can set something up."

Eric snorted. "When you have kids, you'll understand."

Chapter Three

"I was sweaty. I probably stunk. I *know* my face was as red as a candy apple, and I wouldn't doubt for one second that he had to go and have a shower after hugging me," Juliet said as she puttered around the studio, cleaning brushes and wiping down tables.

Stella shot Juliet a look, complete with an exaggerated eye roll. A small party of two mothers, each with their preteen daughter, had just left, and Stella was carefully moving their painted ceramic pieces to the "to be fired" shelf across from one of their many kilns. "I *highly* doubt you were as gross as you think you were. Was there a breeze coming off the water?"

"Yeah," Juliet said, grabbing a rag and wiping a smear of clay off the counter.

"Then I bet you weren't sweaty at all. Any perspiration evaporated before your skin touched his. All is well with the world," Stella said.

God, she loved Stella.

Her best friend since they were kids, Stella had gone to New York after they graduated high school. She did a year at NYU, trying her hand at acting, but by ten months in the Big Apple, she realized she hated it, hated her classmates and took off to travel the world. She was a vagabond for years, living in India at an ashram, in Thailand working at a hostel, in Argentina at a winery, and in Korea running a karaoke bar. She spent two years in Australia picking avocados and mangoes, then touring around the country in a camper van. The woman had lived so many lives in her thirty-one years.

And yet, when she found out Juliet was moving back to Cinnamon Bay to open up an art studio, she didn't hesitate to move home and demand her best friend give her a job. It may have also been the fact that Stella's mom had been diagnosed with multiple sclerosis and Stella wanted to be closer to home to help her mother.

In the end, it worked out for everyone.

The space Juliet rented was huge, and she divided it into two big rooms. One room was dedicated to painting—canvas and pre-fired mold-made pottery pieces that tourists only here for a few days could paint and come pick up their gnome or mug a few days later. The other side of the space was where the wheels and clay work happened.

She offered pottery classes Wednesday and Thursday nights between six and nine; otherwise, people could reserve wheel time and do their own thing on one of the four wheels she had.

She wanted to offer a variety of options for people so that whether canvas was your calling, the pottery wheel, or you preferred to paint a mug or plate that had already been pre-sculpted, Kiln or be Kilned offered a little bit of something for everyone.

She'd hired Stella before the studio even opened—not that Stella gave her any choice—and Stella was the one who helped customers with their painting concerns since, during her nomad years, Stella had taken a bunch of art courses in Italy and was now an accomplished painter.

Juliet also had a few other staff, too. Jill was an art student at the college, Rosa was a stay-at-home mom looking to work part-time while her kids were in school, and Terry was nearly Juliet's parents' age but a quick learner and apprenticing in ceramics under Juliet.

She had a great mix of people working for her.

"Even a sweaty, smelly mess and you'd still be a gorgeous person, worthy of making his tongue fall out of his mouth," Stella added, glancing at the three old birds who were sitting at their usual table. "Don't you agree?"

Three wrinkled faces lit up, and perfectly coiffed heads bobbed.

Every Friday at three fifteen, Hattie, Birdie and Trixie's golf cart rolled up onto the sidewalk, they tottered into the studio, claimed their unofficially reserved table and painted something. Today, they were each painting a dessert plate.

But Juliet could tell by the slow-motion brush strokes and the way each woman leaned in toward Stella and Juliet that they weren't paying attention to their artwork. They were here for the gossip.

"And how did he react to finding out that you're Eric's little sister? Or should I say *remembering* that you're Eric's little sister?" Stella asked.

"Flabbergasted is the word that comes to mind," Juliet said. "He kept blinking at me like I'd gone through this massive metamorphosis and all he could remember was this ugly little grub before. Now—"

"You're a beautiful, educated and successful butterfly?" Trixie Raines, one of the old birds, piped up. "Because you are, darling. You always were. You just needed time for the real world to help you see your beauty."

Juliet shot Trixie a bashful smile. "Thanks, Trix."

"Just telling the truth, honey," said the sassy woman who looked like Mrs. Claus-looking waving a paintbrush covered in blue paint around and causing a few drops to land on the hands and smocks of her friends.

Birdie and Hattie glared at her.

"Watch where you're swinging that," Hattie said, always the no-nonsense one of the group. And also the only one who refused to wear a hat—given her name and all.

Trixie usually sported a floppy hat of some sort, often styled at a flirty angle, while Birdie didn't go anywhere without her red dyed hair covered by a tan beret and a plethora of bangles and other glittery accessories.

"I think the thing we're *not* focusing on here, dearie, is the fact that NOW he knows and remembers who you are," Birdie added. "Which was the big problem, right?"

"When did this become a five-person discussion?" Juliet asked, glancing around the studio to see if anybody else—because there were other patrons doing pottery and painting in the place—were listening.

It didn't look like anybody else gave two figs about Juliet's love life or lack thereof, but then again, they might just not be as vocal as the meddlesome trio.

"When you decided to discuss all of this out in the open and not in the back room," Birdie said, that dry sense of humor coming at Juliet whether she liked it or not.

Juliet narrowed her gaze at the bejeweled old bat. "Touché."

Birdie smiled smugly.

"I'm just here for the poster," Hattie said with a shrug, her eyes turning all swoony.

Juliet's own eyes went wide, and she whipped her head around to face the older woman. "Is *that* why you keep ducking off to the bathroom, to go and stare at Patrick Swayze?"

Hattie shrugged again but then her face turned sad. "Gone too soon, that one. So handsome. I know some people preferred him in *Dirty Dancing*, but I'll always love him best in *Ghost.*"

Stella snorted and turned to Juliet. "What did you expect, putting that poster up?"

Juliet glanced at her friend and the older women, who were all grinning. She was about to open her mouth and say something along the lines of "maybe she needed to bolt that poster to the wall so Hattie didn't steal it" when the bell at the front door jangled and who should walk in but Evan Spencer of Evan Spencer and the October Coyotes.

Had his ears caught fire? Did he know they'd been just talking about him?

All three sets of old-lady eyes went wider than the plates they were painting.

Evan spotted her, smiled a smile she had dreamt of far too often and headed straight for her.

Of course, her apron had to be covered in clay from the seniors pottery class she'd taught earlier, and she had her glasses back on and that stupid broken pencil holding up her hair.

Minus the braces and a bit more shine to her hair, and she looked just as he probably remembered her. No wonder he'd looked through her at the concert. That wasn't her. The woman in the mosh pit getting groped by Handsy Harold wasn't the real Juliet Clarkson. This was the real her.

Evan approached her near the counter, his smile still so big, so sexy. "Hey," he said, reaching out and running his hand down her arm. "How's it going?"

Juliet swallowed. "Hey, um, good, thanks. What—"

"Is that Evan Spencer?" Trixie asked, cutting Juliet off. "Joan and Glenda's boy."

Evan glanced over at the three old birds. "Hi, Trixie."

Birdie crooked a wrinkled and boney finger at him. "Come on over here, young man. Let us get a good look at you. See if rock and roll has corrupted you too much for Cinnamon Bay." The woman left zero room for negotiation.

With a huff of a laugh, Evan shrugged and headed over to the women's table to stand in front of them. "Not corrupt, I swear, Mrs. Dupre."

"Call me Birdie," Birdie said. "Heard you helped Juliet out when some Summerfield guy was getting a little too audacious for his own good."

Juliet could see from where she stood on pins and needles that Evan's complexion had changed color. It was probably close to her own crimson cheeks, or so she assumed, given the rising temperature in her face.

Evan scrubbed at the back of his neck and glanced away. "Only an asshole wouldn't have stepped in. I'm just glad Jules is okay."

Hattie narrowed her steely gaze at him. "As are we all. Tell me, Evan, what are your plans while you're here in Cinnamon Bay?"

Evan glanced back at Juliet, his eyes beseeching her to rescue him from the over-curious trio.

"Hmm?" Trixie probed.

He turned back to face the women. "I just needed a break after our big tour. Need some downtime. Time to write some new songs, to hang out with old friends and family."

"And what, in September you're back off chasing the waves of fame, fortune and flippant fornication?" Birdie asked.

If Juliet had been drinking anything, she would have spat it clear across the room. As it was, she choked on her spit, and it sounded like Evan had, too.

Stella was just standing there trying not to snort while she silently laughed, tears forming in the corners of her eyes.

Juliet nudged her best friend and told her to knock it off.

"I can't," Stella mouthed. "This is pure gold."

"I, um ..." Evan said. "I'm waiting to hear back from my manager. I'm here until *at least* September. But I'm looking forward to the next three and a half months of hanging out in the bay. I've missed it."

"Indeed," Hattie said slowly.

The three birds exchanged looks with one another. A slow smile spread across each one of their faces.

"Evan, dear," Trixie started, "We've placed an order over at Brewed with a View. Need our afternoon pick-me-up if we're going to make it to mah-jongg later tonight. Would you be a dear and run and pick it up for us? Won't take you more than ten minutes to walk there. Feel free to get yourself something and Juliet as well and put it on our tab."

Evan glanced back at Juliet with another "help me" expression.

This time he actually did mouth "Help me."

She shrugged and grinned. "The ladies start to get sleepy if they don't have their afternoon pick-me-up. I usually run and do it for them, but—"

"Excellent idea, Juliet," Hattie said. "You can both go. Stella is more than capable of running the place while you're gone. And we'll help her if things get busy."

"Help me do what?" Stella asked.

But the three birds ignored her and did no more than a *harrumph* before turning their attention back to Evan and Juliet.

Birdie flicked her hand out, dismissing them like this wasn't Juliet's shop and she was some mere peasant girl annoying the queens during their afternoon high tea. "Yes, please, both of you, if you wouldn't mind grabbing our pick-me-ups. And like we said, put your own order on our tab."

"What about me?" Stella asked.

"Yeah, sure, get a macchiato for Stella," Trixie added.

"I prefer chai lattes," Stella said, sticking out her tongue.

All three birds rolled their eyes.

And before she knew how it had actually all happened, Juliet and Evan were walking down the road toward The Boardwalk and the famous Brewed with a View.

"So now that we can chat without being interrupted, how have you been?" Evan asked, shoving his hands into the pockets of his cargo shorts.

Juliet glanced down at herself, only to realize she hadn't even bothered to remove her apron. Normally, when she went to retrieve the birds' drink order, she untied her apron. Sure, she probably had paint or clay on her arms or maybe even a smudge on her face, but at least she wasn't wandering around with layers and layers of dried paint and clay on her stomach.

Ugh!

Earth. Hole. Swallow. Now.

"Hmm?" Evan asked, bumping her shoulder playfully. "How have you been?"

She glanced at him. "You mean since yesterday when we ran into each other on the beach? Or in the last fifteen years?"

He lifted a shoulder and offered her a boyish smile. "Both?"

That made her laugh. "Well, since yesterday I've been fine, thanks. And in the last fifteen years, well, I've had a few ups and downs, but I think I'm living my best life now. I'm back in The Bay. I'm running my own studio, which has always been my dream, so the fact that I'm literally living *my* dream is pretty cool."

He was quiet for a moment, and that made her start to overthink what she'd just said. Had she offended him in some way? Had she said anything, or was that all in her head and they'd actually just been walking down the sidewalk in awkward silence? She hedged a glance at him.

His mouth was open.

"Was that not what I was supposed to say?" she asked sheepishly.

He closed his mouth, and a small but genuine smile spread across his full lips. His brown eyes glittered down at her. "It was the perfect thing to say. And something I've felt guilty for feeling myself because I'm living my dream, too. But because so many people *aren't* living their dream, I don't feel like it's okay to say it out loud. If that makes sense."

She blinked up at him. "It makes perfect sense. And for what it's worth, I'm really happy that you're living your dream."

"I'm happy you're living yours."

He was studying her again, but this time his brows pinched and he reached out with a finger toward her face.

She reared back.

31

"Sorry," he said with a chuckle. "You've just got a fleck of clay on your cheek. Hold on. Let me get it."

She made sure to keep her groan of embarrassment inaudible and merely thanked him. "I'm always covered in paint and clay."

"I remember," he said, throwing her that unforgettable smile. "Remind me where you get your artistic talents from?"

She smiled small and kept her gaze focused straight ahead and not on his chiseled features and dreamy brown bedroom eyes. "My mother—she was a professional potter before she passed away. I found her potter's wheel in the crawl space when I was nine, demanded my dad set up a small space for me to practice in the basement, and between videos online and checking out every book on pottery in the Cinnamon Bay library, I taught myself."

"But your dad didn't buy you a kiln, so ..."

"The college has an art program, and my dad worked out a deal with the art teacher there. I could use their kiln and just had to pay twenty bucks a month. The teacher put my pieces in with the art students' pieces—as long as there was space—so I was basically just renting some kiln and shelf space."

"And then you went to art school and turned it into a career." It was impossible not to detect the sense of marvel in his tone, and it made her heart soar and her belly butterflies take flight.

They reached Brewed with a View, and for once there wasn't a line nearly outside the door. He held the door open, and they stepped inside, hit immediately with the delicious scents of freshly brewed coffee and yummy baked goods.

Juliet's belly rumbled.

She'd forgotten to eat lunch.

Not the first time.

An entire second-grade class had come in for an "experience" field trip, and between Juliet, Rosa and Stella, they managed to help all twenty-eight children hand-sculpt their own bowl. The cleanup alone had taken nearly two hours, at which point lunchtime had come and gone and they were getting the afternoon rush.

"Why do you think they sent both of us?" Evan asked, stepping forward when the line moved.

She moved with him. "Oh, you know those three. They're always up to something."

"I had drinks with Eric last night," he said, changing the subject. "We're planning a boys' trip to see Tony."

"Isn't Hope the most adorable thing ever? I mean, my nieces are *pretty* adorable, too. But those baby cheeks, ugh! So. Cute." They moved again, and she waved to Kolby, who offered her an enthusiastic wave in return as he was heading into the kitchen in the back.

"Friend?" Evan asked.

"Yeah, it's Kolby. He's friends with everyone. And his husband owns—" And as if he knew he was being talked about, Kolby's husband, Craig Reeves, made the door jingle as he entered the café. The atmosphere instantly shifted, and all the patrons in the café couldn't stop themselves from glancing at Craig.

He spotted Juliet immediately and walked right to her. "Darling, so good to see you."

"My tulips are still dazzling my kitchen, Craig. Thank you so much."

He bounced on his toes for a second, then turned his attention to Evan, brazenly giving him a thorough head-to-toe once over. "Mm-mm-mm. I heard the rock star was back in town." He held out his hand. "Craig Reeves, owner of Petal Pushers and husband to that handsome *thang* back there." He waved at Kolby, wiggling the fingers on his other hand.

"Nice to meet you," Evan said. "Yeah, I'm home for the summer. Just getting the lay of the land again and meeting all the locals."

"Well, I'm always around, so if you have any questions or want to just come by and have a chin-wag, don't hesitate."

"I appreciate that," Evan said with a smile.

Craig squeezed Evan's arms. His eyes widened when he obviously found some muscle, then he sashayed his way over to where Kolby was standing, waiting for him.

"He seems nice," Evan said.

"Very nice. You, sir, have a lot of catching up to do. A lot of the same locals but some new ones, too." She approached the counter first, only to be greeted by the raven-haired beauty and café owner herself, Eva Hollaway.

"Hey, Eva," Juliet said.

"Jules, so good to see you," Eva said, her sapphire eyes all a-glitter as they bounced between Juliet and Evan.

"This is Evan Spencer, Kate Rodriguez's older brother." She tipped her head sideways toward Evan.

"Nice to meet you, Evan," Eva said, her eyes still doing their glittery little bouncy thing.

"And you, Eva," Evan said.

"We got shanghaied into picking up the trio's order," Juliet added.

"They said we could get ourselves whatever we wanted and put it on their tab," Evan said, reaching into his back pocket for his wallet. "But I'm fine paying for myself."

"All your drinks are already ready. They called and placed it special. One for each of you, their three, and Stella's chai latte. I tossed in a few spiced cookies, too." She stepped to the side for a moment, only to return with a cardboard six-cupholder tray and a paper bag. "Here you go."

Juliet handed the drink tray to Evan but kept the cookies for herself. She planned to eat at least one on the walk back. Her stomach hadn't stopped growling since they stepped into the café.

"Oh, those women are sneaky," Juliet said with a laugh.

"The sneakiest," Eva said. "See you at Zen Bodies tomorrow morning?"

"Wouldn't miss it," Juliet called back as she and Evan made their way toward the door. He held it open for her as she opened the bag and pulled out a cookie.

"That's huge," he said. "Nearly as big as your face."

"I know." She took an unapologetic monster-size bite. Then came the moan.

Yeah, it was that good.

Evan smiled down at her. "Well, if they're *that* good, give me one, too. I forgot to eat lunch."

She opened the bag, and he leaned over and shoved his hand inside to grab one. Once he had the cookie between his teeth, he located her drink and passed it to her. She was grateful for the sip since, although the cookie was delicious—super cinnamony and with just a hint of orange zest—it also had a bit of heat to it, probably the cayenne, and her tongue felt like she'd just stuck it on an ember.

Wait a second—cayenne.

Cayenne was in the love spice.

Her drink tasted a lot like her cookie.

She knew this drink.

She'd wanted to drink this drink with Evan every day for the last fifteen years.

This was café amour!

With a gasp, she glanced at Evan.

He was happily chewing away, and then she watched him juggle everything in his hands and take a sip from his to-go cup.

Her bottom lip dropped open. Calliope Halloway, the local "witch," made a spice blend known throughout Cinnamon Bay as "the love spice," and legend was if two people consumed the spice together, they would fall in love within the year. Eva's drink, the café amour, was a folklore-chasing tourist's absolute must. And Juliet had to admit, as a hopelessly in love teenager, she'd been sucked into the legend as well, hoping that one day she and Evan could drink the drink together.

With a little bit of milk froth on his upper lip and in his scruff, he turned to her and scrunched his brows. "What?"

"Ummm ..."

Oh, those meddling women.

She should have known what they were up to.

He cocked his head. "Hmm?"

But this is what you've wanted nearly your entire life. You used to dream about the two of you drinking the love spice drink together, and it's finally happening.

She swallowed and shook her head. "Nothing. Nothing. You've got a bit of"—she tapped her lip—"milk there."

He grinned and used his sleeve to wipe it off. "Thanks."

Juliet bit her lip and stared straight ahead. "Yeah, no problem."

No problem at all.

Chapter Four

E van couldn't get over how much had changed in Cinnamon Bay since the last time he'd stuck around long enough to check things out.

Usually, when he came home, it was for a whirlwind of a trip, and he didn't do much besides hang out with his moms, sister and nephews or have a quick beer with a buddy. The last time he'd spent more than two nights in The Bay had been for Tony's wedding, and even that had only been three nights.

Usually, he was passing through between gigs or projects or had two midweek days off where he'd jet up to surprise his moms.

But on those trips, he didn't have time to wander or catch up with the locals. And most of the locals that he remembered growing up in Cinnamon Bay had either died or moved on like he had.

Sure, there were a few regulars he remembered, like the trio, and Bee Brewster, Marvin's grandmother. He remembered Marvin from school. The guy now worked at a bank and was part of Blazers, the volunteer firefighters at the Cinnamon Bay fire station. He'd bumped into Delilah Wilke yesterday as he and Eric were leaving Shenanigans. She was now running her family's business, Antique Alley, and had her man, Chace, on her arm.

Evan was sure that by the time his summer came to a close, he'd know all the locals that he was supposed to know, their quirks and probably even their coffee orders.

He hadn't anticipated that he'd be stuck playing delivery boy and fetching the trio's coffees, but he was happy that they insisted Juliet join him.

Although their conversation had yet to go in the direction he'd hoped it would.

She surprised him with her "I'm living my dream" statement.

He believed that he too, was living his dream.

He'd always wanted to be a famous musician, and here he was doing what he loved. Sure, he was no Mick Jagger or Paul McCartney. Hell, he wasn't even Justin Bieber. But he made good money, got to travel and, most of all, he was doing what he loved, which was writing and playing music.

The reason he hadn't eaten lunch was because since running into Juliet yesterday, lady muse had not left his side. Song idea after song idea just kept popping into his head, to the point where he struggled to write them down fast enough.

And the best part about lady muse was that she wasn't total crap like before.

The stuff he was cooking up was actually really good.

The studio came into view, and he touched her arm with the back of his hand holding the drink tray. "Hey, Jules?"

She turned to face him. "Yeah?"

"I actually popped into the studio to ask you if you wanted to—"

"Ring! Ring! Ring!" His cell phone started to go off. The ringing sound was actually one of his bandmates, Omar, saying in a deep, goofy voice, "Ring!" over and over again. One drunken night in a Boston bar after a gig, the entire band thought it would be hilarious if they all made their phones have the same ringtone— Omar saying "Ring! Ring!" Needless to say, the only one who still had it as his ringtone was Evan. Things had gotten confusing fast when they all had the same ringtone.

He handed her the tray. "Hold on a sec."

She nodded and took the tray from him.

He didn't recognize the number, and he was about to let it go to voicemail when a voice in the back of his head said, "Answer it."

"Hello?"

"Evan Spencer, please," said a woman with a thick Southern accent.

"This is he."

"Mr. Spencer, this is Anastasia Dwyer from Ridley Valley Child Services. I'm calling on behalf of Hope Drake, the ten-month-old daughter of Anthony and Jacqueline Drake."

A huge, heavy ball of dread formed in the bottom of Evan's stomach, weighing down his insides until he thought he might trip over them. "Is she okay? Is the baby okay?"

"She's fine, sir. But you are listed here as her legal guardian should anything happen to her—"

"What happened to Tony and Jacqui?" he practically screamed into the phone. "Why are you talking to me about Hope's legal guardian? Where are her parents?"

Evan's vision grew blurry, but the reassuring touch of Juliet's cool hand to his forearm brought him back and made him focus his eyes.

"Mr. Spencer, I thought the police already called you. I am so sorry. Mr. and Mrs. Drake were killed in a motor vehicle accident late last night. They were hit by a drunk driver. The baby was with a sitter, and when Mr. and Mrs. Drake didn't come home when they said they should, she called the police, and that's when—I'm terribly sorry for your loss, sir."

Evan glanced at Juliet. She was staring at him in horror. Her eyes darted across his face, and her mouth was open in shock. "What happened?" she whispered.

"Mr. Spencer, Mr. and Mrs. Drake listed you as next of kin for Hope. Should anything happen to them, you were put down as her legal guardian. She's currently with a foster family, but we're hoping you might be able to come and get her in the next day or two. A Mr. Eric Daigle has been listed as the executor of the estate as well as the person to contact if we couldn't get ahold of you. I believe the police are contacting him."

At this point, Evan was no longer listening to a word the woman said.

He knew she was just doing her job, but he didn't care.

One of his best friends in the world was dead.

His friend's wife was dead.

And now their daughter was an orphan.

Where was the justice in the world? A car crash had claimed Tony's parents' lives, and a freak diving accident had claimed Jacqui's parents. And now Hope was going to grow up without her parents as well.

Where was the freaking justice in that?

"I—I'm sorry," he said, cutting the woman off. "I just need a second to process this."

Hell, he needed more than a second.

"Of course. Do you have an email address I can send some information to? We don't have one on file."

Nodding, for some stupid reason, he rattled off his email address, then said goodbye to the woman, a hollow gesture he made before he realized he'd said it.

Tears filled Juliet's eyes as Evan stared into their brilliant emerald color. His knees were beginning to liquefy. His throat burned with a silent scream as his vocal cords became a tight knot.

His stomach felt like someone had come at him with Thor's hammer and sent him flying across the street and into a wall.

He had no air in his chest.

His blood was frozen in his veins.

He wasn't sure he'd even blinked.

Everything inside of him was splintering. All the hope and joy and anticipation for a carefree summer shattered. For a boys' weekend and getting to catch up and reminisce about the good old days, obliterated.

He would never get to have that weekend with Tony and Eric.

Never get to see his friend again. Hear his laugh or see his smile.

His best friend was dead.

Tony was dead.

"I'm so sorry," Juliet said, setting everything in her arms down and drawing him in for a hug. "So, so sorry."

Somehow, they found themselves on a bench, and although he didn't cry, she just held him there, her arms around him as he fought the roaring in his ears and the devastating burn that slashed through his body. His brain felt like it was going to explode.

As much as he knew he should be sad, sobbing over the death of his friend, all he could feel at that moment was disappointment. Disappointment and anger.

He was disappointed that he'd never get to hear Tony's unique belly laugh again.

It was the kind of laugh that made others laugh, no matter the context.

Hearing Tony Drake laugh was hilarious in and of itself.

But when the man told a joke and laughed so hard at his own joke that tears formed in his eyes and he had to hold onto his stomach like it might fall off his body—that was the best thing in the entire world.

It didn't matter if it was a joke he'd told a dozen times before and quite possibly to the same audience; when Tony got on a roll, everybody stopped to listen.

And just like Evan had a knack for writing songs, and Eric was some *Good Will Hunting* math savant, Tony could tell the most wicked and engaging stories.

Stories that involved Evan and Eric most of the time—anecdotes from their younger, foolish and mischievous years—and yet, when Tony told them, it was like Evan was hearing them for the first time.

Tony rarely made it to the end without tears in his eyes or having to pause because he was wheezing as he struggled through the laughter to get to the punchline.

And that was one of the things Evan would miss about his friend the most.

Rage continued to mix with the disappointment until it turned into a choking froth inside him.

That kind of joy, that pure, wholesome, incomparable joy, had been snatched from all of them. Nobody would hear Tony's stories again. Nobody would hear his laugh. And all because some stupid, selfish, arrogant bastard had gotten behind the wheel and thought he was invincible and above the law.

How careless, how thoughtless, how positively narcissistic could people be?

Now, because of one person's inability to follow the rules, to think beyond their own needs, a little girl was going to grow up without her mother and father. Hope was going to grow up without her parents, without her family.

He wasn't sure how long they sat there, but eventually, he lifted his head from Juliet's shoulder.

She hadn't held back the tears, and her eyes now glimmered. Her mouth turned down into a pout. "I'm so sorry, Evan." Her bottom lip trembled. "Poor Eric. I have to call him."

Evan nodded. "Right. Eric. Yeah, I should call him, too."

"Are you going to go pick up Hope tonight?"

Right! Hope.

Dear God. Hope was his responsibility now.

He was Hope's ... parent?

Guardian?

Everything?

The weight of sudden responsibility landed on his shoulders like two obese parrots. Their claws dug into his flesh and sent the agony coursing through his chest and out into his limbs.

"Maybe we can drive down there together to pick up Hope," he said, his voice sounding robotic to his own ears.

Juliet sniffed and wiped the back of her hand beneath her nose. "Yeah."

He cleared his throat and stood up. "I need to get these drinks to the ladies, apologize that they're cold and then start making some arrangements."

Without another word, they grabbed the probably cold coffees and the bag of cookies and booked it back to the studio.

He knew they were probably in sight of everyone in the studio when they stopped a moment ago, but at that very moment, Evan didn't care if he became the sole fuel source for the Cinnamon Bay Gossip Train. He had bigger things to deal with.

He stepped inside and set the cardboard tray down in front of the birds. "Thank you for the drink, ladies."

Their faces were all wary, and not an ounce of mischief sparkled between them.

"What happened?" Hattie asked slowly.

"Tell us," Birdie encouraged.

41

"We're not the gossip hounds you think we are, truly," Trixie added. "Everything we do is for the betterment of Cinnamon Bay. We love this town and the people in it. Tell us ... please."

Evan sucked in a deep breath, but it snagged in his lung, and he coughed. "Tony Drake and his wife, Jacqui, were in a car accident last night, and neither of them survived."

People in the studio, and not just the birds, gasped.

"I am Hope's legal guardian now, so I need to go and pick her up." He felt like he was speaking into a tunnel, the way his words echoed strangely back into his ears. It was like someone else was saying them and he was hearing them from a distance.

All three of the birds now had their hands over their mouths and tears welling up in their eyes. Birdie was trembling. The Drake family had been a well-known and well-liked family in Cinnamon Bay. Even though it was just the three of them, Tony and his parents had been active members of the community. His father was high up on the police force, and his mother taught Spanish at the high school.

And even after they passed, until he graduated high school and went off to college, Tony continued to be active in the community. He tutored kids in math and science, and every Sunday, without fail, he worked at the local soup kitchen.

Trixie stood up and reached for Evan's hand. "Anything you and that little girl need, you don't hesitate to ask, okay? Don't even ask. Just assume we'll say yes, because we will."

Hattie and Birdie nodded and sniffed.

A few other people who had known Tony and Jacqui were sniffling around the studio, too.

All Evan could do was nod. He had bitten the side of his cheek hard enough he now tasted blood.

He needed to get out of there. Away from people and all their concerned and curious eyes.

Normally, he didn't have a problem being the center of attention with all eyes on him. At least when he was on stage.

But this wasn't a stage, and he wasn't performing.

This was his life.

This was a tragedy, and at the moment, he wanted to experience it alone.

"Did you walk here?" Juliet asked, coming up behind him and holding his shoulders with her hands. Her presence and touch were a small but not insignificant dose of comfort. One he was grateful for. One he needed for fear of crumpling to the ground without it.

He nodded. "Yeah."

"Let me take you home." She encouraged him to follow her around through the studio, past the *Employees Only* section, three big kilns next to each other, and then finally out into the fresh air and hot sun.

"I'm right here," she said, pointing to a white Jeep with the top off.

Nodding because he honestly couldn't begin to think of what words to say, he followed her and climbed in.

They were on the road in no time, and thankfully, she didn't press him to talk.

He stared blankly ahead as she drove the short distance through town to his beach cottage.

She pulled off the road and down the long single-lane driveway. A dilapidated old fence ran on either side, and he heard the dry, overgrown grass brush against the sides of her Jeep.

When she reached the cottage, she put the Jeep in park then turned off the ignition.

She unbuckled her belt, then he unbuckled his, and at the same time, they hugged. It seemed like the most natural and normal thing for them to do.

This time, though, unlike on the street, he let the tears fall.

The harder he sobbed, the tighter she held him. The more she absorbed his pain, transferred her kind, sweet energy into him, lending him her hope and positivity. Because at the moment, he had none left.

All his dreams for the summer had been zapped and now lay charred and smoking when the social worker called.

And it had nothing to do with the fact that his carefree summer was now going to be interrupted by a baby—it was the fact that his friend, his *best* friend, was dead, and now it was up to Evan to figure out a way to give Tony's daughter a good life. A normal life. The kind of life her parents had dreamed for her—for their family.

The pressure buried him.

He couldn't fail Tony.

He couldn't fail Hope.

As he sat there in Juliet's Jeep and cried on her shoulder, and she cried on his, the growing weight of his impending responsibility became nearly unbearable. The parrots tripled in size, and their claws dug in even harder until they touched bone.

And with that weight—with the knowledge and understanding that he'd gone from a not-a-care-in-the-world bachelor to a dad in the blink of an eye—so too came back the fury.

It was an easier emotion to feel—rage. Sadness came with a vulnerability and one that made his body tighten and his senses become overly alert.

When he was sad, even if it was alone in a vehicle with Juliet, he felt exposed.

Anger gave him a shield to hide behind. It gave him armor.

It gave him a reason to channel the tendrils of hate that prickled along his arms and sizzled within the synapses of his brain.

The hate he felt toward the drunk driver was a suit of armor for his grief. If he wielded a shield of anger, his sadness could crouch down and hide behind it.

Juliet's sobbing ebbed eventually, as did his, and at the same time, they pulled apart, untangling their arms and wiping beneath their eyes.

She blinked spiked lashes at him, and her bottom lip trembled as her head shook. "It's not fair."

Evan's nostrils flared and he nodded. "Not in the slightest."

"Let me know what I can do to help with Hope. Anything, just name it."

He swallowed. "Come with me to get her, please. I can't do this alone."

Chapter Five

They drove through the night to Ridley Valley. Juliet had to take care of a few things at the studio, and Evan wanted to see his parents and Dave, so it was nearly ten o'clock before they hit the road. The town was three hours south in South Carolina and slightly inland. Evan knew that they could stay at Tony and Jacqui's house, but he couldn't bear the idea of having to wander around his best friend's house, look at all of his stuff and all the pictures of the happy family without putting his fist through one of their walls.

They grabbed a hotel room—one with two single beds—and both of them crashed almost the moment they stepped inside.

Crying was exhausting.

There was also no sense going and bothering the foster family that had Hope. Evan had already made arrangements with the social worker to pick Hope up Saturday morning. Juliet offered to go to Tony's house and gather a few necessities for Hope, along with the spare car seat from Jacqui's car.

"Does she sleep in a crib, a bassinet, a bed, what?" Evan asked Saturday morning as he and Juliet awkwardly fumbled around each other as they tried to share the tiny bathroom and brush their teeth and get ready for the day.

Juliet spit into the sink, lifted her head and glanced at him in the mirror. "Crib. Guaranteed. But we can just buy one in town or ask to borrow one. No sense disassembling the one here and loading it all into my Jeep. I'll just grab the necessities for now. We can always come back."

But Evan didn't want to come back.

He knew that for some people, going through a deceased loved one's things could be a way to obtain closure, but Tony's death was still too raw. And at this point, Evan wasn't sure he'd ever be able to go through his friend's stuff.

"I don't know the first thing about babies," he said. "Why on Earth did they think that *I* would be a suitable legal guardian for Hope? Why not Eric? Or ..."

"Or?" Juliet probed. "Tony and Jacqui didn't have a lot of people in their life that they trusted implicitly. They were both only children, remember? We—your family and mine—were his family. And as far as we know, the only family Jacqui had has also died."

"Why didn't he leave Hope to your brother and Isla, though? At least Eric *has* kids. He knows how to do the whole dad thing. He knows how to change a diaper, how to burp them and heal booboos with a kiss."

Juliet shrugged. "They obviously saw something in you. They knew that you'd step up to the plate, provide for Hope and give her a great life."

Yeah, but Eric and Isla would do the same and they had a stable life in Cinnamon Bay. Evan was a nomad musician. That was no life for a kid. At least not a kid he didn't want to see wind up in therapy during her formidable teen years.

He shook his head and scratched the back of his neck, struggling to make sense of it all. Glancing down at his lap he was reminded of the fact that he was hardly wearing any clothes.

Although he normally slept in nothing but a pair of boxers, he'd kept a white T-shirt on last night. When he'd shown up at the studio yesterday—which felt like a lifetime ago—he had every intention of asking Juliet out, but things were different now, and stripping down to nothing more than his black boxer briefs felt weird.

She'd slept in a pair of soft-looking shorty shorts and a figure-hugging tank top. He could also tell she'd gone braless, which he tried not to think about but failed miserably.

But she was in the bathroom now, applying some cream to her face, and he needed to change out of his white T-shirt and into his black one.

Stupid, he was well aware of that.

But he also knew he was too damn clumsy when it came to food for him to ever be able to keep a white shirt white from dawn until dusk. He never had, and he never would.

He showed her his back, peeled off his white shirt and was about to tug his black one over his head when his phone on his nightstand started to ring. He abandoned his shirt on the top of his suitcase and beelined it around the beds to grab the phone from the charger.

"Hello?" he said, putting it to his ear.

"Hello, Mr. Spencer, this is Anastasia Dwyer. I'm just confirming for nine o'clock this morning."

Evan nodded. "Yes, yes. I'm just getting dressed, then we'll be there."

"Very well. Do you need the address, or did you get everything in my email?"

"Got the email," he said shortly.

"All right. I will see you soon. Goodbye."

Evan grumbled. What was the point of that call? She could have just texted him. Or given him the benefit of the doubt that coming to pick up his dead friend's kid was important enough for him *not* to forget.

With another grumble, he tossed his phone onto his unmade bed and stalked back toward his suitcase, only to run smack dab into Juliet, who was exiting the bathroom.

"Oh! Sorry," she said, her voice several octaves higher than normal. A girlish giggle escaped her.

Then there was the dance of them trying to get around each other. He went left. She went left. He went right. She went right.

He smiled stiffly, gripped her by the shoulders and gently moved her to the right so he could go left.

"Sorry," she said again. He grabbed his black shirt, but before he pulled it on, he caught her watching him, keenly. Avidly. Heat swam behind her eyes, and she bit her bottom lip.

He shoved down a groan.

Aside from the fact that all he felt inside of him right now was grief, doubt and fury, Juliet deserved more than some cheap hotel room.

He didn't think she was a virgin, but if what Eric said was true and she'd pined after Evan for years, when he finally asked her out, if they got to the point where they fell into bed together, he wanted it to be romantic for her.

His ego told him to get over himself, that he was building up her dreams of him more than they probably were.

But what if he wasn't?

What if Juliet *had* dreamt of him for ages? Been in love with him since she was a kid?

He didn't want to let her down. He didn't want to be less than what she'd built him up to be. He didn't want to disappoint her.

He tugged his shirt over his head, and turned away from her, running his fingers through his hair and scrubbing a hand down his face. He wasn't going to bother shaving.

"We'll grab coffee and breakfast on our way to meet the social worker," he said, still showing Juliet his back.

"Okay," she said behind him.

He tugged on a pair of cargo shorts, only now keenly aware of the fact that he'd been parading around in front of her in his boxers.

Idiot.

Grabbing his wallet from his suitcase, he spun back around to face her.

Somehow, while he was deep in his own thoughts and his ego was attempting to give him a reality check, she'd changed out of her pajamas and into a pair of denim shorts that hit her mid-upper thigh and a baby-pink tank top that hugged her curves. When a red bra strap peeked out on one shoulder, it was all he could not to picture himself biting that shoulder and slowly peeling the strap down her soft, slender arm.

This was not the time or place.

He wasn't going to act on his feelings right now.

That was disrespectful to not only Tony and Jacqui but Juliet as well.

However, when he saw her last month and then again on the beach, something inside him shifted. His goals. His motivations.

Thoughts of Juliet had consumed him for this past month. The green-eyed girl in the crowd.

And then realizing she wasn't some stranger but rather his best friend's little sister, it all just seemed meant to be.

They were meant to be something.

They were meant to take a chance.

The question was, did she still feel the same way about him as she did all those years ago? Or was he starting from scratch? Was this adoration one-sided, or did she still, deep down, harbor feelings for him?

"Ready to go?" she asked, slinging her purse over her shoulder and flicking her long, dark hair behind her.

He nodded. "I suppose. Though—"

"You can never be *ready* to go and collect Tony's kid. I get it." Her hand fell to his back. "I get it."

He grabbed his phone off the bed and followed her out the hotel door.

They were in her Jeep—with Juliet driving—less than five minutes later. He needed something on his stomach before he faced the music. Before his life changed forever.

One cup of coffee and a mediocre breakfast burrito was all that stood between Evan and the rest of his life as a single dad.

Did the man know what he was doing when he pranced around the hotel room in those ball-hammock-style boxer briefs of his? Did he know that she saw practically *everything* he had to offer? Did he know?

Did he?

He had to know.

How could he not?

He'd slept in a T-shirt, which she was grateful for, but then ran around the room that morning without a shirt. What was his angle?

Was he trying to torture her?

Did he know it was torture?

Probably not, since Evan didn't know he'd tortured Juliet for five freaking years. So many summers, he'd run around in the backyard playing with Super Soakers with her brother, wearing nothing but his board shorts, while Juliet sat at her window chewing her nails down to the quick and watching as his torso glistened in the sun.

Or when the boys were older and he'd show up without a shirt on and he, Eric and Tony would head down to the beach with nothing more than their towels and a volleyball.

Pure. Torture.

She'd easily take electrodes on her nipples over the kind of emotion and sexual anguish Evan had routinely thrown at her for so many years. No question.

A part of her had hoped that they'd get to the hotel and there'd be some mix-up and then there would only be one room left, a room with a double bed and no couch, not even a cot down in the hotel storage.

They'd be forced to sleep in the same bed, and through grief and heat and meandering hands ...

Wasn't that a universal fantasy for every young, hopeless romantic?

The hotel was actually as full, but the only room they had left had two twins, not the king-sized bed taunting them to dirty things on it.

A baby has just been orphaned. Get your mind out of the gutter and off his nothing-left-to-the-imagination boxer briefs.

Right!

After stopping for coffee and breakfast, they made their way to the address the social worker provided them.

It was a nice neighborhood. The houses and yards were maintained, and even at five minutes to nine on a Saturday, people walked the sidewalks and waved at each other as they let their dogs do their morning business.

"Sixty seventy-two," Evan said, pointing to the red brick house at the end of the cul-de-sac.

She nodded, slowed her roll and came to a stop on the side of the road.

A woman with dark gray pressed pants and a canary-yellow sleeveless blouse was waiting in the driveway along with two people—a man and woman—who were probably in their mid- to late forties. All of them had grim expressions on their faces as they chatted. The other woman, wearing a blue dress, was holding a baby.

Hope.

Juliet reached across the center console of her Jeep and grabbed Evan's hand. "It's going to be okay. We're going to figure this out."

His mouth couldn't form a smile. Rather his lips just pressed together into a thin line, and his eyes closed for a few seconds.

It felt natural to reach out and touch him. To make a connection. Just like it'd felt natural to hug him in the street yesterday and again in her Jeep when she took him home.

He didn't shy away when she reached out or act all weird, and she'd be lying if she said a small zing of hope and excitement didn't careen through her when she did touch him—not that she did it too often. She didn't want him to think she was some gropey weirdo.

When he opened his eyes, sadness swirled deep behind the soft brown, and her heart ached for him. If only she could do more. If only she could ease the pain that she so easily saw was rattling inside him.

They each took a deep breath, she pulled her hand from his, and they opened the Jeep doors.

"Mr. Spencer?" the woman in the yellow blouse called out from the driveway.

Evan nodded. "I am."

She smiled and offered him her hand. "Anastasia Dwyer. I am so sorry for your loss. And for Hope's." She glanced at the baby who was happily chewing on a small rubber bunny.

Evan nodded again. "Yeah, me too."

"This is Theresa and Fredrick Martindale, foster parents, and they've been looking after Hope," Anastasia said, gesturing toward the couple.

"She's such a good baby," Theresa said. "Good-natured, easygoing. And very smiley."

"Just like her parents," Evan said through what Juliet could see was a clenched jaw.

She slid her hand into his and gave it a gentle squeeze before letting go and stepping forward. "I'm Juliet Clarkson, a friend of Evan's. Eric Daigle is my brother. I've come to help Evan collect Hope and some of her things from her home." She approached Theresa and held out her arms for the baby. "May I?"

"Of course," Theresa said, handing over Hope.

"Hello, baby," Juliet said, propping a round-faced Hope on her hip. "What have we got here?" She tapped the rubber bunny that Hope was gnawing on like a dog chews on a soup bone.

51

"She's got a couple of teeth," Theresa said. "And I think a few more are on their way, hence all the drool and chewing."

Juliet smiled, bouncing Hope on her hip a bit until the baby smiled around the bunny. "That's okay. We've all been through it."

Theresa handed a very stoic and slightly robotic Evan a diaper bag and rattled off a few instructions about bottles and solid foods. Juliet absorbed it, but she knew by the blank expression on Evan's face that he hadn't heard a word.

After some proof of identification and some signed papers, along with Fredrick helping Juliet install the car seat in her Jeep, they were on their way back to the hotel with a drooling and cooing baby in the back.

"I should probably put the canvas back on the roof and sides, huh?" she asked Evan as she helped Hope out of her car-seat buckles and turned the baby inward to Juliet's chest. "Don't want to blow this peach-fuzz hair of hers clean off." She chuckled at her own dorky joke.

Evan didn't laugh.

He slung the diaper bag over his shoulder, and they walked into the hotel and rode the elevator up to their room.

"I guess we'll need a crib or cot or something if we're going to stay another night," she said, closing the door behind her. Was the floor clean enough to put down a crawling baby?

She glanced at it.

Definitely not.

"I should probably go to Tony and Jacqui's place to get a few more things. Like a stroller, some bedding, blankets, more clothes, and toys. Do you want to come with me?" She adjusted Hope in her arms and narrowly dodged a chubby baby finger up the nose.

He was sitting on the edge of his bed staring blankly at the wall. He shook his head.

"Sooooo, you want me to leave her here with you, then? I don't trust that these floors are clean, and even though she's not an infant, I also don't really think she should be left on a bed unattended. What do you plan to do with her while I'm gone?"

He slowly, almost in a creepy way, but not quite, turned to look at her. "Do with her? Can't you just take her with you?"

Juliet's mouth dropped open, and she almost dropped Hope, too. "You want me to take Hope with me while I run around Tony and Jacqui's house and collect stuff? While you just sit here doing ... what?"

As much as she knew beyond a shadow of a doubt that she was still in love with this man, she was also realizing he still held some of his oblivious tendencies from when they were teenagers. Only instead of being oblivious to her existing, he was oblivious to how much he was trying to impose on her.

She got it. His best friend in the world had just died.

But!

But that didn't give Evan license to behave like a spoiled jerk who was just going to sit and watch television in the hotel room while she carted Hope around, gathered all her stuff and then hauled it all back to the hotel.

Not that she minded, but Juliet had already taken two days off work, and she drove them down to Ridley Valley.

He was asking a lot of her right now.

She was prepared to do anything she could to help—as were both of their families—but Evan also needed to snap out of his stupor and do things, too. They weren't all going to bend over backward for him while he sat back and did nothing. They were all grieving, all dealing with the loss of Tony and Jacqui and what this would mean for Hope's future. But shutting down and doing nothing while others did everything just because you were grieving wasn't productive, and it was fertilizer on the soil of an invasive vine of resentment.

She turned to look at Hope, smiled at the rosy-cheeked little lamb, took a deep breath and then faced Evan. "All right, here's the plan: You're coming with us. You can hang out in the yard or Jeep with Hope. Or I can find the stroller, then you can take her for a walk around the neighborhood while I pack up. You don't have to go inside the house, but I can't do this by myself. Got it?"

Evan tipped his eyes up to hers.

She smiled a wide fake grin at him. "Great! Now get in the Jeep!"

Chapter Six

It took them two hours to load up everything at Tony and Jacqui's. It probably would have taken them less time if Evan hadn't continuously stopped Juliet from what she was doing to ask for help with Hope.

But he had no idea how to "fix" a fussy baby.

He'd never spent much time with babies, so the fact that Tony had left *his* baby to Evan just made Evan scratch his head to the point where he was sure people thought he had fleas.

"She's not *fussy*," Juliet said. "Just go through the checklist."

"Checklist?" he'd asked. "I didn't see any checklist in the diaper bag."

Juliet rolled her green eyes. "Is she wet? How's her diaper? Is she hungry? Is she tired? Go through the checklist. It's *usually* one of those. She's also teething, so it could be that."

Turned out, it was all of the above, just at separate times.

First, Hope had been hungry. That was easily solved with a bottle of formula premade by Theresa. She also ate a pouch of apple sauce, some Cheerios, and Theresa had been kind enough to send along a banana, some of Hope's leftover toast from breakfast and some cut-up strawberries. Hope ate it all.

But just when Evan thought he'd sorted things out and Hope was smiling in her stroller again, she lost her mind five minutes later.

So he raced back to the house.

"It's her diaper this time," Juliet said. "In one end, out the other. Have you ever changed a diaper?"

He looked at her like she'd asked if he'd ever hopped on a space shuttle for a weekend trip to Mars. Because those questions had the same answer.

"I'll show you," she said, settling down on the grass and pulling things out of the diaper bag, one of which was a blanket where she laid down Hope.

"How do you know how to do all of this?" he asked, once Hope was all cleaned up and sporting a fresh diaper under her purple striped pants.

Juliet shrugged and squirted hand sanitizer on her hands. "Eric and Isla *do* have two kids, you know? My nieces. Even though I was living out of state for most of their infancy, I tried to come home as often as I could. Besides, it's all kind of common sense, really."

He shook his head. Apparently not, since he didn't even know where to start.

Once he *saw* her change a diaper, it all made sense. But he wouldn't have thought to lay the baby down on a blanket, rather than the bare grass, or to tuck the clean diaper under the dirty one so that nothing spilled out onto the blanket. These things seemed like hacks a parent would figure out along the way, not common sense.

Unless his common sense ended at knowing to look both ways before he crossed the street.

He put Hope back in her stroller and headed off again, but they weren't gone ten minutes before he was booking it back to the house with a wailing baby nearly going red in the face as she showed off her two bottom teeth to the world.

"What did I do now?" he asked, exasperated and sweating like a pig.

He'd forgotten how brutal the heat could be. And it was only May.

Juliet scooped Hope up and held her against her chest but away enough that she could look into the baby's eyes. She glanced at him. "My guess is that she's tired. Just let her cry for a bit longer, keep pushing her in the stroller, make sure the sun is off her, and I bet you she falls asleep."

"That's it?" he asked. Surely there had to be a much greater reason for a person to scream the way Hope had. A broken bone, a nail to the hand, something.

"I think so." Juliet smiled at him. "You're doing great. She's clean. She's fed. Now she's ready to sleep."

"Then why'd she scream her head off?"

Juliet snorted and tried to hide her smile. "It's what babies do. They fuss when they're tired, and then they fall asleep. Maybe the sun was in her eyes. Maybe she was hot or uncomfortable. Who knows? But if you look at her now"—she turned Hope toward him—"her eyes are starting to droop. She'll be out before you reach that stop sign up there, I guarantee it."

She handed him Hope, patted him on the back and turned to go back into the house.

Into Tony and Jacqui's house.

Evan hadn't even bothered to come and check out their new digs or to fly up and meet Hope when she was first born.

What kind of a best friend had he been? Not a good one, that was for sure.

And yet they still thought he was good enough to take care of their daughter. To *raise* their daughter.

He just didn't get it.

"Shall we try again?" he asked Hope. "Third time's the charm?"

She blinked her blue eyes at him, then her face cracked into a smile and she did one of those iconic baby-style giggles. The air sucks in and a squeak out.

He grinned at her, kissed her cheek and put her back in her stroller.

Of course, Juliet had been right. Hope was out before Evan reached the stop sign.

By the time he got back to the house, two hours had passed since they arrived and Juliet was just finishing loading up her Jeep. It was packed!

"Man, babies do not travel light," he said, turning the stroller a bit so a still sleeping Hope wasn't in the sun. He'd had to be strategic in where he walked so that the sun was always in front of him and not beating down on the slumbering baby.

"No, sir, they do not," Juliet said with a smile. "You guys ready to go?"

"She's sleeping."

"Would you like to take a walk-through on your own?" Juliet asked. "I can watch her outside if you'd like a moment. Or I'm sure we can wheel her into the foyer if you want company."

A hard, sticky wad of peanut butter was lodged in his throat. He couldn't speak, and it hurt to even nod. He didn't *want* to go in there. He didn't *want* to see all of Tony and Jacqui's things—their life. The life they'd dreamed of, then made into a beautiful reality. But he knew he had to.

He hadn't come to see their life earlier, witnessed their perfect happy family when it was a living, breathing entity, so now he had to see it after the fact.

That was his punishment for being a crappy friend.

For not being there for Tony when it mattered. When Tony became a dad—something he always wanted to be.

When they bought their first house.

Besides their wedding, Evan hadn't been around for any of the big moments in Tony's life.

And now, he had to pay for that folly.

He had to experience, had to walk through and witness everything he'd missed. Everything he'd declared himself too busy to make time for. Everything that had been stolen from Hope.

He tried to swallow but couldn't.

A cool, delicate hand slid into his and tugged. "Come on," she said, tilting her head.

With his free hand, he pushed the stroller up to their front stoop, and she helped him carefully lift it over the threshold.

He checked on Hope.

She was still sawing logs.

Taking a deep breath, he stepped into the house.

As he expected, it was homey, welcoming and perfect.

And not perfect in that it was immaculate; perfect in that it was the perfect family home. The quintessential two-story, suburban family home with three bedrooms, a brick fireplace, a mantel full of family photos, cereal under the couch, baby toys stuffed in random corners and a big pile of clean, unfolded laundry sitting in the hamper on top of the kitchen table.

It was a lived-in home.

Because up until a couple of days ago, a family had lived here.

A happy family.

A beautiful family.

A family that didn't deserve to have their world ripped apart by a careless drunk driver.

He slowly wandered through the kitchen and was stopped by a picture on the fridge. It was a picture of Eric, Tony and Evan at Tony and Jacqui's wedding. All three of them were in gray suits with lavender-colored ties. Each of them had a bottle of beer in their hand and their arms looped around each other. They were standing on the deck of Tradewinds, which was the restaurant in Cinnamon Bay where Tony and Jacqui had their reception, and all three of them were smiling.

Evan remembered that moment—even though he shouldn't, given how drunk he got at the wedding—but he did. The photographer came around and said, "Hey, let's get a shot of the three most handsome guys in the room."

To which Evan replied, "All right, hold on. I'll go see if I can find two other guys to stand beside me."

That prompted Eric and Tony to tackle him until they were all laughing, then that was when the photographer took the picture. All of their mouths were open because they were mid-laugh. But it turned out to be a fantastic picture.

Had that been the last time he'd seen Tony?

Evan grabbed the photo off the fridge and stared at it closer. Dammit, it had.

"I felt so bad I couldn't make it to the wedding," Juliet said, coming up behind him, her voice soft and almost angelic. "That was the same day as a huge art exhibit, and I had four pieces featured in it. I sent a gift, though."

She stepped behind him toward the dining area of the kitchen, then stopped and pointed to an enormous painting—a beautiful painting—of a beach scene. But it wasn't just any beach scene. It was Cinnamon Bay, the tall beach grass and endless horizon right at dawn.

"I asked them if there was something specific they were saving for and if money would be okay." Her brows pinched for a moment. "That seems to be the way things are going these days. Couples getting married just want cash for a house or the honeymoon. But they said they wanted a painting—if I was willing. I sent them a copy of my portfolio and what I had, and they picked out this one. Said it reminded them of home."

"Because it is home," he said. "It's gorgeous."

Her complexion pinked up, and she averted her gaze from his.

Still holding the photo in his hand, he walked toward her but kept his eye on the painting. "I've never seen any of your work. This is incredible, Juliet."

She shrugged. "It was an earlier piece. I was dabbling with water-based paint. But I'm really more of an acrylic girl. Acrylic and clay."

He shook his head. "Don't sell yourself short. It's stunning." He glanced out the window at her Jeep. "Do we have room to take it back with us?"

Her green eyes widened. "Y-you want to take it back? But it was a—" She stopped herself for a moment, then her expression turned sad. "It was a gift," she finished saying. "But I guess they ..." With slumped shoulders, she carefully removed it from the hooks on the wall. It was roughly three feet tall by two and a half feet long. He could only imagine how long that took to paint.

"What would something like that cost?" he asked.

She set the canvas down on the ground at her feet and lifted her head to look at him. "This piece here would run for roughly two thousand dollars."

Evan's mouth dropped open. "That's amazing."

She didn't say anything but just picked up the painting and jerked her chin toward the rest of the house. "You go finish doing what you need to do. I'm going to see if I can wrangle this beast into my Jeep. Otherwise, we'll have to leave it for the second trip."

The second trip.

He hadn't really thought about the fact that they'd probably have to come back. Eventually, they'd have to go through all of his friends' belongings. Throw things out, donate them, sell them.

All of that money, of course, would go to Hope, the same with anything that came out of the sale of the house and Jacqui's car.

She didn't wait for him to respond but just headed toward the living room and front door again. He glanced out the kitchen window a second later to find her pulling a few things out of the Jeep to rearrange and accommodate the canvas.

A chirp, a warble and a grunt echoed through the house from the entryway.

More grunting followed by squeaking.

Shoving the picture from the fridge into his back pocket, he went to go check on Hope.

She was wide awake and squirming in her seat, making all kinds of goofy faces. He unclipped her buckles and pulled her out, cradling her against his shoulder the way he'd watched Juliet. "Did you have a good nap?" he asked her, kissing her head. "Feel rested and less cranky?"

The baby's eyes were wide, and she smiled a gummy grin at him, then pointed behind Evan and went, "Oooo."

He turned to see where she was pointing, and his heart stopped beating. It was at a picture—a recent one, too, since Hope looked very similar to how she did now—of the three of them. It was framed and hanging on the wall that traveled up the stairs. In fact, the entire stairway was full of family photos.

She pointed more enthusiastically, and her noises grew more intense. With concrete in his shoes and an ache so alarming in his chest, if he didn't know it for the crippling grief that it was, he would have thought he was having a heart attack, he walked her closer to the pictures.

As soon as she spotted her parents, her face lit up like a birthday cake for an octogenarian.

"That's right, Hope. That's Mama and Dada," he said through a painfully tight throat. "And they love you so, so much."

He pressed his lips to the side of her head and held them there as the backs of his eyes began to burn. Soon his vision was blurry, and he buried his face in the crook of Hope's neck.

"I think we could hit the road now and head back to Cinnamon Bay. Plenty of time to get there before dinner." Juliet's soft, melodic voice grew closer as she stepped back into the house.

Evan sniffled, wiped his eyes, swallowed as best he could and turned to face her. "We should probably double-check that Hope's not hungry again and that her diaper is clean. But yeah, sounds good."

There was no hiding his emotions from Juliet, though. She knew that he'd been crying. The sympathetic tilt to her head and the softening of her gaze said as much.

She approached him and took Hope, but she didn't step back. "We'll get through this. We will. *You* will. You have an entire town of people behind you. Your family, my family. Everyone is willing to pitch in. There will be a legitimate village raising Hope. Trust me."

Then before he knew it, she had gathered him in for a hug, with Hope still in her arms and now squished between them. They stood there, with the front door open, surrounded by Tony and Jacqui and Hope's life—or what was left of it—and even though he drew comfort from Juliet's words, he couldn't stop the feelings of dread and inadequacy from careening through him.

Even with a village helping to raise Hope, she was his responsibility now.

Tony and Jacqui had left Hope to Evan.

Her life, her well-being, her entire everything and how she grew up was up to him.

And he didn't have the faintest idea where to begin.

Chapter Seven

They arrived back in Cinnamon Bay shortly after dinnertime.

Unlike when adults drive and are able to just keep driving, arriving at their destination in the estimated time, when you had a baby in the car, Google's ETA ceased to exist.

It felt like a dozen but was probably closer to four or five times that they had to pull over and go through the checklist to figure out what was making Hope lose her marbles in the backseat.

They quickly realized that it was the fact that she felt lonely and couldn't see anything because her car seat was rear-facing. So Evan climbed into the back seat with her, and they tossed a bunch of shit in the front with Juliet. After that, Hope was as happy as a clam, smiling and giggling at all of Evan's funny faces.

He wasn't sure how driving solo with her was going to be, since he couldn't exactly sit in the back seat if nobody was driving, but he'd cross that bridge when he came to it. For now, he was going to call this a win.

They stopped the baby from crying and arrived back in Cinnamon Bay in one piece.

When they arrived at his beach cottage, he was surprised but also not surprised to find three other vehicles parked there besides his own rental—one of his moms' cars, Eric's truck and Ron Clarkson's SUV. They were all hanging out on the back porch but made their way around the wraparound when they heard Juliet's Jeep pull up.

Each one of them wore a similar look on their face.

Sadness. Pain. But also ... determination.

Evan and Juliet glanced at each other in the rearview mirror.

"You ready?" she asked.

"Nope. But that's never stopped me before."

He could only see her eyes, but the way they glimmered back at him, he could tell she was smiling.

She got out of the Jeep first, then came around the right back passenger door to help get out Hope.

Evan got out himself and made his way toward the small gathering of people. Both his moms were there, along with his sister, Kate, his brother in-law Rick, Eric, Isla, and Eric and Juliet's parents, Ron and Sandy.

His mother—Joan or Mom-J as he called her—was the first to break through the wall of people, and she ran down the few steps and threw her arms around him. "I'm so sorry, honey," she said, her voice croaky from emotion. Even though he'd gone to see his moms, sister and Eric yesterday after getting the news, it was good to see them all again. To feel the presence of family and people he knew loved him—loved Hope.

More arms wrapped around him, which he knew to be his other mom Glenda, or Mom-G, as she was called, and his sister, Kate.

They stood there, all four of them hugging for a moment, the women crying.

"Has everyone met Hope?" Juliet asked, breaking the painful tension in the yard, something Evan was grateful for.

His moms and sister released him from their grasp and stepped away, all of them wiping their eyes and turning to Juliet.

"Oh my, the little darling," Mom-G said, stepping forward first and asking if she could hold Hope. Juliet handed her over.

Joan was Evan's birth mother, and Glenda was Kate's. They shared the same sperm-donor father, but each mom had carried one kid.

Though they all knew that if Mom-G had her way, they would have had a dozen kids. She'd always loved babies. It was probably why their joint business venture, an online kids' clothing store, did so well. Her heart was in it one hundred percent.

Everyone else stepped off the porch as well.

Eric and Evan locked eyes. They went to each other and hugged.

Neither of them said anything.

They didn't have to.

Evan knew what Eric was feeling, and Eric knew what Evan was feeling.

Each man cleared his throat and stepped away, glancing to the side and swiping his hand beneath his eyes.

Nobody said a word for a moment.

It seemed everyone was trying to gather their thoughts and rein in their emotions. Bringing Hope to Cinnamon Bay had made everything, the whole tragedy of it all, seem so much more real. Tony and Jacqui were gone, and Hope was now Evan's responsibility.

"Are you hungry after the drive?" Sandy, Eric and Juliet's mother, asked. "I brought a seafood lasagna that's still warm with foil on it."

Heads bobbed, and several of the group headed toward the house. Evan snagged Juliet's gaze, and she walked toward him. He held out his keys. "Let them all in, please. I ... I just need a couple of minutes. I'll start unloading."

She nodded. "I can do that."

She accepted the keys, and their fingers touched.

They'd touched countless times over the last couple of days, but this time it felt different. There was a spark, a longing he hadn't felt until now.

Yes, he was attracted to Juliet and had been planning to ask her out when he went into her studio yesterday—dear God, had it only been yesterday? It felt like a lifetime ago. But up until now, nearly every one of their touches had been done under the pretense of grief and consoling. Maybe not their first hug on the beach or when they bumped shoulders as they walked down the street to get the trio's coffee order. But as soon as he got the call about Tony and Jacqui, any deliberate touching was made with a veil of consolation over it.

Her fingers held his for a moment.

A small smile curled one side of her mouth, and her green eyes lit up.

"Thank you," he said. "For everything."

The other side of her mouth lifted as well. "We've got this. Don't worry." Then she took the keys, broke their contact and headed toward the front door.

Thankfully, everyone else had wandered around to the beach side of the house, so they hadn't watched Evan and Juliet's exchange.

She opened the door and disappeared inside, leaving Evan with the task of unloading Hope's things.

Thank God he'd rented the two-bedroom cottage and not the studio carriage house he'd also looked at.

By the time he was done getting everything out of the Jeep and onto the porch, dusk had settled in and laughter could be heard from inside the house.

A quick glance at the sky showed no dark thunderclouds, so for the time being, everything could stay on the deck. He'd run out and grab what he needed for Hope for the night, then tackle finding a home for everything else tomorrow.

He opened the front door and was greeted by lots of voices and the delicious scent of Sandy's *famous* seafood lasagna.

And it was famous.

At least in Cinnamon Bay.

Even Evan remembered people talking about Sandy's lasagna at potlucks and dinner parties. She brought it everywhere. And if she was told to bring an appetizer instead of an entrée, she just made lasagna cups in muffin tins and she was good to go.

"Beer, son?" asked Ron, Juliet's father, approaching Evan and offering him a frosty-looking bottle of some microbrew.

Evan nodded and thanked Ron.

"Been a hell of a couple of days," Ron said, shaking his nearly bald head. "Can't even begin to imagine a world without Tony." Evan watched the older man's throat move as he took a swig of his beer. Ron's bottom lip quivered when he moved the bottle away from his face.

Evan had nothing to say. He one hundred percent agreed with Ron, but at the moment, he could barely say Tony's name out loud, let alone think about him for too long.

Eric sidled up to them, along with Evan's brother-in-law, Rick. All four men stood quietly, sipping their beer. Eventually, they all somehow turned to face the window that looked out onto the water, which was now a dark indigo color.

The women continued to chat in the kitchen, and every so often he'd hear Hope coo or giggle.

"I'm meeting with an estate lawyer next week," Eric said, breaking the silence. "I don't even know where to start with all of this."

"The best thing you can do," Ron started, "is ask for help. And we're all here to help. The next best thing you can do is try to get as much money out of all the assets as you can so that that little girl in there is set up as best as she possibly can be."

Evan and Eric nodded.

"I'm happy to help organize anything in the financial territory," Rick said, since he was an accountant, after all. "Do you happen to know if they had life insurance?"

Eric's eyes slowly closed. "By the looks of things, they didn't. But I'm going to dig a little deeper."

"She'll want for nothing," Evan said, his throat hoarse. "I'll make sure of it."

"Still, it'd be good to know if there is life insurance out there. Raising kids isn't cheap," Ron added. "They only just bought that house, might not get much for it if they haven't paid much into the mortgage."

"We brought over one of the spare play yards that Kate uses for the daycare for Hope to sleep in until you get her set up with a crib," Rick added. "I've already put it in the spare room all set up."

Evan glanced at his brother-in-law. "Thank you."

Rick slapped him on the back. "It's what family does."

Evan's throat was tight. His grief had him wanting to be alone, but his fear of now being responsible for a baby had him wanting everyone to stay, to stay over even. What was he going to do if Hope woke up and started crying, wanting her parents, and he was unable to console her?

A plate was placed in front of him, and he glanced down, then over, to see Sandy smiling at him. "You need to eat," she said.

With a deep inhale through his nose and a nod, he took the plate from her.

"She won't let you refuse her lasagna," Ron said with a brief chuckle. "Not even if you're full, gluten-free, lactose-intolerant or vegetarian."

Eric snorted. "She's not *that* bad." His father side-eyed him, then Eric nodded. "Well, almost. But she respects allergies because of her own peanut allergy."

Slowly, over the course of the next few hours, everyone came up to Evan to offer their condolences, a hug and to say that they were available to help whenever he needed it. He thanked them all, but before too long, it was just him, Hope and Juliet left in the cottage.

Hope was asleep on Juliet's shoulder, while Juliet stood in front of the sliding glass door to the back deck. She swayed and hummed, and the tune in her head was, to his surprise, one of his songs, "Night of My Life."

He'd written that song after his high school graduation party. It had been epic and something that stuck with him even to this day. Sure, there were a few moments that he couldn't remember—since it'd been a kegger, after all—but that night on the beach still ranked as one of his top five favorite nights of his entire life.

Had Juliet been there?

He almost slapped his face to his palm. Of course, she hadn't been there. She was three years younger than him and Eric, and although there were some juniors and sophomores at the party, he would have remembered seeing Juliet there—wouldn't he?

The waves lapped against the shore as he slowly approached her. She was still humming.

Hope's cheek rested against Juliet's shoulder, her little mouth partly open and her lips so perfectly pouty—like a little cupid's bow.

"She's changed, fed and in her pajamas," Juliet said, glancing over at him when he came to stand beside her. "Nothing left to do but put her in her bed and cross your fingers."

Yeah, right. Cross *all* of his fingers. And his toes, and his eyes. Because he was damn tired and also feeling overwhelmed.

"You want her, or should I just go put her in the other room in the play yard?" Juliet asked.

"No sense transferring her more than necessary," he said.

She nodded and walked past him and down the hall. Moments later, she emerged and headed toward the front door that led out to her Jeep.

"Where are you going?" he blurted out, eating up the distance between them in only a few long strides. Panic rippled through him.

She was leaving.

Why was she leaving?

Her dark brows scrunched, and her lips twisted in a curious way. "I'm going home?" She worded it as a question.

"But why?"

"Because that's where I live?" Another question.

"But what if Hope wakes up?"

"Then you go through the checklist. She's ten months, not a newborn. Chances are she's sleeping through the night now that she's on solids. Theresa said she was a great sleeper, remember?"

Slowly, he nodded. Yeah, he did remember Theresa saying that. But it wasn't reassuring now. Not when a night alone in a house with a baby he'd only just met loomed over his head.

"And what about in the morning?" he asked. "What do I do then?"

She huffed a laugh through her nose. "You pick her up, change her diaper, feed her and play with her."

"Are you coming back?"

Juliet's head cocked to the side, and she looked at him with a puzzled expression. "I have to work in the morning, but I can pop by on my way."

Evan's eyes, although sore and tired, darted down the hall to where Hope slept. He wasn't afraid of much. Not scary movies, not roller coasters, not spiders or snakes. But he was afraid of being left alone with that small, dependent creature sleeping in his guest room.

Juliet's face softened, and she smiled, reached out and rested a hand on his shoulder. "You've got this. It'll be okay." She squeezed his shoulder and then turned to go. "Call me if you need anything."

What he needed was for her not to leave.

He couldn't do this.

He didn't know *how* to do this.

"Can't get you to stay, can I?" he asked, shoving a chuckle onto the end of his question. "I can take the couch. I'll put clean sheets on my bed."

She glanced at him over her shoulder. "Go to bed, Evan. I'll see you in the morning." Then before he could get down on his hands and knees and beg her to stay, she opened the door and stepped out into the cricket-song-filled night.

He accompanied her out, but neither of them said anything. She also didn't turn around again.

She got in her Jeep, stuck her hand out the window and waved.

He stood there, leaning against the door jamb until her tail lights disappeared, then he stood there a bit longer.

A cry from down the hall shook him from his tired fog, and at first, he wasn't sure what it was. Then he remembered—Hope!

He booked it down the hallway to find her standing up in the play yard, her mouth open, two bottom teeth exposed, and her eyes were filled with tears. The moment she saw him, she lifted her arms in the air, but that only made her lose her balance and fall back onto her butt.

He bent down, picked her up, and held her against his chest.

"Shhh," he murmured, pressing a kiss to the side of her head. "I'm not sure if I'm doing this right, but I'm here. I'm here."

Hope stopped crying and rested her head on his shoulder.

"I'm here," he whispered again, gently bouncing her and making his way out to the living room. "I'm here." He headed to the porch overlooking the dark ocean and reclined in one of the lounge chairs with Hope's chest to his. "I'm here," he said again, running his hand over her head. "And I'm not going anywhere."

Chapter Eight

J uliet had cursed herself out more than once on her drive home last night.

"Stupid, stupid, stupid!" she'd said as she hammered her hand on the steering wheel. "Evan Spencer asks you to spend the night and you turn him down? YOU TURN HIM DOWN? What are you? Crazy? On crack? You must be to turn down the man you've loved most of your life when he invites you to spend the night. That or certifiably insane."

But he wasn't inviting her over because he was *interested* in her as a romantic partner, a girlfriend or the other half of his heart, like she wanted him to. He had asked her to stay over because he was terrified of being home alone with a baby and he needed her help.

As much as it had pained her to leave him, she knew she had to.

He and Hope needed to figure this out on their own. She would be there to help, but she wouldn't always be available. She had a job, a life, and unless Evan wanted to make her part of his in another way, she wasn't going to let him use her as a buffer between him and Hope. He needed to get to know Hope without the interference of anybody else, including Juliet.

But as she said she would—because she never broke a promise—she showed up the next morning on her way to work. She even swung into Brewed with a View and grabbed them each a café amour (hey, she might not be willing to stay over at his place if he just wanted help with Hope, but she *could* give him a nudge to want her to stay over for another reason, couldn't she?) along with some pastries.

She knew better than to ring a doorbell with an infant inside, so she knocked gently.

No answer.

She knocked again.

Still no answer.

Now she was starting to worry.

With her heart rate picking up and panic in her steps, she walked briskly around the veranda to the back side of the house that faced the beach. She was hoping to just peer in through the sliding-glass doors but what she stumbled upon instead left her speechless.

Evan was lying down, asleep in the lounge chair, and little Hope was also asleep on his chest.

She couldn't stop herself, and she quickly yanked her phone out of her purse and snapped a couple of adorable photos.

Had they had a rough night?

When did Hope wake up?

How long had they been out there?

Neither one of them seemed distressed or cold.

Her heart melted, and warmth spooled through her.

She shifted on the porch and reached for the handle of the sliding-glass door, but just as she put her foot down on the board, it squeaked, then groaned.

Evan stirred, and his eyes fluttered.

He lurched slightly and inhaled. His eyes flew open, and he pivoted his head to look at her, shock streaking clear across his face.

"Morning," she whispered. "Rough night?"

He squeezed his eyes shut, cleared his throat, then gazed down at Hope. "She woke as soon as you left, then we wandered out here, passed out and never moved." His eyes lasered in on the cardboard tray with two drinks in it.

She lifted the tray. "Brought caffeine and sustenance."

Relief came out in his smile. Relief and appreciation.

71

Juliet held up a finger, telling him to wait. She opened the glass door, stepped inside and set everything down, then came back outside and gingerly removed a noodle-limbed Hope from his chest.

The baby squirmed, made a bunch of delicious baby sounds, then snuggled into Hope's chest. Juliet snuggled her right back.

It made sense for Hope to sleep a lot right now. She was processing and going through her own kind of stress. She didn't know if she'd ever see her parents again, didn't recognize these new people in her life and had screamed for a good portion of the drive to Cinnamon Bay before Evan went and sat in the back with her. Screaming like that would tire anybody out.

Evan pried himself off the lounger, scratched the back of his head and wandered in through the door. He picked up one of the to-go cups and took a sip. "Mmmm. Same drink as before. It's good."

She grinned. "Eva brews the best." Holding Hope in one hand, she stepped into the house and grabbed the other to-go cup. "Go have a shower. I'll watch her. I can't stay long, but I figured I'd give you a break to at least go make yourself presentable."

He snorted. "Thanks." She watched him move his frame—broad shoulders, narrow hips, long legs—down the hall. A second later, just as she was taking another sip of her own café amour, Hope started to wiggle and grunt in her arms.

The baby opened her eyes and lifted her head, gazing at Juliet for a moment, then smiling a gummy, two-tooth smile.

"Good morning, sweet thing," Juliet said. "I bet you're hungry, too." She glanced around the kitchen. Evan hadn't brought the bottle warmer or the formula in from the porch last night.

With a heavy sigh and still holding Hope in one hand, she headed out to the front deck and went on the hunt for where she'd stashed the bottle warmer.

She heard the shower click on.

Hope started to get fussy as Juliet sifted one-handed through the piles of stuff they'd brought back from Ridley Valley. Would it have killed the man to bring in just a few things?

With Hope now screaming her head off and right in Juliet's ear, she finally found the bottle warmer and ran back into the house.

Only the ONE bottle that Evan had brought into the house and they'd fed Hope with last night was sitting dirty in the sink.

Come on, man, seriously?

Still doing everything one-handed because she had a shrieking baby in her other hand, she washed the bottle, added the powder formula and water, and stuck it in the warmer.

"While that's heating up, let's go change your bum, huh?"

But Hope was having none of it.

While continuing to scream, she fought Juliet at every turn as she tried to change her diaper. She kept crawling away, nearly kicked a soiled diaper onto Juliet's foot, and when that wasn't proving effective, then she took to growling.

Juliet could honestly say she'd never heard a baby growl before.

It was probably no more than five minutes, but it felt like fifty by the time she had Hope in a new diaper. And just a diaper, since trying to put a three-piece suit on an octopus would have been easier than attempting to redress that enraged baby.

She left Hope on the floor in the living room, made sure the doors to the outside were all closed, then quickly grabbed the now-warmed bottle from the warmer. She passed it to the squalling child and nearly burst into tears of her own when the crying abruptly stopped and Hope started to drink the bottle.

But that wouldn't satisfy her for long. She needed real food.

"Hey, she's awake," Evan said jovially, wandering back into the living room freshly dressed, smelling scrumptious and drying his hair with a towel.

Juliet shot him a look she hoped conveyed her irritation with him.

He remained oblivious.

Classic Evan.

"Do you have any Cheerios or some small finger food like cereal in your cupboards? What about fruit?" Without waiting for him to reply, she ducked back into his small kitchen and started raiding his pantry. She found some instant oatmeal—that would work. An orange. That would work. A clamshell of strawberries and a loaf of bread.

"Can you make her breakfast?" Evan asked, appearing behind Juliet and sipping his café amour.

Exasperated, Juliet dropped down to her feet from her tiptoes and turned to him. "No. But you can. Oatmeal. Wait until it's cooled. Cut up oranges and strawberries. Little pieces no bigger than your pinky fingernail. Toast, finger-length."

His carefree, charming smile fell. "Bu—"

"Look, Evan, you two need to figure each other out. I have to get to work. I'm happy to help and am willing to help, but you also need to figure out just what it is you *need* help with and what it is you're just *afraid* to try to do yourself. You can make a ten-month-old breakfast. You can change her diaper. You can get her dressed and take her for a walk down the beach in the stroller.

"You can get the freaking bottle warmer out from the porch and clean a freaking bottle. These are not things you are *incapable* of. They are things you are just choosing to remain oblivious to. Things that you don't understand *need* to be done but you are capable of doing." She plopped her hands on her hips and let out a sigh, her shoulders feeling impossibly heavy and slumping from the invisible weight.

The look on his face had her instantly feeling like a colossal bitch for everything she'd just said.

Dammit.

Should she take it all back?

Should she stay and make them all breakfast?

Should she call into work and help him sort through everything they brought with them in her Jeep?

Stella's voice popped into her head. "*No, you should not. He's a grown-ass man, and they obviously thought he was capable enough on his own if they left their baby to him. Give him an inch, and he'll take a mile. Set some boundaries right away.*" Not that Stella had actually said any of this to Juliet, but it was something she *would* say.

And of course, Stella was right.

Evan nodded. "You're right. I'm sorry. I just—I'm feeling overwhelmed right now. But I'm asking too much of you. You have a job and a life." He scrubbed his hand down his face, but when he pulled his arm away, his gaze was caught by someone very cute crawling into the kitchen. "Well, hello there, naked baby," he said, bending down to scoop her up. "We need to find you some clothes." He glanced at Juliet, the look in his eyes asking if she knew where Hope's clothes were.

With a sigh and a smile, Juliet pointed to the porch out front.

Evan nodded. "Right! That is something I am *capable* of doing on my own. I can locate baby clothes and get a baby dressed."

"You absolutely can," she said with a nod before taking Hope from him.

With a final sip of the café amour, he headed to the front door, returning seconds later with a big blue tote that Juliet had labeled "Hope's Clothes."

He opened the tote and started sifting through items, coming up with a cute little romper with lemons all over it and ruffled sleeves. "Does this work?" he asked.

Juliet nodded. "Wish they had it in my size. It sure does." She passed Hope to Evan and watched as he laid the baby down just like Juliet had yesterday when she showed him how to change a diaper, and he got Hope dressed. It took longer than it would the average parent, but he'd get the hang of it.

When he did the final snap up between her chunky little thighs, he picked her up by the waist and held her hands while she stood on his couch, grinning at both of them. "There, presentable for the day."

Juliet tapped her hand against her to-go cup in a small applause.

"Now breakfast. Can babies have eggs?"

Juliet's head bobbed. "Scrambled would be great for her. I'll grab the high chair from the porch, but then I gotta run."

Of course, she grabbed way more than just the high chair for him, and before she left for work, she'd brought in everything that was on the deck, including the canvas she'd painted and Evan had insisted they bring back to Cinnamon Bay.

"I really appreciate you coming by and helping," Evan said, putting a bunch of small strawberry pieces on the high-chair tray for a ravenous-looking Hope. The baby went to town on them.

Juliet finished her café amour and tossed it into the recycling bin at the end of the counter. "I told you I was here to help, and I am. But you two need to get acquainted, too. You need to figure out what it is you actually need help with." She ran her hand affectionately over Hope's head. "I think you'll surprise yourself with just how capable you are."

His smile was small as he cracked eggs into a bowl and whisked them together with a fork. She was just about to say her goodbyes when there was a knock at the front door.

"I'll get it," she said, bending down and plopping a kiss to Hope's head as she maneuvered around the high chair.

The cottage was small, so she was at the door in under five seconds, hauling the thing open with a squeak to find four faces—all of which she'd come to recognize since moving back to the Bay—staring at her.

They all looked at her with wide, surprised eyes.

Particularly since it wasn't even eight o'clock and she was opening up the door at Evan's house.

Ohhhh, the rumor mill was going to be busy in Cinnamon Bay.

"Juliet," Addison Ford said with an upward inflection to her voice.

Juliet rolled her lips inward and shrugged. "Addison, Travis, Raleigh, Brock, what are you guys doing here? And so ... early?"

All four of them exchanged looks, and then their expressions turned sheepish.

"It is a little early. I realize that now," Addison said, glancing at her man Travis and swatting him in his hard marine chest. "I told you we should have waited."

Evan came up behind Juliet. "How can we help you guys?"

"I'm Addison Ford," Addison said, sticking out her hand. "This is my husband, Travis, and this is Raleigh Carmichael and Brock Gibson."

Evan nodded and took Addison's hand. "Nice to meet you all." His words were slow, cautious, and he took in each person with equal measures of hesitation.

"We heard about what happened ... about the accident and Tony and Jacqui Drake," Addison went on, her crystal-blue eyes turning sad.

A squeal of delight punctured the awkward silence that was blooming among them. Everyone smiled.

"About baby Hope," Addison added.

Evan's nod was stiff.

"We'd like to host a charity event to raise money for her," Addison continued, tucking a strand of her poker-straight blonde hair behind her ear. "The Carmichaels own The Factory, and we think it'd be the perfect venue for a music festival. I'm an event planner for Aggie Hall, which is in The Factory. Everything would be donated." She glanced at Travis and Brock. "Travis runs Top This, the pizza place on The Boardwalk, and Brock owns—"

"Tradewinds, I remember," Evan said. "Tony and Jacqui had their reception there."

"That's right," Brock said, recognition dawning on him. "That was a crazy night."

Evan's head bobbed. "I don't understand, though. Why a charity event?"

"The Drakes meant a lot to Cinnamon Bay. Tony meant a lot to Cinnamon Bay," Raleigh said. "We want to do something to help their little girl. To help *them*."

Addison nodded. "All the food would be donated by Top This and Tradewinds. Since you're a musician, we were thinking a music festival."

"Isn't there already a music festival in August? I saw a poster for it. *Summer in the Sun* or something?" Evan's voice was tired and sad and made a fist squeeze around Juliet's heart.

"There is," Addison confirmed. "But that one is on The Boardwalk and a little different. We'd hold this one at The Factory, on the grassy field behind it."

Evan's forehead scrunched, but he didn't say anything.

Addison seemed to take the fact that Evan didn't immediately dismiss the idea as encouragement to keep talking. "We want to call it *Rock the Shores*. We could call on talent from The Bay, adjacent towns, but maybe ..." Addison's nose wrinkled, and she twisted her lips, glancing up at Evan hopefully from beneath her lashes. "Maybe Evan Spencer of the October Coyotes could be our main attraction?"

"We'd sell tickets to the festival, charge for the food—Eva wants to donate coffee, tea and pastries, the same with The Rolling Pin. And then all the proceeds would go into a trust for Hope," Raleigh added. "We're also looking at approaching local businesses to donate things for a silent auction." He glanced at Juliet and grinned. "Perhaps a free pottery class or a canvas from a local artist?"

Juliet nodded. "I can donate whatever." Evan shifted back and forth on his bare feet. He didn't look as jazzed about this as the rest of them. Juliet waited until he lifted his head and their eyes met. "What's wrong?"

"I've got money," he said. "I can provide for Hope."

Now it was everyone else's turn to shuffle awkwardly.

"We understand that," Brock said patiently. "And we're not trying to step on your toes. We just want to help. Raising kids is expensive, and we don't know what kind of a trust, life insurance or otherwise Tony and Jacqui had for Hope. We just want to help."

"Think about it," Addison said. "We'd like to hold it at the end of July. Gives us two months to plan it since we're mid-May now. A little rushed, but we can pull it off."

Travis squeezed his wife's shoulder. "If anyone can pull it off, it's this woman."

Addison glanced up at him over her shoulder with affection in her blue eyes before turning back to face Evan and Juliet. "We understand if you're reluctant to take money when you don't think you need it, but look at it as a way of the town banding together to help when one of their own has been hurt. Because we know Tony was a dear friend of yours. That you're hurting."

"And besides," Raleigh added, "people of The Bay love a good festival. They're not going to complain if we give them another one this summer. They'll probably just complain if it doesn't become an annual thing."

The back of Juliet's eyes stung and her throat grew tight as she continued to watch Evan and his reaction to Addison and the other men's words.

"You're probably going to take some time off from work, right?" Travis asked. "So consider this money as a buffer. We don't want to you to have to suffer financially because you've—"

"I've been what?" Evan snapped. "Saddled with a baby? With my dead best friend's baby?"

Juliet's eyes went wide. She'd never heard Evan's voice take that tone before. Never experienced his venom.

But the hard-chested, retired military man didn't bat an eye. If anything, his expression softened. Juliet knew the tall, dark-haired man had seen his fair share of tragedy, so he probably understood—better than most—where Evan's ire was stemming from. Travis was also a very laid-back man. Not much rattled him. Or so she'd witnessed during the dinner rush when people were lined up down The Boardwalk for pizza and there was Travis, whistling and smiling and joking with every person who walked in. Not a bead of sweat on his head as he dished out pie after pie to happy, hungry patrons.

"What I was *going* to say," Travis said slowly, "was that you've been handed a very difficult situation. Difficult all around. You're grieving, you're not a father, and yet now, *while* grieving, you're supposed to care for that little girl. A little girl who, every time you look at her, reminds you of your dead friend."

Evan's Adam's apple jogged in his throat, and he murmured, "Sorry."

Travis waved his hand. "Forget about it. I understand what you're going through."

"Me, too," Brock said softly.

Addison held out a card. "Just give it some thought, okay? We only want to help."

Evan took the card and thanked her.

Her smile was grim, as were all of theirs, but Juliet hoped that by following them all outside, she'd be able to smooth the waters a bit more.

She stepped out and closed the door behind her, waiting until they were all down on the driveway before she started speaking. "He's just really overwhelmed right now. I found him and Hope sleeping on the lounge chair on the porch. Apparently, that's the only way she would sleep last night. On his chest."

All their eyes turned sympathetic and understanding.

"I'm sure once he's given a bit more time to adjust to this new way of life and he and Hope get into a routine, he'll come around." She hoped. The music festival was a great idea. They had no idea what Tony and Jacqui had in the bank or whether they had life insurance. Eric was under the impression that they didn't, that they'd "planned" to but forgot.

Addison, a soft-spoken, kind woman that Juliet had only met a few times since being back in The Bay, nodded. "I appreciate that, Juliet."

Raleigh's eyes narrowed. "Are you and Evan—"

"Just friends," Juliet said quickly. "I was with him—getting coffee for the trio, I mean—not *with* with him—when he got the news about Tony.

He asked me to accompany him to Ridley Valley to collect Hope and her things. Then I popped in this morning on my way to work to check on them."

Coy smiles coasted across all of their faces.

"Did the trio get you drinks, too?" Brock asked, lifting his thick brows.

Juliet rolled her eyes and nodded. "Sure did. Had Eva throw in some of her spice cookies, too. They weren't *too* obvious," she said sarcastically.

"And you don't seem to mind?" Addison probed.

Juliet shrugged her shoulders, hoping her cavalier attitude was being bought by the people in front of her. "I mean, you don't believe in that *love spice* mumbo jumbo, do you?"

They all glanced at each other.

"We'll see where we are and where you're living this time next year," Travis said with a chuckle. "Those three know what they're doing."

She wasn't about to tell them that she actually *did* believe in the love spice and had doubled her chances by bringing Evan another café amour this morning.

She didn't want them thinking what Stella already knew—that she was still hopelessly in love with Evan Spencer and probably always would be.

The four people in front of her chuckled, waved, and headed to the black pickup truck. Brock swung in the driver's seat, and they all waved again as he backed down the grassy lane to the main road.

She didn't head back into the house until she saw the vehicle disappear.

A quick glance at her phone made her pulse jump. She was going to be late opening up the studio if she didn't get a move on.

Chapter Nine

I t was mid-June. Evan and Hope had been figuring out their new normal for a month now.

And what a time to create a new normal and try to "keep your cool" around a teething baby, then in subtropical temperatures.

If it wasn't for all the fans he had going in his cottage and the breeze off the water, they both would have melted for sure.

She was uncomfortable in the heat, and so was he.

He could understand her discomfort, having to wear a diaper all the time. Her poor butt was a hot box. But he'd grown up in this heat and yet it still got to him, even at thirty-four.

He'd also like to think that over the last four weeks, the two of them had fallen into a pretty awesome routine.

They woke up, had breakfast together, discussed world events—her position on global warming was fascinating—then before the heat of the day got *too* bad, he'd put her in the stroller and run down the beach.

After that, they'd return home, have a snack, and she'd play while he strummed his guitar and worked on a few new songs that had been flying around in his head.

She seemed to really like it when he played.

Then it was more food, followed by a nap—then they headed into town and visited people.

He had a standing date every Monday, Wednesday and Thursday with the trio. It was always in a different place, since those three were very busy, but he knew their schedule and met them where they told him to. Sometimes the visits weren't more than ten or fifteen minutes, but they always managed to sneak in some words of wisdom and a gentle *nudge* of a question about Juliet.

"What's the holdup?" Hattie had asked earlier that morning. "We thought for sure you two would be strolling hand in hand down The Boardwalk by now."

He chuckled awkwardly and rubbed the back of his neck.

Birdie tutted. "He hasn't told her how he feels yet, that's why."

"And why not?" Trixie asked, plopping a hand on her round hip.

Evan shrugged. He really didn't have a good answer, except for the fact that the month had flown by and he was spending all his time getting his footing when it came to Hope.

"You're not getting any younger," Hattie said.

Evan's eyebrows pinched together. "Thanks."

She was holding Hope but turned the baby outward and set her on her knee. "Now you tell Uncle Evan that he's being a procrastinating fool for not telling Juliet how he feels. That he's just wasting time."

"All right, that's enough," Evan said, swooping in and picking up Hope. He shook his head. Man, he knew these three were meddlesome, but did they have to rag on him about his love life? It was his business. His and Juliet's business.

He put Hope back in the stroller, shot the trio a confused and frustrated look, then continued on down The Boardwalk toward Top This.

Hope was his kindred spirit. They both loved mushroom pizza with alfredo sauce instead of marinara sauce. Of course, he gave her tiny little morsels, but she devoured them happily, her little limbs just a-going as he pulled off bite-size pieces for her.

After they shared a couple of slices, they made their way up a few blocks to Juliet's studio.

They popped into Kiln or be Kilned nearly every day, and the way Hope lit up when she saw Juliet's face was similar to the way Evan felt inside when he saw Juliet.

The trio was right. Things between them, however, hadn't progressed at all.

He was dragging his feet.

He hadn't asked her on a date, hadn't made a single move.

And she was getting more and more difficult to read.

Did she still have a thing for him after all these years? Or had her teenage crush come and gone like a fallen leaf on a gust of wind?

Many afternoons, he pushed the stroller to Brewed with a View, he and Hope shared a spiced scone, then they grabbed two café amours and headed over to Kiln or be Kilned.

It was weird how every time he showed up and Stella was there, she asked him, "Is that another café amour?" What was her beef with the drink?

He thought it was delicious, and so did Juliet.

When he would nod or say "Yes," Stella's mouth would break into a big grin. Even some pottery customers would snicker and whisper to each other.

He needed to ask Juliet what the deal with the drink was.

Was there some secret ingredient in it? Like a laxative? Or an illegal drug?

No!

Eva wouldn't be able to put the items on the menu if they had an illegal drug in it. Besides, he never felt loopy after he had the drink. Just satisfied, if not a little more attracted to Juliet, but that was probably just because he was itching to finally take her on a date. She was busy shaping her bowl on the wheel when he went there today, so he just set the drink down on the table and watched her, loving her serene smile as she sculpted. She caught him watching her and her smile grew, the twinkle in her green eyes reminding him of cut gems in the sunlight.

Yeah, he really needed to ask her out on a date.

Later that Friday afternoon, he was just getting home from a busy day around The Bay. Hope was asleep in her stroller, her rubber bunny clutched tight against her chest, and Evan was feeling good.

He could do this dad thing.

Sure, he and Hope had experienced their ups and downs. A few long nights, a lot of crying over teething, but now, a month later, they were running like a well-oiled if slightly poopy machine.

He needed to ask Juliet out.

It'd taken him about two weeks to call Addison Ford and agree to the music festival fundraiser. Juliet kept on him about it, as did his moms and Eric.

As they all suspected, Tony and Jacqui did not have life insurance. The forms had been filled out but never filed. In fact, they were sitting in an envelope on their counter ready to be mailed out, but they hadn't gotten the chance.

The sale of the house, vehicles and contents was proving to be a lot of work for Eric, since Ridley Valley was three hours away and he was also running his electrical company. Even so, no equity from their estate would go to Hope until the estate was out of probate, so they had to wait for that.

Evan wasn't worried about money, though. He made decent coin and had invested and bought stocks when his broker told him to. But he wanted to make damn sure that even if *he* lost every dime if the stock market suddenly crashed, Hope would still want for nothing. He'd popped into the bank and spoke with Marvin Brewster who walked him through setting up a life insurance policy. Now that he had a dependent, he needed to make provisions for her in case the worst happened—as it had to her parents.

A morbid thought, to orphan a child twice, but it could happen, so he needed to make sure that no matter what Hope would always be looked after.

After a trip to the bank, he stopped in and touched base with Addison Ford and how everything regarding the music festival was going.

Addison, ever the professional, told him not to worry about a thing, that she would take care of everything. That he just needed to show up with his singing voice and his guitar.

She did walk him through some of their plans though, which he appreciated. They walked around the property at The Factory and she pointed out where everything would go. They were going to set up a portable stage outside and hold the silent auction and put all the food stalls inside the Aggie Hall.

After a visit to The Factory, they swung into see Juliet and the way his heart kicked up when he saw her he knew that tonight had to be the night. He was going to tell her how he felt. That the crush was no longer one-sided.

Or maybe it was and she didn't feel anything for him anymore.

But even so, he wanted to tell her how much all her help and care meant to him and that ever since that night at his concert in Summerfield, he hadn't been able to get her out of his head. That she'd inspired him to write at least four new songs and his muse hadn't waned yet. He hoped by the end of the summer he'd be on his way to a full new album. The band hadn't released a new album in nearly three years. They'd been so busy touring that they hadn't had time.

It also didn't help that every new song Evan had tried to write over the last year had been garbage.

But not anymore, and it was because of Juliet.

Hope was asleep in the stroller again, so he rolled her onto the porch and plugged in an oscillating fan in front of her to keep her cool, then, leaving the door open, he went about cleaning his place.

He'd heard from his sister and Eric that once you had kids, your house was never clean again. But he'd never believed it.

Until now.

Not that Hope had a lot of stuff, but the stuff she did have was sprawled all over the place. Not to mention all the sticky hand- and fingerprints everywhere, since the now eleven-month-old was cruising around the furniture and trying desperately to walk.

He needed to think about baby-proofing the place. She'd be walking in no time, then she'd be into everything.

Were guitar picks something a baby could choke on?

He needed to make sure he didn't have any lying around.

After he gathered all of her toys from the living room and put them into a basket, he went about wiping down surfaces.

How did she manage to get jam *under* the kitchen table?

He was go-go-go for a solid hour when the ear-piercing scream of Hope from the deck made him drop the disinfectant spray bottle and scrubber onto the kitchen tile and run like he'd never run before out to the deck.

That was not a normal scream.

That wasn't like any scream he'd ever heard before.

Did the stroller fall over?

Did the fan tip into the stroller?

Had a bird landed on her stroller and was now pecking at her?

His brain went wild with ideas until he got to her and realized none of those things was happening. She'd just woken up.

He unbuckled her from her straps and held her against his chest. "Shh, I'm here. I'm here."

But unlike other times, there was no consoling her.

Her wail became even more intense now that he'd picked her up.

Something wasn't right.

He went through the checklist.

Diaper? Clean.

He offered her a bottle. She shoved it away.

She wasn't tired. She'd just woken up.

He soaked a baby washcloth in cold water and offered it to her for her gums. She tossed it on the floor.

Was she just bored? How long had she been awake in the stroller before she started to scream? Maybe she just needed to be entertained?

He set her down on the floor, picked up his guitar and started to play.

But not even that seemed to work.

Big, fat tears rolled down her round cheeks, cheeks that had grown red. She blinked spiked lashes over watery blue eyes and stared at him like he should know what was wrong and fix it already.

But he was out of ideas.

He didn't know how to help her.

"Mum mum mum!" she cried out, making him pause and nearly drop his guitar. "Mumma. Mum mum mum!"

It was like Hope had taken a broadsword and stabbed him through the heart with it. She was upset, inconsolable because she missed her mother. Her parents.

Of course, she still remembered them.

He'd be a fool to think four weeks with him would be able to erase ten months with Tony and Jacqui.

And he didn't even think that. He didn't want Hope to forget her parents. Not ever.

But she hadn't ever called out for them, and they'd fallen into a routine, so he just assumed she had accepted this as her new normal. As her new life.

She was still processing though. Still looking for her parents. Waiting for them to come back to her.

How could he tell an eleven-month-old that she was never going to hear her mother's voice again? Never going to smell her mother's scent or feel her mother and father's arms wrapped around her.

No wonder she was screaming.

She was screaming for them.

She missed them.

Guilt and pain brewed into a nauseating cocktail inside Evan's gut, and he sank to the floor, where Hope continued to wail. Her cries were a near tangible essence that wrapped around his heart and tugged until he thought she was going to rip it clean from his chest.

He tried to hug her. Rub her back, sing to her. But nothing worked.

She just kept crying, just kept repeating, "Mum mum mum."

"If I could take her place, I would in a heartbeat, peanut," he said softly, though she probably couldn't hear him. And definitely didn't understand what he was saying. "I'd give up my own life to bring your mama back to you. I wish she was here. I wish they were both here. What happened wasn't fair."

Tears burned his eyes, and he stroked the back of her head.

Then something clicked inside him.

Where was her rubber bunny?

She'd had it with her when he left her on the porch sleeping, but he didn't see it when he went to get her after she woke up.

Leaving her sitting on the floor, he got up and raced back outside.

The bunny was on the ground beside the stroller.

He snatched it up and took it to her, but not before taking a quick detour into the kitchen and washing it under the sink.

He handed it to her, but already her wails had turned into moans, and her tears weren't falling nearly as fast.

Had all of this fuss been about the rubber bunny?

She held it in front of her face, and he held his breath.

Please let this just be about the bunny. Please let this just be about the bunny.

Hope gnawed on the bunny's flexible ear for a moment, and just as Evan was about to exhale, she tossed it across the room and started crying all over again, calling out for her mama.

Juliet pulled up in front of Evan's cottage shortly after nine. She hadn't eaten anything, and her gut told her he hadn't either, so she'd ordered takeout from Shenanigans and picked it up on her way over. Two turkey burgers with onion rings on the side. She also swung into Bottles of Bliss, chatted for nearly half an hour with her old high school chum Joanna Miles—the owner—before buying a bottle of pineapple wine and heading home for a quick shower.

Every time she came over to Evan's, she made sure she was freshly showered and wearing nice clothes. She didn't want to remind him of the paint-covered teenager she'd once been. She hoped she'd either get the nerve to tell him how she felt or the love spice would kick in and he'd kiss her. And maybe more—hence the shower and freshly shaved legs.

With the wine in one hand and food in the other, she gently knocked on the front door.

There was no answer.

Was he putting Hope down?

The stroller was on the deck, so she didn't think they were in town.

Maybe down on the beach? Maybe on the back porch?

She made her way around the side of the house, her cork wedges making a clunking noise against the old wooden planks.

The black cotton wrap dress with the ruffled shoulders hit her shins as she moved. Stella had convinced her to buy the dress a few weeks ago.

She rounded the corner to the back portion of the porch, and if she hadn't been looking at the lounge chairs since she'd found them there once before, she would have missed him.

Only this time, he was alone.

Well, besides the bottle of beer he was holding by the neck.

The energy around him was unnerving.

Not frightening, but she could tell something was wrong.

Something was eating away at him.

His face was tight, his eyes laser-focused straight ahead. A muscle ticked in his jaw.

The sliding glass door was open, but the screen was pulled so no bugs could get in.

"Hope asleep?" she asked.

He nodded and tipped the beer up to his lips.

She opened the screen, walked in and set dinner and the bottle of wine on the table before heading back out to the porch.

She didn't bother to ask and just slid onto the end of the lounge chair, facing him.

He didn't make eye contact with her but continued to stare out at the sea and the shorebirds tittering along the surf.

"How many beers have you had?" she asked cautiously. She'd never been around Evan drunk, and based on the vibe he was throwing off, she wasn't sure if she should stay or go. But she also wasn't sure that she should leave Hope with him if he was drunk.

"One," he said, his voice hoarse. He lifted the bottle up. "Just this one."

Phew.

She lifted her eyes from the bottle to his face, and that's when she saw the tear hidden along the crease of his nose.

He'd been crying.

Thinking about Tony?

Probably.

"I brought dinner," she whispered. "I can put it in the fridge if you've already eaten. I wasn't sure—"

He lunged forward, grabbed her by the back of the head with his free hand and crushed his mouth to hers.

Everything inside her exploded.

Her brain didn't know what was happening.

Was this a dream? She'd surely had enough dreams in her life about kissing Evan Spencer that she could understand if her brain was unable to distinguish fact from fiction.

But this here was not fiction. It was no dream.

Not even dream men kissed this good.

This kiss was the real deal.

Evan Spencer, the man she'd loved since she was eleven years old, was kissing her.

And the man could kiss.

Boy, oh boy, could he kiss.

Her body rioted, trying to figure out just what was happening. *Evan's kissing you, you idiot.* She opened her eyes and pulled away.

Why did you pull away?

"Evan, I ..." With her fingertips, she touched her lips. They still buzzed from his kiss.

"I have feelings for you, Jules. Even when I didn't know who you were, just a girl at the concert, I couldn't get you out of my head. Still can't." His throat moved. "I had no idea you ..."

She smiled and stared down at the cushion of the lounge chair; her cheeks were probably splashed with pink. "Had a giant crush on you for five years? Yeah, I kind of figured you had no idea."

He cupped the back of her head again and ran his big, strong thumb over her cheek. "Had I known ..."

She scoffed. "I was Eric's dorky, paint-covered, brace-faced little sister. Had you known, you probably would have done nothing about it because I was"—she shrugged—"I was who I was back then."

He shook his head. "You don't know that. And who you were back then wasn't dorky. I was just caught up in my own shit."

That dragged a smile from her. "Yeah, you were."

He snorted a laugh, and she lifted her gaze up to his eyes. "You've been incredible through all of this. Helped me so much, *taught* me so much. Hell, since I saw you at the concert, I've been hit by inspiration. I'm writing songs again, and I haven't written a decent song, a song I was willing to take to my band, in over a year."

He was writing songs about her?

About *her*?

"When I came into the studio a month ago, on the day we—"

She nodded. "Yeah. That day."

"Yeah, that day. I was going to ask you out. But then life ..."

"Went sideways."

"Boy, did it ever. And I procrastinated. I wanted to get things right with Hope. Get a handle on my grief but ..." He set his beer between his legs and reached for her hand with his free one. "But grief doesn't just disappear, and after the day I had today with Hope, I don't know if things will ever be right."

Oh no! What happened with Hope? Was she okay?

"What happened?" she asked.

He shook his head. "I couldn't console her. Couldn't get her to stop crying. I tried everything."

Oh. Poor Evan. Poor Hope.

His frown made her chest hurt. "I just know that, when I'm with you, I'm happier. I don't hurt so much about Tony, and I feel more capable with Hope. Even if you're not helping with her, your presence gives me strength."

She'd never had a man open up like this to her before. Never knew Evan to be such a talker. But then again, he was an artist. A musician. Musicians, particularly those who wrote their own songs, and the kinds of songs that Evan sang, poured their feelings into their lyrics. He knew how to say them in a way that made sense and properly tugged at the strings of her heart. Because boy, were they tugging.

He pressed their palms together and spread her fingers with his, prying them apart and then squeezing.

"I'm sorry I didn't notice you back then. Or recognize you at the concert ... or even the beach." His head shook. "God, I'm a tool."

An adorable, oblivious tool, though.

She chuckled to herself, and rather than agree with him, she shook her head. "We were all a little wrapped up in ourselves as teenagers. I think it's just a rite of passage."

"Have I lost my chance? No more crush on your brother's best friend?" His boyish, lopsided smile made her heart sing and dance and do a little twirl. Butterflies took flight in her belly, and her lips still tingled from that kiss.

She brought her gaze down to their intertwined fingers for a moment and how his big hand engulfed hers. His fingertips were calloused from playing the guitar, but she didn't mind. She actually kind of liked it. Lifting her head, she bit the corner of her bottom lip. "Maybe kiss me again and we'll see if we can reignite that crush. I'm sure it's still in there somewhere."

His smile was electric, and he grabbed the back of her head and pulled her close, claiming her mouth yet again.

Their tongues tangled and tangoed. He led the kiss, and she followed along, keeping up and tilting her head when she needed to, sucking on his tongue and moaning when he bit her lip.

She was in heaven.

Finally, at long last, she was making out with Evan Spencer.

Where were a closet and a bunch of friends on the other side with a stopwatch, making sure they locked lips for at least seven minutes?

Heat radiated through her and down between her legs.

Her breathing grew ragged, and her need for this man, her long, *long-awaited* need for him, began to grow fierce inside her. If she had her way, she'd rip off his clothes right there.

This was fifteen years in the making. Fifteen years of pining, of crushing, of dreaming, and the way he held her—with such ferocious need, a need that mirrored her own—only added fuel to the fire that burned hot inside her.

When he broke the kiss, they were both panting wildly.

His gaze was hooded, his lips puffy.

"I wanted to take you on a date," he said, almost out of breath. "Do this the right way."

She shook her head, her chest heaving. "The right way would have been you noticing me back when we were in high school and asking me to prom. Spinning me around the dance floor in front of our peers. The *new* right way is us going to your room."

His eyes widened. "Jules ..."

"Evan," she said, the warning to not make her beg hopefully evident in her tone.

Resolution shimmered in his brown eyes, and he helped her stand up, then stood up himself, and before he was even fully upright, she had him by the neck and was kissing him again.

He didn't fight it.

He grabbed her by the waist and kissed her back, guiding her over the threshold of the sliding door and through the house, their lips never unlocking, unless it was to shed clothing like breadcrumbs through the house.

His tongue made possessive sweeps through her mouth, and his hands roamed her body, cradling her frame against his, making her feel safe and desired.

By the time they got to his room, she was in nothing but her black bra and panties and he was in the same boxer briefs he'd worn in the hotel room. The same pair that left very little to the imagination, and this time, there was even less left to the imagination. His need for her pressed into her inner thigh as he spun them around and lowered her down to the bed.

Heat and need swirled in his eyes, the gold flecks in his irises muted by the lack of light in the room. But it didn't matter. She knew what his eyes looked like. Knew every gold speck, every swirl. She'd stared into those eyes, imagined them looking back at her with the need he looked at her with now, for years. And then when she was at art school and he was off living his dream, she'd look into those eyes again when she brought up pictures of his band and their concerts online.

She knew those eyes, the masculine planes of his face and the scar on his chin from when he fell off her parents' roof, like a roadmap home.

He cupped her breast with his big, warm palm and kneaded, pulling a groan from the back of her throat when he tugged the bra cup down and gently pinched her nipple.

She sucked in a breath and smiled into their kiss, her hips lifting in search of more friction.

Her fingers grazed down his muscular back, his skin smooth to the touch. She'd dreamed of this. Imagined countless times what it would be like to kiss Evan. To feel his weight on top of her. To touch his skin in such a way, feel the gooseflesh rise and his muscles bunch and flex.

But reality was so much better than the dream.

The scent of him, manly and slightly salty from the day, along with the beer on his breath—it made her pulse pick up and her body tingle.

He broke their kiss and dipped his head low, wrapping his lips around one of her nipples and gently sucking. Her back bowed, and she pushed her breast against his face, closing her eyes and biting her lip as he drew the tight peak deeper into his mouth and flicked it with his tongue.

Her hands continued to explore his body, her fingers committing every inch of him to memory. She reached the elastic waistband of his boxers and tried to shove them down. She was anxious. Needy for more.

This wasn't *just* happening.

For Juliet, this was fifteen years in the making.

Releasing her nipple, he lifted his head. His eyelids were at half-mast, and his pupils were dilated.

She swallowed.

He swallowed.

His eyes never left hers.

A small, mischievous smile curled one side of her mouth, and she reached for the front of the waistband of his boxers and tugged.

His gaze flicked to his nightstand, and he stood up and leaned over, opening the drawer and grabbing a condom packet.

"Jules," he said, standing in front of her with a circus tent for underwear and a weary look in his eyes, "you're sure?"

Lifting her eyebrow at him, she twisted on the bed, unhooked her bra and tossed it at him, then she shimmied out of her panties and tossed those at him, too.

Then there she was, completely naked in front of a man she'd loved for half her life. "Does that answer your question?" she asked with a small but playful smile.

"Guess it does," he said, returning her grin. "But first ..." He sank down to a crouch on the floor, spread her legs apart where they draped over the side of the bed, and he put his mouth on her.

Juliet's hips shot off the bed, and her hands fell to his head, where she gripped his hair.

"Oh God," she cried when he swept his tongue across her clit.

This was better than she'd ever imagined.

Evan was better in every single way.

Even though she tapped him on the head several times, the man refused to quit until his mouth and two of his fingers inside her brought her to the most glorious, soul-shattering climax of her life.

She was panting, boneless and still seeing stars when he swept his hand across his mouth and levered himself over her.

She hadn't even been paying attention, but he'd ditched his boxers and sheathed himself in the condom. She glanced down between them where his erection bobbed heavily, and she could have sworn her wildly beating heart skipped a beat.

His mouth dropped to hers, and his tongue swept inside.

She tasted herself and beer on his lips, but all it did was turn her on even more.

Bending her knees and planting her feet on the mattress, she reached between their bodies, took him in her palm and guided him home.

When he slid inside her, fully seated, they both paused. He broke the kiss, and she opened her eyes wide.

Evan was staring down at her.

Evan Spencer was inside her.

It was so surreal.

"This isn't just sex, Jules," he said softly. "I care about you. I want you ... I want *us*."

I want us.

She wasn't expecting him to profess his undying love for her.

This wasn't a star-crossed mutual unrequited love kind of deal. Just because she'd been madly in love with him for fifteen years didn't mean he felt the same. But wanting an *us* was a start.

"I want *us*, too," she said, blinking up at him.

He smiled that smile she would never forget, would never tire of. "You mean you still have a crush on me?"

Even with him inside her, his weight on her, she shrugged and twisted her mouth. "I mean ... maybe a little."

His grin just grew wider, cockier, and more handsome. "I can work with a little."

She wiggled beneath him. "Doesn't *feel* little."

That made him toss his head back and laugh, giving her a glimpse of his straight, white teeth and those creases around his eyes when he really allowed himself to smile to his fullest. She hadn't seen a lot of those smiles in the past month—which was understandable—but seeing it now made her chest constrict.

His brown gaze settled on her again, and his expression turned serious, avid and aroused. "I want you, Juliet."

She reached for him, wrapped her hands around his neck and pulled him down to her until his mouth hovered just over hers. When their lips were just a hair's breadth apart, she whispered, "And I've wanted you forever, Evan." Then she kissed him, lifted her hips, and he started to move.

To say that sex with Evan was everything that it was cracked up to be would be the understatement of the millennium.

The man had moves.

The man had stamina.

The man had a body that drove her absolutely wild.

And when he grabbed her wrists, held them above her head with one of his big hands and moved his hips in that oh-so-wonderful way, Juliet was pretty sure she heard a few angels singing somewhere.

His lips were like velvet as they caressed her skin, and he peppered hot kisses across her collarbone and neck. His teeth knew just how hard to scrape to push her closer to the edge.

For their first time together, their bodies moved in sync, and when she wrapped her legs around his hips and he drove into her harder, faster and deeper, she knew she wasn't going to last much longer.

He stilled, and then they barely moved, but somehow, some way, the pleasure inside her intensified to almost unbearable heights. She squirmed and wriggled beneath him, moaned out as his subtle hip tilts drove her mad with need, pushed her so close to the edge she was teetering, windmilling her arms to keep from falling over the cliff.

What was he doing to her?

Why did it all feel so good?

Evan lifted his head from where he'd been laving at a nipple, and he once again bored into her with those soulful brown eyes.

Neither of them said a word.

They didn't have to.

Their bodies were doing all the talking.

Speaking a language as old as time.

He lifted his hips, hovered, and her eyes went wide. His grin was salacious. He knew exactly what he was doing.

She drew in a shaky breath and stared up at him as he slowly, torturously so, dropped his hips again and slid back inside.

She shattered.

Squeezing her eyes shut, Juliet pushed her head back into the bed and tilted her chin to the ceiling as the orgasm took hold of her body and the waves of ecstasy consumed her.

Evan's mouth dropped to her neck, where he nipped and licked.

He paused his movements for a moment, stiffened and exhaled hard against her bare, sweat-misted skin, finding his own release as she rode out her own.

She threaded her fingers into his hair and tugged, lifting his head from the crook of her neck and taking his mouth. Ragged pants came out of his nose, and she felt every warm puff against her upper lip as she swept her tongue into his mouth and challenged his to a duel. She wanted to ride this high, this decadent feeling of pure bliss for as long as she could. The feeling of being one with Evan.

Finally.

At long last.

But all good things must come to an end eventually, and when his orgasm ended, he broke their kiss and lifted his head to look at her.

She opened her eyes, and what greeted her made her heart soar.

He was smiling.

But it was an Evan smile she'd never seen before.

And this Evan smile made her tingly all over. It made her want to run into the streets and sing and dance and shout from the rooftops how madly in love she was with this man.

It wasn't cocky. It wasn't arrogant. It wasn't even a contented smile.

It was boyish, maybe even a little relieved, and there was definitely a whole lot of affection in those eyes.

"Jules?" he said, his throat moving on a swallow.

"Yeah?"

"I'm really sorry I didn't *see* you sooner."

She blinked a few times and smiled shyly.

"But I see you now."

Chapter Ten

S till naked but now lying the proper way in bed and under the covers, Evan kissed the back of Juliet's hand, keeping their fingers intertwined. "Stay the night?"

"I'll have to leave extra early in the morning to run home and grab work clothes," she said tossing him some side-eye but adding a gorgeous smile along with it.

"I'll set my alarm so you're not late for work."

"Thank you. The boss is a complete tyrant, and if I'm even a minute late, she'll have my hide."

He kissed her hand again, then opened his mouth wide and pretended to bite her. "Cheeky."

Her smile wobbled for a moment, and she turned onto her side. "What happened with Hope?"

Sighing, he ran his thumb over the back of her hand, then lifted his gaze to hers. "She kept crying out for Jacqui. Kept screaming, 'mum mum mum mum,' and no matter what I tried, I couldn't console her."

"But you did eventually, right? I mean she fell asleep."

He nodded. "She fell asleep crying. I'm sure she'll wake up tonight starving since I couldn't get any food into her. She just cried and cried and cried. It was gutting." He released her hand then flipped over onto his back and tucked his hands behind his head. "And here I thought we were getting into a routine. That we'd finally found our footing."

He couldn't see her face, but he heard her sigh. She reached out and rested a delicate, long-fingered hand on his chest. "And you have, and you will continue to get into a routine and continue to find your footing. She's eleven months old. She's got a lot of change and development ahead of her—and so do you. You've been thrown into this parenting without a manual. But she's still a baby, and I can tell by the way Hope looks at you that she loves you. That she trusts you."

His hand landed on hers, and he glanced at her. "I just felt like I failed her today."

She shook her head. "You stuck around. You stayed with her, let her know that no matter how hard she screamed, how upset and sad she was, that you weren't going anywhere. She felt safe enough to feel that pain and miss her parents. You're doing an amazing job with her, Evan, truly."

"I still don't understand why Tony and Jacqui thought that *I* was a good choice as a guardian for Hope."

"Well, you're not blowing the job, so I'd say they were spot-on in their decision."

That pulled a smile from him, and he brought the back of her hand up to his mouth again.

Her smile was small, but encouraging. "It'll get easier. Then harder. Then easier. Then harder. Then way harder. Then crazy-hard, then easier again. Then harder and so on and so forth until she's an adult and you hopefully have raised her right. Then you can become friends. Or at least that's what my mom told Isla and Eric after they had Ruby and neither of them had slept in three days. You don't have kids to be friends with them. You just cross your fingers that by the time they're old enough, that you've raised them to be someone you'd *like* to be friends with."

The difference here, though, was that Evan didn't *have* Hope. He was supposed to be the cool uncle who flew in with presents and wild stories. Who took her backstage to her first concert and introduced her to her favorite musician, then put her in a limo home before he went back to the after-party. Because no way in HELL would he let Hope go to a concert after-party.

But he kept those thoughts to himself and merely smiled down at Juliet. "Thank you. I guess I just figured that once we got the hang of things, we'd have the hang of things for good."

She chuckled a sexy, throaty laugh that stirred all kinds of things between his legs. "I'm pretty sure parents of like ten kids will tell you even they don't 'have the hang of things' come baby number ten. You just learn how to adapt. You learn their tells, and then you improvise until something clicks."

Evan sucked in a deep breath through his nose, making his chest lift. "Well, nothing clicked tonight. She fell asleep on me, soaked the shoulder of my shirt with her little tears. Then I put her down, and she's been out ever since."

"You were there for her, and that's what matters."

"I hope you're right."

She drew her bottom lip into her mouth with her top teeth and gazed up at him with a look he couldn't quite place. He recognized the glimmer of arousal—that was evident—but there was also curiosity there, too, perhaps even a bit of bewilderment.

She had him intrigued. What was she thinking? What was she planning?

"Can we, um ... can we talk about that *thing* you did earlier?" she asked, her words coming out just a touch shaky.

He furrowed his brow. What *thing?* "Huh?"

"You know ... that *thing*. Where you like almost stopped moving completely and yet everything just suddenly felt like a trillion million times more amazing than it had a second before. What was that? I have never experienced that before."

Call him conceited, but what man on the planet would be able to hold in his cocky smile after a question like that?

Certainly not Evan.

And his smile caused her to roll her pretty green eyes and swat his chest, which only made him smile even more.

"Come on, what was that?" she asked, attempting to be serious.

He looked down at her and picked up a lock of her hair, holding it between his thumb and finger. She really was the most incredible, most gorgeous thing he'd ever seen. And in his opinion, she hadn't changed that much from high school. How had he not noticed her before? "It's this thing called grinding the corn."

"Grinding the what now?" she asked, sitting up, which caused her silky hair to slip from his fingers.

Now it was his turn to roll his eyes. "It focuses on getting you there, just put it that way. You're welcome to google it." He reached for his phone on the nightstand and handed it to her.

She shook her head and sank back down into the bed. "That's not a great name."

"I think it's also called the coital alignment technique. But to me that sounds so technical. Meanwhile, I'd like to think we created enough heat and friction to pop a pan of Jiffy Pop." With a growl, he rolled on top of her. "Or at least, I'm pretty sure we could get there."

Her legs spread, and he settled between them. He was already hard again.

Juliet looped her arms around his neck and grinned up at him. "I did bring burgers from Shenanigan's, you know. They're probably cold by now."

"Onion rings, too?"

She nodded.

He groaned. "Oh man. Okay, first we make Jiffy Pop, then we go eat burgers and onion rings on the deck. Deal?"

"Deal!" Then she pulled his head down, and he claimed her mouth like he owned it, because now, he did. Jules was his, and no way was he letting her go.

It was late June now, and the Pirate Festival in Cinnamon Bay was in full swing. Locals and tourists alike raced around town, ducking into participating shops to grab scavenger hunt clues, designed as rolled-up book pages tied in jute, that would lead them to the coveted prize.

Of course, Juliet participated, but she kept a bowl of clues—she was clue number eleven—at the front of the studio so that if she was with a customer or had her hands caked in clay, she didn't have to worry about making the participants wait.

Every year, Cinnamon Bay hosted the Pirate Festival in honor of the legend—Captain Lionheart DeVane. There was live music, skits and entertainment at the bandstand down on the beach in the evenings, along with a potluck dinner.

The studio was busy, which made sense since it was the weekend and the town was packed to the brim with tourists. It seemed everyone within a hundred-mile radius had heard about Kiln or be Kilned and wanted to try their hand at painting their own garden gnome or throwing some clay and hand-sculpting a mug. The "to be fired" shelves were overflowing, and they had to clear space on the counter for more pieces that were in the queue for the kiln.

Business was booming. Which meant Juliet was happy.

Oh, and Juliet and Evan's romance was *booming* too—which meant Juliet was ecstatic. One might go as far as to say that their relationship was all-consuming. Spectacular would be another accurate description. In essence, it was everything she'd ever dreamed it could be.

The sex ... don't get her started on the sex. She'd never had her world rocked so thoroughly in all her life, and to have it rocked by a rock star was just icing on the love spice cake.

Had the spice helped?

They'd certainly consumed enough of it together that it probably had some effect on Evan finally seeing her as more than just Eric's little sister.

Did the effect of the spice wear off then? Did she have to keep pumping it into his veins to keep the affection there? He seemed to like the drink as well and brought her one at the studio several times a week.

She hated the notion that a legend and a few ingredients thrown into a drink were all that made Evan see her differently—see her at all. Joanna at Bottles of Bliss said that many a Cinnamon Bay couple had sipped or eaten the love spice and were happy as could be. Including Eva and her man Mac.

But then, Eva and Mac ran the café, so they were always consuming the spice, right?

She shook the idea clean out of her head.

She needed to believe that it wasn't *just* the spice that made him see her for who she really was. That he saw her for her, liked her for her, because at long last, Evan Spencer had opened his eyes.

Outside the studio, teams ran around as part of the scavenger hunt, all dressed as pirates with eye patches, stripes and ruffles.

By the time the day was over, they'd all have some pretty healthy appetites.

She already knew her mom's seafood lasagna would be at the potluck—with a dash of cinnamon in it, since everything at the potluck had to have cinnamon in it. The thought of the bechamel sauce and lobster made her belly rumble. Juliet herself planned to bring a bunch of deviled eggs—with the most modest sprinkle of cinnamon—that she made last night and had stored in Evan's fridge since she'd spent the night at his cottage. It was where she spent most nights these days.

She left work, ran home, showered, changed and headed to Evan's around nine. They fell into bed, and there they stayed, talking, laughing and making love until she fell asleep with her head on his shoulder and his arm wrapped around her.

It was just like she'd dreamed. Just like how she'd imagined a life, a romance with Evan Spencer would be.

Then, in the morning, they'd wake up, have breakfast with Hope, and off to work she would go.

She never thought domestic bliss could be so ... blissful.

She was just ringing up another happy customer who'd come in and painted Old Blaze, the lighthouse, on a platter when the bell for the front door chimed. "Clue is in the bowl," she called out.

"Take your time. We don't mind waiting," the person replied. Only it wasn't just any person. It was Evan, and the moment she heard his voice, her pulse picked up the tempo, her heart did a little *thump-thump* in her chest, and she felt her cheeks get warm.

Even though they'd technically been together for almost two weeks now, the excitement she got from her *boyfriend* coming to visit her at work hadn't diminished at all. If anything, it had intensified.

She lifted her head from where she'd been putting Mrs. Bentley's platter into a reusable fabric shopping bag and smiled at Evan as he wheeled Hope through the studio toward her.

Mrs. Bentley said goodbye and happily took her new platter out the door and down the sidewalk. But Juliet's attention was no longer on her happy customer. It was on the man only five feet from her with lips so kissable, she was struggling not to lunge at him and plant a big sloppy one on his face.

They'd moved Hope out of her car seat adapter rear-facing stroller, and now she was forward-facing. The little girl loved how much more of the big world she could see now. Her blue eyes were wide open and limbs just flapping with delight.

"And to what do I owe the pleasure?" Juliet asked, stepping forward, pressing her hand to Evan's hard chest, lifting up on her tiptoes and brushing her lips across his. A thrill raced through her that she could actually do that now. That she could actually walk up to Evan Spencer and kiss him—and he wouldn't think it was weird in the least.

"Just came to say *hi*," he said, wrapping an arm around her waist. "But also, my moms mentioned to me that Hope's birthday is coming up in a week—she's a July Fourth baby, wouldn't you know it. So I'm wondering if we should throw her a birthday party. What do you think?"

"I think it's a fantastic idea."

He beamed. "Good. I was also wondering if we could do like a footprint or handprint thing for her to, you know, commemorate her first birthday. It might be kind of cool if we could do something like that every year." He sighed, then made a scrunched-up face that she recognized as self-doubt. It was a face she made a lot growing up. "Unless you think that's a stupid idea? I'm so lost. I don't want her to have nothing to look back on, to think she didn't have a childhood, because her uncle slash dad slash guardian or whatever I am couldn't get his shit together and do the things that normal parents do to make memories and mementos for their kids." He shoved his fingers into his hair and glanced at her with a helpless look. "What do you think?"

She rubbed his back affectionately—because she could do that, too, now that they were dating. "I think it's a fantastic idea. And I have just the thing."

He blew out a breath and glanced down at Hope. "See, once in a while Uncle Ev has some good ideas."

Chuckling, Juliet wandered behind the counter and pulled out what to the average person would look like a six-inch subway tile. It had only been fired once, so when they put any paint and a glaze on it, it'd need to be fired again.

"Let's paint her little tootsie, press it onto the tile, date it and then fire it. We can do one every year, and then I have these really cool wooden frames—they hold twelve of these tiles—and you glue the tiles in and it'd make a neat art feature on a wall. What do you think?"

He grinned at her. "I knew we came to the right place."

Sticking her tongue out at him, she wandered over to the wall of paint bottles and grabbed a turquoise bottle.

He gathered Hope out of her stroller. She was happily gnawing away on a baby rice cracker and didn't have any issues with her soft, barefoot being shoved into a sloppy, cold puddle of paint.

But that wasn't where the challenge lay.

Oh no.

After doing over a thousand handprints and footprints over Christmas last year, Juliet and her staff had quickly realized that kids didn't so much hate putting their hands and feet in cold paint—well, some did, and they screamed their faces off—but most of the time, once the paint was on, they either made little fists that were almost impossible to pry open or scrunched their toes up so tight it made any kind of artistic print damn near impossible.

But Juliet had learned a trick quick. She grabbed a paintbrush, turned it around so that the pointy end was sticking toward Hope's feet, then she ran the tip of it up the middle of her foot from her heel to her middle toe.

The baby instantly unclenched her toes and splayed them out.

Juliet was Olympic-runner-fast, and she grabbed the tile and pressed it to Hope's foot before the little nugget had time to re-clench her Jelly-Belly-size toes.

"You've perfected your craft, Ms. Clarkson," Evan said adoringly. "I never would have thought of that."

She held up a nearly perfect but slightly smudgy baby footprint. "I did close to seven hundred baby footprints and over three hundred handprints last Christmas. If I'm not an expert at getting kids to unclench their fists and toes by now, then I shouldn't be running this studio."

He gave her a thumbs-up and accepted the baby wipes she gave him to clean off Hope's foot. He put her back in the stroller and handed her another rice cracker while Juliet went about writing Hope's name and all her birthday details on the tile.

Once she was finished, she put it in the "to be fired" queue and turned back to her man. "Taking in the festivities today?"

He lifted his brows and blew out a breath that had made his cheeks puff up. "And then some. This Pirate Festival thing is crazy. People really get into it. Costumes and everything."

"Why not embrace it all than just go half-assed, hmm?"

He did a quick glance around the studio before closing the space between them. Her belly did another little flip-flop, and her heart thumped hard. Even though the studio was busy, everyone was in their own little artistic world. Nobody was paying them any attention.

And Juliet entirely understood.

When she was in the zone, either on the wheel making a new bowl or vase or standing in front of a canvas with inspiration coming out of her pores, she barely acknowledged the world around her.

The room could be on fire, and if she was in the zone, she probably wouldn't even be able to smell the smoke.

"Listen," he started, looping his arms around her waist.

She tilted her head up to look into those beautiful brown eyes. "I'm listening."

"I still haven't taken you on a proper date, you know. And that feels wrong."

She twisted her lips and glanced away. "It's okay. I get that your life is sort of upside down right now. We don't have to do dinner and a movie to be dating. Things are different these days."

"But some things shouldn't change. Like taking a girl—nay, a *woman*—you like out on a date. My parents have agreed to watch Hope tonight so that after the festival we can go on a date. What do you say?"

Evan Spencer was asking her out?

Evan Spencer was asking her out!

She lifted one shoulder. "I mean, are we going Dutch or ... I need to know if I need to run to the ATM and take out cash." She stuck her tongue out at him. "This is so last-minute. I seem to remember a book called *The Rules* that said you should never accept a weekend date after Wednesday. Now, what kind of woman would I be if I—"

But he didn't let her finish. He swooped in and took her mouth, shut her up and made her moan.

She wrapped her arms around his neck and pressed her body against his, lifting up onto her tiptoes and deepening the kiss.

A throat cleared behind them, but Juliet barely heard it for the roaring of her pulse in her ears.

But Evan heard it, and he broke their lip lock and loosened his grip on her.

They turned to face whoever was pooping on their makeout party.

It was only Stella.

Juliet had almost forgotten that her friend was even in the studio. She'd been over on the other side of the room and around the corner helping some tourists from Long Island with their stenciling.

"Hey, Stel," Evan said, releasing Juliet's hip but only with one hand so that she could turn and face Stella. Her hip knocked Evan's.

"This is a place of business, you two. All *flippant fornication*, as Birdie calls it, must be done in the storage closet. Come on, now, be respectful." The twinkle in her dark brown eyes was there the whole time, but she managed to keep a straight face until one of the patrons snorted at her joke, then a smile cracked her serious veneer.

Stella walked past Evan and swatted his shoulder. "About time you woke up and smelled the acrylic, man. I was telling Juliet for years to tell you how she felt."

Juliet shot her best friend a look that said, "Shut up."

But either Stella was truly oblivious or she was pretending she didn't notice. Or she didn't care and was going to flap her gums anyway.

"Yeah, well, we all make mistakes when we're young and stupid," Evan said, squeezing Juliet tighter against him. "But I've learned from them." He kissed Juliet on the side of the head. "And I won't make them again."

Stella lifted a brow at him. "You've got to convince the BFF, though, buddy. And right now, I still think you're a flight risk."

Juliet's head whipped around from where she'd been making faces at Hope to stare at her friend. If she had a hard candy or gum in her mouth, she would have choked on it.

Where on earth did Stella get off?

"Ummm ..." Evan said, glancing at Juliet, then back to Stella. Juliet could see his cheeks getting red beneath his scruff.

"Stella!" she said, releasing her hold on Evan and plopping her hands on her hips.

But Stella wasn't backing down. She'd never been the type to stir up shit, but she also never threw in the towel and shied away from confrontation or standing up for what she believed in.

Juliet just wished Stella had brought her concerns about Juliet's relationship with Evan to her privately rather than bombarded Evan with them and announced them to a studio full of people. What did she mean Evan was a *flight risk?*

Did she think he was going to do a midnight run? Leave Hope with Juliet and take off to go travel the world and play music? Avoid responsibility?

Juliet glared at her friend, but Stella ignored her.

"I like you, Evan. I always have," Stella went on. "But I also watched my best friend pine after you for five years, and you didn't so much as smile her way, let alone take notice. And then you didn't even recognize her at the concert, even after you looked RIGHT at her when we were being accosted by those Summerfield guys. I mean, I always knew you were a bit oblivious, but ..."

"You don't think people can change?" Juliet asked.

"I do," Stella said with an innocent nod. "And I'm not saying that I don't support this union. Because I do. But Evan needs to figure out what he wants and where he wants to be. Have you guys thought about what happens when the summer bubble pops?"

Juliet stalked over to her friend, grabbed her by the shirt sleeve and hauled her toward the employees-only section.

"What the hell?" she said with a hiss, glaring down her nose at Stella.

"I'm just looking out for you, Jules. Have you thought about what happens when the summer is over? Is he planning to go back on tour? Move back to wherever it is he called home before coming back here? Is he going to move to Cinnamon Bay for good? Get a proper place for him and Hope? What's he doing with Hope if he doesn't stay in Cinnamon Bay? Can a rock star be a single dad, too? I know they fabricate that shit in romance novels, but we're living in the real world here. Have you guys thought past the end of August, or are you all caught up in orgasmic bliss?"

Juliet didn't have an answer for any of those questions, and it just made her all the more frustrated with her friend.

Why was Stella popping their love bubble?

Because she's your best friend and looking out for you.

Yeah, well ...

Stella rested a hand on Juliet's shoulder. "I'm just asking the questions that I think the two of you should be asking yourselves and each other. I'm sorry if I overstepped, but ..." She shrugged. She wasn't really sorry.

Juliet glanced back out into the studio. Evan was twisting the cap off one of those applesauce squeeze pouches for Hope and handing it to her. How easily he'd fallen into the role of dad made her body pulse and her lady parts tingle.

Hell, the man just had to look at her—or not even look at her—and her lady parts would start to tingle.

Stella's hand on her shoulder squeezed, drawing Juliet back to her friend. "Just talk to each other. I know this is new, but it's not a normal summer romance. There's a baby involved, and he's said from the beginning that he's just here for the summer. I don't want to see you get hurt. To see you get crushed by the man you crushed over for years. It's one thing to help you pick up the pieces of your broken teenage heart over unrequited love. It's another thing to try to help you pick up those fragments when you're thirty-one and the whole reason your heart is broken in the first place was that you two never bothered to discuss anything."

Juliet understood where her friend was coming from. More than once, Stella had been there handing Juliet the tissues when Evan would have a girlfriend in high school, or Eric would come home saying he wasn't going out with Evan that night because his friend had a date.

Juliet would then run up to her room and cry into her pillow.

Stupid, yes. She knew that now.

But tell that to a hormonal teenager who was sure that Evan Spencer was the man she was supposed to marry and grow old with. She'd doodled his name all over the inside of her binder, for goodness' sake.

Along with more than a few scribbles of "Mrs. Juliet Spencer." Yeah, she was that lame. That head over heels.

"I get where you're coming from," Juliet said to Stella, most of the rancor gone from her tone. "But next time, maybe address us in private and *not* in my place of business."

Now Stella actually did manage to look remorseful. "Duly noted."

Juliet smiled at her friend, thanked her for her concern, then turned to walk back to Evan. He was near the front door though.

What?

She raced through the studio to catch him, the pencil that held up her hair coming loose and causing strands to fall around her face. "Where are you going?" she asked, stopping in front of the stroller and tucking hair behind her ears.

Evan's expression was grim, and her heart instantly sank. Oh no! He was thinking about what Stella had said, too. Not even two full weeks in, and their love bubble had officially popped. "Hope's diaper needs changing, and I don't have any more in the diaper bag. I could have sworn I filled it up last night."

She wasn't sure if he was telling the truth. Maybe he was but he was just using it all as an excuse to get out of there.

Nodding because she didn't want to come across as desperate and needy, she stepped out of the way. "I'll see you at the potluck tonight? Remember to bring my deviled eggs, please."

He nodded, the look on his face still making her insides get all twisty. "Sure thing."

She glanced down at Hope, said goodbye and held the door open for him so he could push the stroller through. Then she watched Evan walk down the sidewalk and out of view, taking a piece of her heart with him.

Chapter Eleven

Where did Stella get off?

She's looking out for her friend. And she's not wrong.

Evan had a full conversation with himself as he pushed Hope in the stroller home. He wasn't lying when he said the diaper bag was void of diapers, but he'd stretched the truth a little saying that Hope needed one.

She didn't.

He just needed to get out of the studio, away from the tuned-in ears of Cinnamon Bay and the judgy eyes of Stella.

The way Juliet had looked at him shifted after Stella basically asked Evan what his intentions were.

By the time they got back to his cottage, Evan was a sweat-dripping mess. He turned on every fan, opened up all the windows that faced the beach and peeled off his soaking wet shirt.

He also stripped little Hope down to her diaper so she could cool off, too.

She was so close to walking. She kept trying to take a few steps, but then she'd grow wary of the world without having something to hold on to and stop herself before she took that first step into the great unknown.

He wasn't going to push her. She'd walk when she was ready.

Before he forgot, he found the new bag of diapers he'd bought the other day, grabbed a dozen and shoved them into the diaper bag that was stuffed in the basket beneath the stroller. More than once, he'd been caught unprepared out and about Cinnamon Bay and been forced to either run home in the heat with a screaming Hope, angry that he was making her sit in her dirty diaper, or duck into the grocery store to buy a new pack.

Juliet said that he'd be forever trying to find his footing, as that was the way of parenting, but he'd just like for this parenting gig to not constantly make him feel like he was flapping his arms on the edge of a cliff trying to regain his balance. Even just one foot planted solidly on the ground would be an improvement on the imbalance he felt in his world now.

Hope was happily playing with her stacking cups and rubber bunny on the floor, so he sat on the couch and grabbed his guitar.

He strummed and hummed the tune to the latest song he'd been working on. But as hard as he tried to get the bridge just right, Stella's words kept interrupting his flow.

He's a flight risk.

Was he a flight risk?

What made her think that?

It wasn't like Evan bailed on people or broke promises.

Where did she get off saying that about him?

Maybe it's not so much that you bail on people but that you still have a career and she thinks you're going to leave Juliet brokenhearted and take off on tour again.

To be honest, he'd been so caught up in his grief over Tony and trying to get his footing with Hope, he hadn't had time to think about what he was going to do when the summer was over.

In his mind, he figured he'd just go back to work.

He was expected to go back to work.

His band expected it.

Their fans expected it.

Their record label expected it.

Their manager expected it.

They'd taken a break, but they didn't break up.

The band would reassemble after some much-needed R&R, jumping back into the recording studio, bang out a new album, make some music videos, then head out on another tour. That was what they'd been doing for the last eight years. Only none of them had taken an entire summer off, and he couldn't speak for any of his bandmates, but Evan was loving the downtime.

He hadn't really thought about what that would mean to his and Juliet's relationship or how he'd figure Hope into everything.

He had the money to hire a nanny, so he could do that, couldn't he?

But Hope would still need a proper home. He would need to set down roots somewhere, right? Even if they weren't the deep roots of a redwood but shallower ones like a mangrove or a young birch sapling. She'd need a house, and a studio apartment like the one he'd had in Nashville wouldn't cut it.

Could he set down roots in Cinnamon Bay?

He'd never really thought about coming home and settling down in The Bay.

Once his career took off, the idea of returning to the sleepy little town he'd called home since he was a kid just seemed like an outlier of an idea on the path to his dreams.

He was deep in thought, playing a tune on his guitar that he hadn't put lyrics to yet and staring unfocused at a spot on the floor, when there was a knock at his door.

Both he and Hope looked up at the same time.

"Yo, it's Eric," called a voice from the other side.

Setting his guitar down on the couch and stepping around Hope and her toys, he made his way to the door and pulled it open.

Sure enough, it was Eric and his four-year-old daughter, Dia, standing on the other side. Eric had what appeared to be a rocking horse—but not a horse, rather an elephant—in one hand, and Dia had a small box of toys in the other.

"We come bearing hand-me-down toys," Eric said with a big smile.

"I'm too old for these baby toys," Dia said, not waiting to be invited and heading inside toward Hope. "Hi, Hope," she cooed. "I brought you some new toys." She sank down to the floor, and Hope immediately abandoned what she was playing with to go and investigate the new stuff.

"Beer?" Evan offered, shutting the door behind his friend.

Eric nodded.

Once they had their beers in hand, Evan pushed the sliding glass door all the way open, and he and Eric sat at the small kitchen table in front of the door while the girls played on the floor.

"To what do I owe the pleasure of your company?" Evan asked with a smirk, lifting his beer to his lips.

"Just wanted to give you an update on Tony and Jacqui's estate," Eric said. "Plus"—he tilted his head toward Dia—"D's been begging to come to visit Hope."

Evan's throat grew tight at the mention of Tony and Jacqui. It had to be hard for Eric to go through all of their friends' personal things. Not only did it probably feel like an invasion of Tony and Jacqui's privacy, but it probably wasn't easy emotionally. Evan knew that if he thought too long or too hard about Tony, or poor Hope growing up without her parents, the backs of his eyes started to burn and his throat made it impossible to swallow.

"What's the latest?" Evan asked, flicking the label of his beer with his thumbnail.

Eric swallowed a sip of his beer and put his bottle down on the table. "They had a decent amount in savings, so that of course will go to Hope. They had only just moved into the house, so not much will come back to them on the sale of it, I'm afraid. Rick is still helping me with those numbers. I've had Jacqui's car appraised, and since they'd paid for it in cash and it was secondhand and about five years old, we can probably get about fifteen grand for it when we turn around and sell it."

Evan nodded. All money that would help with Hope's education, set her up when she turned eighteen and decided to strike out on her own. He wasn't going to touch a dime of her inheritance to help raise her. He didn't need to, and the idea of it made him ill.

Taking another sip of his beer, Evan leveled his gaze on his friend. "Can I ask you something?"

Eric lifted a thick, dark brow.

"Why me?"

Eric's brow twitched. "What do you mean?"

"Why leave Hope to me? I don't get it. Why not you and Isla? You have a family. You know what you're doing. It's a nuclear family with stable parents with stable jobs. Why me? The bachelor. The nomad.

The never-around friend?" He shrugged and glanced down at Hope on the floor. She was gazing up at Dia like the older girl was neater than a banana-flavored rice cracker.

"Because I told him to," Eric said, drawing Evan's attention back to his friend.

Evan's mouth dropped open. "What?"

Eric brought the mouth of his beer to his lips. "When you're with kids, you're amazing. With my two, with Kate's two. I've seen it. You're present, you're engaged, you're involved. You are meant to be a dad. Not just a cool uncle. And honestly, I thought if something like this ever did happen, you'd have settled down somewhere, made your millions, and be living off royalties. I figured you'd be able to give Hope a better life than Isla and I could. No, we're not struggling, but we don't make mad rock-star money either." He lifted a broad shoulder under his lily-white T-shirt. "Honestly, though, it was because I knew—and Tony knew—that you are a loyal, good, honest, decent, and kind person, and even though you're busy, when you're needed, you step up."

"I thought Tony was upset with me for not being around. That was why he was avoiding my texts. I mean, I never came and saw their new house. Never even bothered to come to meet Hope after she was born. What kind of a friend does that make me?"

Eric shook his head. "He knew you were busy. And so was he. What matters is that you asked for baby pictures. You commented on them. Messaged him back. He knew—we both knew—that no matter how busy you got, you never forgot your friends. When you were nearby or passing through, you reached out and swung into The Bay. Sometimes our schedules didn't align, but I know for a fact that you always let us know when you were in town."

That was true. Evan always did. Even if he was only around for half a day, a day, or just passing through, he let his friends know in case they were able to carve out twenty minutes for a bullshit and a beer.

"And that was why we both decided that if something happened to Tony and Jacqui, you were the best person for the job to give Hope a good life. And I think we were right," Eric said. "You might be oblivious to some things, like how hard Jules was crushing on you for all those years, but you're a good friend, and even with your success and fame, that hasn't changed. You sent a housewarming gift. You sent a baby gift. You're oblivious to obvious things, but you know how to be a good friend where it counts."

Evan glanced out the open door through the screen and blinked back the threatening tears. His throat was tight again. He couldn't speak if he tried.

Not that he knew what to say anyway.

His friends saw him in a way that he didn't see himself at all.

Not that Evan was an overly selfish person, but he knew that in comparison to many of his friends, he led a carefree life. He only had to take care of himself for the past fifteen years. Take care of himself and his band. Yes, he made a point of keeping up with his two best friends from childhood, but in his mind, it wasn't enough. In his mind, he'd failed Tony and thought Tony was all wrong leaving Evan with the responsibility of raising Hope.

And yet, Tony and Eric saw him as a man who stepped up and stepped in when he was needed. They saw him as loyal.

The two versions of himself, his version and his friends' version, didn't add up.

"You guys going to the potluck and bandstand tonight?" Eric asked, having changed the subject because he obviously had no clue how Evan was reeling inside with what his best friend had just laid on the table.

Evan swallowed through the tightness in his throat and nodded as he brought the beer to his lips.

"Isla's making apple cinnamon turnovers for the potluck." Eric rubbed his belly. "I've already had three."

Evan smiled at his friend, though it was a challenge to bring the corners of his mouth up. After hearing why Tony and Jacqui put Evan in charge of raising Hope and everything Stella had said at the studio, Evan's brain just wasn't down with throwing on a big grin and meaning it.

His brain was close to short-circuiting.

"Something's off," Eric said. "And it's not just what I said about why Tony decided to name you Hope's guardian. What's going on? Trouble in paradise with Jules?" There was a chuckle tossed at the end of the sentence but also a protective brotherly glint in Eric's brown eyes. Say what he would about being a feminist but Eric was still a big brother, and he couldn't just turn off his protective instincts.

Evan's gaze drifted back out to the beach. "Stella called me a flight risk."

"What does that mean? I wouldn't say you're a flight risk. You've never bailed on anybody, on anything—not that I know of, anyway."

"She asked if we've thought about what's going to happen after the summer is over. Am I going to run back out on tour? Leave Juliet here in Cinnamon Bay all alone? She doesn't think we've thought everything through."

"Ah." Eric nodded. "Have you?"

No.

"I mean, you two are getting close fast, and there *is* a kid in the mix. Hope's getting attached to Jules, too. Are you going to go back out on tour, take Hope with you and rip her from the only *other* mother figure she has? Or do you plan to leave Hope with Jules and go do your rock-star thing, popping home once a month for a weekend? Because as much as my sister has become attached to that baby, that's also not what she signed up for. She has a business that she's still trying to get off the ground."

Evan lifted his arm and scratched the back of his neck. "I know, I know."

"And I can tell you right now, if you *did* saddle her with Hope and just took off back on tour or whatever, she would have every right to think that you only hooked up with her because you needed the childcare. And you know others would think that, too. How convenient your relationship with Jules started just when you needed help with Hope." Eric eyed Evan warily over his beer bottle. "I mean ... it *was* pretty convenient, no?"

Evan surged to his feet, sending his chair skidding noisily across the tile floor, then crashing into the wall behind him. "It's not like that at all, and you know it."

Eric's gaze slowly slid up Evan's body to his face. He was unflinchingly calm. "Okay."

Evan glared at his best friend. "I would never use Jules. I went to her studio the day we found out about Tony and was going to ask her out.

Hope wasn't even in the picture and I already had feelings for her." He ran his fingers through his hair and stalked out from behind the table and started pacing in the kitchen. "Did she tell you what happened at the concert in Summerfield?"

Eric nodded but didn't say anything. His calmness was bugging Evan.

"Since that night, I haven't been able to get her out of my head. I didn't even know she was Jules that night, but I couldn't stop thinking about her."

"And you didn't know she was my sister, someone you saw nearly every day for over five years, because ..."

Evan stopped his pacing and rounded on his friend, tossing his hands up in the air. "Because I'm an oblivious asshole with his head up said asshole and never saw your sister when she was right in front of me. There. Is that what you wanted me to say?"

Eric shrugged, nodded and sipped his beer. "Yep." He rolled his finger forward in the air, telling Evan to continue. "Continue with your tirade that I'm sure will lead to an epiphany. This is honestly quite entertaining."

"You're a dick."

Eric's gaze slid sideways to the little girls playing in the living room. "Little ears, bro."

Right, shit!

"Anyway," Evan continued, the fire in his veins having died down to more of a crackling ember, "you know damn well that I'm not the type of guy to use a woman. I would never do that and certainly not to Jules. Not your sister. I care about her. I l—"

Eric's brows shot up.

But Evan caught himself before he finished that sentence. Like hell was he going to tell Eric that he loved Jules before he even told Jules.

A smug smile slid across his best friend's face, Eric's white teeth gleaming through his dark lips. "You know I'm mostly ribbing you, right? But I wasn't wrong about that epiphany."

Evan's gaze narrowed on his friend.

Eric's smile only widened, which angered Evan all the more.

"I'm not using Jules, and no, I haven't thought about what we're going to do come September. I need to talk to my band. Jules has inspired me to write music again. I'm itching to get back into the recording studio, to play and watch others sing along to my music." He faced Eric, confusion heavy in his chest. "I haven't written a decent new song in almost three years. But since that night in Summerfield, I can't stop writing new songs. New *good* songs."

"So you're keeping my sister around so that you have some song inspiration, that's why," Eric probed, one side of his mouth lifting, along with one brow on the same side.

"You know damn well it's not. Now you're just being a goading ass."

"Or I'm just being a good friend helping you realize your feelings. I mean, you two have consumed enough of the damn love spice, I'm surprised you're not married with a baby on the way already."

Evan's heart stuttered. "Love spice?"

Eric's chuckle was more of a rumble as he tossed his head back and showed off more of his teeth. "Man, you really are oblivious. You grew up here and you don't know the legend?"

Heat and unease wormed through Evan, coiling around his insides. "Legend?"

Eric rolled his eyes. "Calliope Halloway makes a spice blend, aka 'The Love Spice,' and the legend says that those who drink it together will end up together within a year. The trio made you two drink it that day you went to pick their order. Why do you think they ordered for you? And then Eva tossed it into the cookies, and then Jules brought it over for you multiple times since. And don't you bring it to her at the studio, too?"

Evan's bottom lip dropped open. "And everyone in town knows about this?"

"Everyone in town, every tourist. They all come here for the café amour at Brewed with a View, hoping that the love spice will work its witchy magic. Jules has wanted to drink it with you since she was a kid."

"How did I miss this?"

Eric shrugged. "If it wasn't right in front of your face or shaped like a guitar, you didn't really know it existed, bro. It was kind of a running joke in our house. I mean, with love of course. But you honestly just never really picked up on shit that most normal people would. Did you know you drove past Jules standing soaked in the rain one day after school and she was in a bright yellow coat and you drove into the full gutter and it all splashed up on her?"

Horror swamped him. "No! When?"

"Your senior year. You'd just bought your car."

"I didn't do it on purpose!"

"I know. I saw it from the library window. I had to stay late to finish an assignment and told Jules to run out and ask you for a ride home. She was too nervous to actually talk to you, you know, massive crush and all. But she did wave at you, stood on the curb in her bright yellow coat, but then you sped past her like she was a telephone pole, drenching her in the process—as she was waving at you trying to get your attention."

"But I ... I didn't see her. I swear. I wasn't trying to be mean. I didn't mean to ignore her."

Eric held his hands up in an effort to get Evan to stop spiraling. "I know. You're not that kind of guy, but what you are is oblivious." He chuckled. "My parents actually thought it was such a funny thing, they kept trying to come up with more elaborate schemes to see just *how* oblivious you were. Did you know that one time when you were over, my dad wore a dress for like nine hours? And not just any dress, like a ball gown. He mowed the lawn in it. You didn't say a damn word."

Evan's eyes went wide. "You're lying. I'd notice big Ron wearing a dress."

Eric grinned and shrugged.

"Tony and I decided to one day test you, and he brought an empty box to school, scrawled the words *books* on it, and just when he knew you were getting out of your car, he pretended to try to get the 'heavy' box of books out of the trunk of his car. Struggled and grunted, made all kinds of noises. You walked right past him, lifted your chin, said 'hey' and kept going."

"I—"

"And it was a big-ass box, man. Like I think he found it behind an appliance store or something. Might have been for an air conditioner or big microwave. And you just kept on walking."

At this point, Evan was sick to his stomach.

He should have done better. Done better by his friends, by Jules.

Jules was Eric's little sister. He should have seen her standing there in the rain. She shouldn't have had to wave him down. He should have just offered her a ride. Asked her where Eric was, then drove her home.

"Why didn't you say anything to me after I drove off and splattered Jules with rainwater?"

Eric lifted a shoulder. "It happened on a Friday. We didn't see each other that weekend because I was studying for an exam, and then by Monday I forgot." He held up his finger. "Oh, and Jules begged me not to. That was it. I was going to. I was going to call you Friday night and bitch you out for what you did, but she begged me to let it go."

Evan pulled out a different chair and plunked his ass into it with a heavy sigh. "Why did she want to drink the love spice with me after I treated her like she didn't exist?"

Eric shrugged. "Beats me. But maybe she saw you the way the rest of us see you. The way Tony and I see you. Yes, you might be oblivious, but when you're *asked* to do something, when you're *asked* to step up, you do. You might not always see it to offer help, but when someone calls upon you, you're there. And we learned that about you quickly."

Evan cocked his head to the side and squinted at his friend.

Eric took pity on him. "Isla says that I don't *see* dirt the way she sees dirt. That I walk past shit that needs to go upstairs or downstairs, that I don't wipe the crumbs off the granite countertop—though, in my defense, that mottled grain makes it impossible to see shit on the counter. You need to get down to it at eye level to see the dirt. However, if she says, 'grab that stuff on the stairs and take it down to the garage to the recycling bin,' I do it. If she hands me the cloth to wipe the counter, I do it." His face pinched. "I mean, this was back when we first started dating. The woman has trained me now, and I do that shit without being asked because I'm a good boy and I like it when she rubs my belly and scratches behind my ears." He winked and grinned cheekily at Evan. "I like it when she does other things, too." Evan rolled his eyes. "But you know what I'm saying?"

He did, kind of.

"We learned that it wasn't that you were unwilling to step up or help. It's more that you just don't see where there is the need to help. You don't see the dirt. But when someone points it out to you or asks you to wipe it up, then you see it and you have no problem pitching in and doing what needs to be done. We just learned to not wait for you to step in on your own accord and just asked you right away. It was an easy fix and one that eliminated any kind of resentment. Just one of your quirks. We all have them. Like I'm just *too* nice and *too* handsome for my own good. Gets me into a heap of trouble." He flashed his pearly whites in a cocky smile, making Evan chuckle and his shoulders relax.

"So you're saying that where someone else might 'offer' to help you lift a heavy couch and take it to the thrift store, I need to be asked because I don't offer." How on earth had nobody ever called him out on this shit before? He sounded like a colossal ass. He was still berating himself for what he'd done to Jules in the rain.

Eric nodded. "Yeah, pretty much. You're loyal and kind and giving, but you just need to be asked to give. If that makes sense. You're Oblivious Evan, and we love you for you."

"Oblivious Evan," he murmured. "And everyone feels like this?"

Eric shrugged again. "I mean, everyone that I know that knows you kind of jokes about how a woman could walk past you naked on the street and unless she said, 'Hey, Evan Spencer, I'm naked. Look at me,' you wouldn't see her at all."

Evan snorted, shook his head and reached across the table for his beer. "And so I never saw your sister because—"

"She was too shy to tell you to look at her. She always hoped you'd just notice her on your own. That she would be the exception to your oblivion."

"She told you all of this?"

"Of course not. My mom did. Isla did. Isla and Jules are close. They go to yoga at Zen Bodies every Saturday."

Yeah, Evan knew that. He loved it when Jules came out of the bedroom wearing those butt-hugging yoga pants. He wanted to peel them right off her, toss her to the bed and give her a different kind of workout.

Eric stood up, finished his beer and took it to the sink. "Time to get a move on, D," he called to Dia in the other room. "We'll see Hope and Uncle Evan at the Pirate Festival later tonight." Eric clapped Evan on the shoulder. "I don't think you're a flight risk. But I do think up until now, you've remained oblivious to what lay beyond the summer. How you're going to fit Jules and Hope into your life. And now, you have some thinking to do."

"Thinking, berating, not opposed to some mental flagellation," Evan grumbled.

"Hey." Eric squeezed his shoulder. "We all love you just the way you are. But if you do *l*— my sister, then you need to really think about how your choices impact her, her heart and your heart."

Evan's head bobbed. But then he glanced up quickly at Eric. "You don't believe in that whole love spice thing, do you?"

Eric's white smile was back. "All I know is that Isla thought I was a cocky jerk before I brought her a spice cookie and a café amour while she was working behind the bar at Shenanigans, and then a month later, the woman was *obsessed* with me. Couldn't peel her long legs from around my waist in the morning to get to work on time if I tried."

That drew a real smile from Evan. "Yeah? And would Isla tell the exact same story if I asked her?"

Eric nodded quickly. "Absolutely, which is why there is no need to ask her at all." He held up three fingers. "A scout always tells the truth."

"Yeah, but you were never in Scouts."

Dia appeared at Eric's side, and he ran his hand over the little girl's dark, wild curls that sprung out from her head. "Still no need to ask her." His smile grew, and he took his daughter's hand. "Ready to go, honey?"

Dia nodded, and the two of them headed to the front door.

Hope was suddenly at Evan's feet, so he scooped her up, and they followed Eric and Dia to the door.

"Thanks for all the toys," Evan said.

"They came with the price of my harsh dose of reality," Eric said, turning the latch. "I hope it was worth it."

Evan adjusted Hope in arms and set her on his hip. "A tall price to pay for some toys, but also much needed. You've given me a lot to think about."

Eric hit the fob for his truck. "We'll see you tonight."

"That you will. I'll be the oblivious guy wandering around wondering how he even got to the beach since nobody *told* him to walk there."

Eric's chuckle boomed against the shiplap siding of the cottage as he made his way to the truck. "Hey, bro, I'm just glad you're not oblivious to when you stink and remember to put on deodorant."

Chapter Twelve

With everything Hope would need for a night at Evan's moms' house packed into a backpack on his back, Evan pushed the stroller, the diaper bag and the cooler filled with Juliet's deviled eggs back into town after a late afternoon of deep thought and a solid two-hour nap from Hope.

He needed to talk to Juliet.

He needed to see her.

He needed to not only tell her how he felt about her but see how she felt about him, where they stood and what she wanted out of their relationship.

He wasn't willing to end this when the summer was over.

But could they have this talk already? They hadn't been together that long.

They had to. Even if it was still in its fledgling state, this relationship—Juliet—was the best thing that had happened to him since his first record deal.

And who said he couldn't have it all?

Dusk was settling in, but the town wasn't quieting down at all.

If anything, it was busier than it had been earlier that day. Probably something to do with the heat.

Now that the sun was going down and not trying to roast the nice people of Cinnamon Bay, everyone was coming out of hiding and enjoying the cooler temperature and all the festivities.

Juliet had texted earlier to say that she would meet him at the tent set up on the beach where they had all the buffet tables. She was in "mad cleanup mode" at the studio and was running late.

Evan pushed his way through the groups of people along The Boardwalk, many of them glancing down and waving back at a happy and waving Hope.

Lights on Main Street highlighted the sky a few blocks away while the sound of folk music echoed around The Boardwalk from the big speakers down on the beach near the band stage.

"There she is," came a familiar voice he recognized to be one-third of the trio. Hattie.

Evan turned around, making sure to put a smile on his face as he wheeled the stroller around, too.

All three women were there, dressed to impress and still sitting in their golf cart.

"And how is our darling Hope?" Birdie asked, adjusting her tan beret just a little, which made her bangles jingle.

"That tooth has finally popped out so we're *all* a lot happier and sleeping better, thanks."

All three women smiled.

"All?" Trixie asked with a wicked glint in her eye.

Evan rolled his eyes. "Yes, *all*."

Hattie clucked her tongue and glanced at her friends. "Took Oblivious Evan a little while to get his butt in gear, but when he did ... this may have been the easiest, most *willing* match we've ever made."

"It helps when one half of the match is all for it and buying her own café amour to up her chances," Trixie said, touching her white curls. "Speaking of, where is Juliet?"

"She's still at Kiln or be Kilned. It was busy today, so she's still cleaning up after all the customers," he said, careful not to add any venom to his tone at their use of his nickname—Oblivious Evan. Did the whole town call him that?

Had he been too oblivious to know?

127

"We were there earlier," Birdie said with a nod. "She got in the cutest little ceramic pirate figurines. I just *had* to paint one before all the tourists snapped them up."

Her friends nodded.

"Well, I'm sure once they're fired, they're going to look great. Are you ladies heading over to the potluck?" He waved at a few people he recognized who were heading toward the beach.

Hattie nodded. "In a bit. Have some things we need to take care of first."

He wasn't about to ask. They were probably scheming and planning another match somewhere in town now that Evan and Jules were together. He only hoped the poor unsuspecting people didn't mind the whole town knowing their business.

"Well, I will see you there, then. I need to get Jules's deviled eggs to the table." He wheeled the stroller back around and was almost home free when Trixie called after him.

"Save some deviled eggs for us!"

He didn't turn around but waved and nodded, pushing the stroller just a little bit quicker toward the beach.

He found his parents and Juliet's parents all sitting at a table with Eric, Isla and the kids, as well as Evan's sister Kate, Rick and their boys. The kids were off in the grassy patch fenced off and in front of the stage playing and dancing, while the adults all had paper plates in front of them loaded with delicious goodies.

He greeted them all, and instantly, Mom-G made to get Hope out of her stroller.

Evan took the deviled eggs over to the buffet table and set them down, then made himself a plate. When he returned to the table, he exchanged knowing glances with Eric, but neither of them did more than smile.

They'd had their talk today.

He'd done a lot of thinking.

There was no need to hash and rehash things.

Eric said his piece, and now it was time for Evan and Juliet to say theirs but in private.

Evan's mother was feeding an arm-flailing and happy Hope, so Evan sat down next to his sister, kissed her on the cheek, then dove into his dinner.

"First night without Hope in over a month. Whatever are you going to do with yourself?" Kate asked, bumping his shoulder. Her brown eyes, the same shade as his, twinkled.

He shoved a piece of Juliet's mother's seafood lasagna into his mouth and lifted a brow at her. "Probably the same thing you and Rick do when the grandparents take the boys for a night."

"Soooo sleep in?" Rick interjected with a chuckle.

"Among other things." Evan nodded and chewed.

A throat cleared across the table, and that's when he remembered that Juliet's dad, Ron, was also at the table.

Crap.

"And by other things, he obviously means reorganize his stamp collection, polish the silver and update his address book," Rick said quickly, taking a sip from a red solo cup. "Right, Ev? That's what Kate and I do when your moms take the boys for a night."

Evan nodded exaggeratedly. "Absolutely. My stamp collection is a mess."

Ron snorted but didn't say anything.

He didn't have to. The look he was giving Evan was deafening.

"Hey, guys. Sorry I'm so late." Another voice he recognized, a voice he loved, came up behind him, and cool, slender fingers landed on his shoulders and squeezed.

Warmth spooled through him at her touch, at her scent, at her nearness.

Glancing up and over his shoulder, he smiled at Juliet.

She did say that she was going to run home to shower and change, and what she wore now made his pulse pick up and his jaw drop: a thin-strapped, white summer dress with tiny little holes in it. He could have sworn a past girlfriend of his who'd been a fashion designer had called the fabric eyelet. Whatever it was, Juliet rocked it. Her dark, thick waves flowed down over her shoulders, she wasn't wearing her glasses, and her naturally bronzed skin glowed beneath the white cotton. She was the most beautiful thing he'd ever seen in his life, and with the lights from the tent behind her, illuminating her head, she appeared almost angelic.

Song lyrics popped into his head like corn kernels puffing up in a bag of Jiffy Pop. And then the thought of Jiffy Pop and grinding the corn popped into his head, and blood began to pool in inconvenient places on his body.

Before he could stop himself and the words fell out of his brain, he spun back around, grabbed the notebook out of the side pocket of his khaki shorts along with the golf pencil he kept in the metal spiral that held all the pages together, and he started jotting down words.

Angelic glow.

Standing under the stars, but you're the only star I see.

Eyes all aglow.

My eyes are only for you.

None of it made sense at the moment, but he'd put it all together later. He just needed to get the words down.

He scribbled a few more notes, as well as a tune that fit perfectly, then satisfied that he'd scraped his brain clean, he stowed his notepad and pencil back in his pocket and lifted his head.

The entire table was staring at him.

He glanced up, and Juliet was staring at him, too.

"Is that how it happens?" asked Sandy. "Suddenly, inspiration hits, and no matter where you are, you need to write it down?"

Evan shrugged, not liking all the attention and eyes on him. "Sometimes. Lately, it's been happening like that a lot. At least when"—he glanced up at Juliet—"at least when Jules is around."

Color filled her cheeks, and she bit her lip, but the curl at either corner of her mouth was unmistakable.

He shoved his sister over, causing Kate to grumble but all while smiling, and Juliet slid in beside him.

"Thanks for bringing my deviled eggs," she said, finding his hand beneath the table and sliding her fingers against his. "Stella offered to stay and finish cleaning up so that I could get here before all the food was gone."

He pushed his plate toward her. "Eat. I'll go make up another one."

She didn't hesitate and reached for a Moroccan-spiced chicken wing.

130

"So Evan talked to you about a birthday party for Hope, right?" Mom-J asked, nibbling on one of Kate's apple cinnamon turnovers.

Evan paused as he got up to go and make another plate.

Juliet nodded. "He did. And I think it's a great idea." She pivoted to face Evan. "Though we also need to think about a celebration of life for Tony and Jacqui. I was thinking about it today after you left the studio. We really should do something to honor them."

"Damn," Eric said, sweeping his hand over his short-cropped black hair. "I completely forgot about a celebration of life. I've been so caught up with their estate and making sure everything is in order so that Hope is taken care of financially that it completely slipped my mind."

Juliet rested a hand on her brother's shoulder, his muscles bunched and tense beneath her fingertips. "It's okay. You've both been busy with other things—taking care of things for Tony and Jacqui."

Evan had been up off his seat, his butt hovering over the picnic table bench, but he plopped down next to Juliet again, a look of pain on his handsome face. "I forgot, too."

"And there is no *rule book* that says when you have to have a celebration of life or funeral or whatever. I think it's old-school to do it early after the people have passed because they didn't want to just keep a dead body around forever. It needed to be buried," Juliet's dad spoke up. "But with more people getting cremated, it frees up the timeline a bit."

Juliet's mom nodded. "Exactly."

"Their ashes are being delivered next week," Eric said, hanging his head low. "I don't know what to do with them."

"Sprinkle them over the water at sunset," Juliet piped up, glancing at her brother. "We all know that was Tony and Jacqui's favorite time of day and favorite place. It was why they got married on the beach at sunset, right?"

Evan's hand found hers again beneath the table, and he squeezed. "How do you know this?"

She lifted her shoulder. "It was on their wedding website."

"She pays attention and isn't oblivious," Ron added with a chuckle at the end.

Juliet glanced at Evan, whose body had stiffened.

"Dad," she warned.

131

Her father merely shrugged and looped his arm around Juliet's mother's shoulder.

"What about a celebration of Hope?" Kate, Evan's sister, offered. "We have a birthday party for Hope down on the beach on July Fourth, and at the same time, we invite anybody from The Bay who wants to come and say a few words about Tony and Jacqui. Then, with Hope, we sprinkle their ashes into the sea at sunset?"

Juliet couldn't imagine a more beautiful way to say goodbye but also celebrate their lives and their daughter. She knew it would be exactly the kind of thing that Tony and Jacqui would want.

"I think that's perfect," she said, blinking back a tear that threatened to slide down her cheek.

Heads around the table bobbed, and people murmured agreements.

Juliet turned to Kate and mouthed a thank-you. Now was not the time or place, but Stella's words this afternoon had bothered her for the rest of the day.

Juliet loved her best friend, but Stella had no right to say the things she said when and where she said them.

Juliet had been short and quiet with her friend for the rest of the day, and by the time they closed up the shop, Stella knew she'd messed up.

They hadn't had it out, and they might not, but Juliet knew that Stella offering to stay late and clean up was her olive branch and asking for forgiveness.

Of course, Juliet would forgive her friend, but the fact of the matter was, Stella had said the words. She'd said the words to Evan—to many people in Cinnamon Bay—and she'd said them to Juliet. And those words couldn't be unsaid.

Evan squeezed her hand again, then he stood up and went to go fix another plate.

She stared at the heaping plate in front of her and picked up a white chili bite and bit into it. Flavor—one of them being cinnamon—exploded across her tongue. Beans and chilis, cumin and oregano, it was all delicious. She didn't know who made them, but they were filling the void, hitting the spot and cruising across each and every one of her tastebuds, making them very happy.

Everyone at the table was in their own little conversation now, which Juliet was grateful for. She was still thinking.

Even though their relationship was new, her feelings weren't.

She'd been in love with Evan since she was eleven, and even though over the last fifteen years she'd had boyfriends and men in her life—had even told two of them that she loved them—she never stopped loving Evan.

This might be a new relationship for him—he might not be ready to say that four-letter word—but she'd been saying it to him in her mind and feeling it in her heart for years.

So she owed it to herself to figure out where they stood.

As much as it angered her that Stella brought all her concerns up in public, her concerns weren't unfounded.

Juliet hadn't wanted to pop their new romance bubble and ask the hard questions, but she knew she needed to.

Tonight, she needed to.

Tonight, she and Evan were going to talk.

She was going to tell him that she didn't want their relationship to end when the long days of summer ended.

Tonight, she was going to lay it all out on the table and finally, at long last, tell Evan Spencer that she loved him.

Chapter Thirteen

The sky was filled with a million stars, all of them winking at Juliet in a coy and knowing way as she and Evan strolled hand-in-hand away from the beach and all the commotion.

Evan's moms had left roughly an hour ago with Hope, then Juliet's parents departed shortly after that. They were watching Eric and Isla's girls for the night so that Eric and Isla could continue to party with the rest of the carefree, childless Cinnamon Bay people. Not that there were very many of those left. In Juliet's opinion, the carefree and childless were dropping like flies. As were the single people. The matchmakers were definitely on a bit of a spree. Juliet hadn't told Evan, but after their first night together, she comped the trio's next visit to the studio. Just her way of saying thank you for the nudge.

When Juliet and Evan took their leave of the tables and tents, Eric and Isla—neither of them sober—were swaying on the dance floor even though the music playing called for a more upbeat and lively style dance.

"Oh to be that caught up in each other that you don't even know your dance doesn't fit the beat," Evan said with a chuckle.

"I don't think they care," Juliet said, tilting her head to the right to indicate that they should head up the block and away from the beach. "I need to pop into the studio for something quick."

He didn't say anything but allowed her to lead the way.

Since Evan had Hope, they actually hadn't spent any nights at Juliet's place. Sure, he'd been there, but since she lived in a studio apartment, there was no place for Hope. She also much preferred to stay at his place since it was right on the beach, while her loft was several blocks up and only lent her a view of the bowling alley.

They came to the studio door, and she unlocked it.

He held it open and then locked it behind them when they entered the dark space.

"Forget something?" he asked, right behind her.

Nodding, she bent down and opened the small square bar fridge she kept beneath the counter for her and Stella's lunches. She pulled out a bottle of pineapple wine from Bottles of Bliss. "I did."

His gaze turned avid, and a sexy smile lifted his lips. "Got a corkscrew?"

"On my keychain, I have a multitool. You never know when you're going to be in a wine emergency and need to open up a bottle to save someone's life."

He took the keychain from her and the bottle. "Very smart. Very resourceful." The cork was deployed in seconds. "I don't suppose you have some cups or glasses somewhere, do you?"

"I run a pottery studio. We have a whole shelf of misfired mugs."

"Misfired mugs?"

"Mugs—or bowls and plates as well—that didn't turn out how people wanted or cracked in the kiln." She grabbed a couple of mugs from a drawer, one of which had a broken handle, and passed them to him.

He poured the wine and passed her a cup.

They clinked and sipped.

"So, why Kiln or be Kilned?" he asked, setting his mug down and leaning back against the counter. "Why not *A Time to Kiln*."

She smiled over the rim of her mug before pulling it away from her mouth. "That name is taken by a studio I used to work at in New Mexico."

"Okay. *Licensed to Kiln*?"

"Belongs to a studio a friend of mine owns in Arizona."

"You artists really like your puns."

She sipped more wine and lifted a shoulder. "Guilty."

"Kiln Bill?"

135

That made her snort. "Believe me, I Googled 'movie titles with kill in it' and there was a lot. But not a lot of them worked. Some were movies that not a lot of people would recognize, so then the pun would be lost. I liked *Kiln Your Darlings,* which is a movie, but my parents didn't think anybody would get the play on words."

"To Kiln a Mockingbird?"

She snorted again. "Yeah, my dad suggested that one."

"Fired Up?"

"I do really like that one, but it's the name of a paint your own pottery place up in Canada. I met the owner and general manager at a ceramics convention one year, and they are fantastic women. I wouldn't want to take their name and use it, too."

"I like Kiln or be Kilned."

"Thanks. You can thank Eric for that suggestion. It was his."

He took another drink of his wine. "Eric's ego is far too big already. I'll keep quiet. Don't want his head to explode or anything."

Juliet smothered her chuckle in her mug before taking a sip. Her gaze drifted over Evan and she took in how delicious he looked.

The man didn't even have to try, and he looked good enough to eat.

Navy polo, dark tan khaki shorts. He'd always had a casual style about him, never put any real effort into his appearance, and yet he always looked put-together. And boy, oh boy, when he threw on that leather jacket, she was a goner.

She kind of wished it was cool enough for him to be wearing it now.

More times than she cared to admit during her days of mega-crushing on Evan, she'd envisioned him wrapping that leather jacket around her shoulders when she caught a chill. Maybe they were at the movies or down at the beach at a bonfire, or perhaps he just saw her walking home one day hugging her arms because she forgot her own coat and he just took it upon himself to stop and give her his jacket to stay warm.

These were only three of the dozens of scenarios she cooked up over the years.

She'd even gone so far—just once—to take his jacket and put it on when he was over hanging out with Eric in their parents' basement.

Evan had hung the jacket up on the hook in the foyer of their home, then gone down in the rec room, where he and Eric were playing video games. Juliet spied the jacket, and before she could stop herself, she'd grabbed the soft black leather and taken off to her bedroom.

Being in that jacket was like being in Evan's arms. His scent wrapped around her, and she never wanted it to go away.

Of course, the moment she heard her brother and Evan ascending the stairs in search of food, she'd raced down the hallway and hung the jacket back up, a mere three seconds before Evan grabbed it off the hook and Eric announced that he and Evan were going to run to the diner for a burger.

"Care to share where your head is?" Evan asked, drawing her back to the present. His husky, deep voice made her shiver even though heat began to pool in her lower belly. He set his mug down on the counter and placed his hands on her hips.

"Do you still have your leather jacket?" she asked, glancing up at him beneath her lashes. "The black one you wore in high school."

His head cocked to the side in curiosity, but a playful smile danced on his lips. "I do ... why?"

Shaking her head, she scraped her top teeth over her bottom lip for a moment. "I just really liked it when you wore it."

"It's back at my cottage. I can put it on for you if you want."

Oh, she wanted. She also wanted to wear it.

She wanted him to wear it, get it all nice and warm with his body, then drape it around her shoulders just like she always dreamed he would.

"Jules," he said, drawing her once again out of her fantasy and back to the now.

"Hmm?" She smiled up at him, feeling almost sleepy from the wine, the long day and the heat that radiated off his hard body.

"I'm in love with you."

Well, now she was awake.

Her eyes flew open wide as he lifted her up and plunked her butt onto the counter, stepping between her legs and causing the hem of her dress to slide up her thighs.

His warm, slightly calloused fingers landed on her thighs, and a frisson of delight swirled through her.

"I know it's early, but I'm in love with you," he went on, looking up at her with hope in his brown orbs.

The teenager inside of her wanted to cheer and holler and run around the studio waving her arms like an idiot. Evan Spencer loved her.

Evan Spencer was IN LOVE WITH HER.

But she was a thirty-one-year-old woman, not a twelve-year-old with no clue how to talk to boys. She needed to play it cool.

Cucumber cool.

So rather than jump off the counter and go nuts and do cartwheels, she looped her arms around his neck and leaned in close, the heat of him hitting her between her legs and waking up the already very aware parts of her that had come to like Evan's attention a whole heck of a lot.

Her lips brushed against his, but she could tell that there was a tension in his shoulders because she hadn't said anything back.

She got a kick out of his unease.

Payback was a bitch.

Not that she really intended to torture him. But the worry in his eyes did give her a bit of a thrill.

She stuck her tongue out and slid it along the seam of his mouth. "What took you so long?" she whispered, watching as his gaze flared and heat and need ignited behind his irises.

"I'm Oblivious Evan, remember? Takes me a little longer than others to see what's been right in front of me all along." His hands slid up her thighs more, and butterflies took flight in her belly. Butterflies with wings of fire. "I was an idiot."

"You were."

He reared back slightly.

She shrugged and smiled. "Don't expect me to tell you that you weren't."

It was his turn to shrug. "Yeah, Eric's given me a bit of insight into just *how* big of an idiot I was." He shook his head. "I feel so bad that I didn't see you standing there in the rain. That my car shot water all over you from the gutter."

"Or when I sent you that Valentine, the one with the Shakespeare quote, calling you my Romeo and saying that your Juliet was waiting for you."

His brows furrowed. "That was *you?*"

"I figured since I was the only Juliet in school, you'd figure it out, but ..."

"Oblivious Evan struck again." He closed his eyes and shook his head. "I'm really sorry, Jules." Even though he was apologizing and she could see the remorse on his face and in his eyes, his fingers hadn't stopped moving along her thighs. They were now beneath her dress and strumming the sides of her panties like a guitar string.

Swallowing, she pinned her gaze on him. "I've never stopped loving you, Evan. Even when I should have. Even when I had other boyfriends, I never stopped loving you."

His eyes opened, and flames of desire flickered inside them. "And even though I only just fell in love with you, what I feel is so real. So strong. I don't want this to end when the summer is over. I want us to figure out how to make it work. How to do it all."

She nodded fervently and smiled, though tears of joy, of relief and satisfaction, tingled behind her eyes, causing a burning sensation to travel down her throat. "I want that, too."

"You, me and Hope, we're going to figure this out, I promise."

More nodding from her, because there wasn't a hope in hell that she would be able to say anything through the heavy threat of tears.

Evan Spencer wanted her. He loved her, and he wanted a life with her.

Clearing her throat, she tightened her hold on his neck and looked into his eyes. "Say it again."

His thick brows knitted together. "Say what?"

"What I've wanted to hear you say for fifteen years."

A smile crept across his mouth, and he leaned in so she could feel the warm puffs of his breath across her lips. "I am in love with you, Juliet Clarkson."

He took her mouth with a need that she felt all the way down to her toes.

She tugged at his shirt, and their lips only came apart long enough for him to ditch the shirt, then he was back to kissing her. Back to pushing his tongue into her mouth, sweeping it around and toying with hers.

She moaned into the kiss and pulled him down to her, biting his lips and letting the frantic feeling inside her take over.

They'd just said, "I love you."

That was huge.

That was a cause for celebration.

Naked celebration.

And if she was being honest, she'd always had a fantasy to have sex in her studio.

His fingers pulled at the sides of her panties, and she moved her butt cheeks up and down until he worked them over her thighs and tossed them to the ground beside him.

They broke the kiss for a moment. He unfastened the belt, button and zipper on his shorts and was about to let them drop when she lifted her brow and said, "Condom."

"Right." He nodded and fished one out of his pocket before letting his shorts—and his boxer briefs—slide down his legs.

Licking her lips, she watched him roll on the condom, her body trembling with the need to feel him inside her.

Once he had the condom on, his hands pushed beneath her dress, cupped her butt, and he pulled her toward him. She tilted her hips so the angle worked, and with a little lift from her, a push from him and a couple of very manly grunts, he was seated inside her.

"Yessssss," she said on a hiss, letting her eyes close and her head tip back.

He tugged a strap of her dress over her shoulder and went fishing inside the top of her dress and bra until he found a nipple. He pulled her breast free and bent his head, latching onto a nipple and sucking until she was forced to arch her back and moan from how good it felt.

His hips continued to move, his body pistoning in and out of her until her whole body began to hum with pleasure.

"I love you, Jules," he said, lifting his head from her breast. "Love you so damn much."

"I love you, too, Evan," she cried out into the dark, quiet studio. She leaned back and rested her elbows on the counter, tipping her head back between her shoulders and keeping her eyes closed.

With her sense of sight deprived, she allowed the others to grow stronger.

The sound of Evan breathing, of his grunts and groans and the knock of his knees against the cupboard door below the counter.

The scent of sex and pineapple wine, salty air, acrylic paint, clay and cleaner filled her nostrils. Of course, she couldn't deny that intoxicating scent of man—of Evan—that seemed to make its way through all the other scents and wrap around her like a comforting shroud.

She tasted the pineapple wine, the beer he'd had from earlier and just a hint of cinnamon and apple from the turnover they'd shared.

And lastly, she felt him.

She felt Evan inside her, above her, consuming her. He burrowed beneath her skin, into her heart, into every cell of her body. He'd changed her genetic makeup so that every part of her also now held a part of him. Her heart beat for him. The blood in her veins ran hot for him. She felt his love in every corner of her body, felt his need for her, his desire flowed through him and into her with every kiss, every caress, every move of his hips.

This wasn't like the other times in his bed, on his couch, or that one time on the lounge chair on the deck. Yes, she'd been in love with him, but he hadn't said it to her. Now they'd both said it. Now they weren't just having sex. Now they were making love, and it was better than she'd ever dreamed it to be.

Pleasure speared through her, pulsing outward from where they were connected and into the rest of her body. Her fingertips clawed at the counter. Her toes curled. Even the tips of her ears began to burn and tingle as he brought her closer and closer to the pinnacle.

A pinnacle she wanted for them to desperately jump off together.

"I love you, Jules," he said again, his mouth falling to her neck, his hips still moving. "So much. I don't want to do any of this without you. I'm better when I'm with you. You inspire me."

His teeth scraped her shoulder and up her neck, and he lifted a hand up to caress her breast, to tug on the still-exposed nipple and send her bliss level up to dangerous heights.

"I'm close," she whispered, wrapping a hand around the back of his neck and encouraging him to lift his head. Their eyes locked. "I don't want to let go without you," she said.

His head shook. "You won't have to." Then he took her mouth again, and together they found their release.

141

Chapter Fourteen

H and in hand with their shoes off and a bottle of pineapple wine being passed between them, Evan and Juliet walked along the now-quiet beach. Nothing but the waves lapping at the shore infiltrated the night. Nothing but the waves and their laughing.

After making love in the studio, they finished the bottle of pineapple wine Juliet had brought out, then to Evan's surprise, she reached into the fridge and brought out a second bottle, waggling her eyebrows at him and saying they needed to celebrate again.

"Celebrate what?" he asked, deploying another cork.

"The fact that Oblivious Evan finally came to his senses and—"

"Realized that loving Juliet Clarkson was the smartest thing he ever could have done?"

She nodded in a cute, slightly drunk little way. "Yuppers!" She lifted her mug to him. "To you not being *so* oblivious anymore and to that great sex we just had. In my opinion, it needs to be toasted to as well."

He clinked her mug and chuckled. "Well, the night is still young—"

"And so are we."

He laughed more. "Not as young as we used to be, but young enough that my parts still work for more than just one roll in the hay a night."

"Ooh, are we going to go find some hay?"

He shook his head and grinned at her. "I can find you hay if you want, my love. I'll find you a whole field of hay if that's what you desire."

She looped her arms around his neck and lifted up onto her tiptoes, her eyes struggling to focus just a little. "I don't need hay, just you naked ... and maybe that leather jacket of yours. I really want to wear it."

"You can wear it, as long as you don't wear anything else."

Her eyes gleamed, she giggled, then she hauled him and their pineapple wine back outside. She locked up, and they headed back to the beach, where they would walk through the sand back to his cottage.

"I wore your jacket once," she said, her speech only a little slurred as she released his hand and went skipping ahead of him, kicking up sand as she went.

"Did you now?"

"Yep. You were downstairs with Eric. I grabbed your jacket and went into my room and put it on and stared at myself in the mirror."

He lunged to save her when she stumbled and nearly ate sand, but she recovered her balance and kept skipping. "I bet it looked better on you than it ever did me."

She lifted her brows at him. "We'll see when we get home."

Home.

She was calling his place home.

She spent most nights there, and had a toothbrush there. Why couldn't he ask her to just move in, and then when September hit, they could find something more permanent. She didn't need to give up her loft just yet, since the cottage wasn't big enough for all of her stuff and his and Hope's, but ... he could ask her to "move in for the summer," couldn't he? They'd already decided that they were going to make it work—whatever that meant—and not break up at the end of the summer.

And no, he wasn't SO oblivious that he didn't realize that saying "they'd figure something out" and "make it work" wasn't an actual plan or solution.

But they both knew that they wanted to continue their relationship. She loved him. He loved her. They were going to do what was necessary to see where their love took them.

Maybe he could do a week on, week off thing, hire a nanny to help Jules with Hope when he was away, or Jules and Hope could come with him and he could help her find more staff for the studio. Maybe he could move his home base from Nashville to Cinnamon Bay or Summerfield. Move closer so the commute wasn't so long.

There were options, and they would explore them.

But not tonight.

Tonight, they were celebrating.

His cottage came into view along the beach, and they started to make their way up the sand, passing the wine back and forth until, when she handed it back to him once more, there wasn't anything more than a few drops left.

"That was quite the sip," he said with a chuckle, setting the bottle down on the porch and reaching into his pockets for his keys to the back door.

"Hydrating for the marathon we're about to do," she said, bobbing her eyebrows up and down.

Laughing, he opened the door and flicked on the light inside, but as soon as she stepped over the threshold, she turned the light back off and was on him.

Clothes were peeled away, lips found skin, and bodies once again united.

He couldn't get over how insatiable she was. How sensual and comfortable in her own skin Juliet could be.

This time, she climbed on top and took control. He liked this side of her. Pineapple wine was liquid courage and allowed her to release her wild side. He was all for it. But when she stopped just before they started, climbed off him, opened his closet and pulled out his leather jacket, he was a goner.

She slid her bare arms into the sleeves and pulled the sides over her breasts before climbing back onto the bed and straddling him, the jacket falling open and giving him the perfect view of her.

"I was right," he said, holding her hips as she slowly lowered herself onto him. "You look way better in that than I ever did."

Then they took each other back to the top of the mountain, more than once that night, and finally, sometime around three in the morning, she collapsed against him, her hair splayed across his chest, and she fell asleep.

Only Evan couldn't sleep. And it wasn't because Juliet snored—which she did, but he didn't mind. It was because he couldn't shut off his brain.

Song lyrics flitted in and out of his thoughts. Thoughts about them and their future. About the band and how music had always been his dream. His path had no forks, no alternate routes.

For Evan it had always been music.

He knew he was going to play guitar and be the lead singer of a band, and since he was a kid, he wouldn't let anybody tell him differently. He'd say it with a straight face and so much conviction in his tone that even the most skeptical adults started to believe him by the end.

Music was his soul.

It ran through his veins.

Only now, something else was also his soul.

Someone else.

And she, too, ran hot through his veins. His heart beat to the tune of her.

To the tune of Juliet.

He needed to figure out a way that they could both live their dreams, take care of Hope and be together.

The sun was beginning to creep in behind the closed blinds before long, and he hadn't slept a wink.

Gently, he rolled her over to her side and off him, pulled on a pair of jeans from the pile of clean laundry on a chair by the dresser. Along with a new T-shirt and the leather jacket she'd shucked sometime around one thirty, he grabbed his guitar and left her sleeping beautifully in the bed.

The clock on the microwave said it was almost seven o'clock as he slid the glass sliding doors open and stepped barefoot on the porch and then down into the sand.

He didn't have to wander too far down the beach before he found a spot that hopefully wouldn't disturb anybody with his playing.

He strummed, getting the tune he'd come up with last night at the Pirate Festival just right before humming.

"Your hand on my shoulder ... takes me back ... takes me forward. Your hand in my hand ... gives me the strength that I need to go on, that I need to move into the future."

He dropped his right thumb over the strings, moving the finger of his left hand over the frets, keeping his eyes closed so he could feel the music, see the notes and the lyrics on the backs of his lids.

"The jewel of my heart ... I didn't know. For too long I've wandered ... the world all alone. Your hand on my shoulder ...your eyes on the stage ... your soul is my soul ..."

He wasn't sure how long he sat there. When he was in the zone, he tended to lose all track of time.

Oblivious Evan.

At least he came by it honestly.

The sun was climbing the sky, and he knew he'd have to pack it up and go pick up Hope from his moms' soon, but the draw of the music, of the shore and of how full and open his heart was kept him from moving off the dune and back toward the cottage.

He'd nearly figured out the bridge when something—nay, someone—wearing nothing more than one of his white T-shirts made her way toward him, smiling.

"That's beautiful," she said, coming to sit beside him, resting her head on his shoulder and yawning.

"You heard it?"

"Only bits and pieces. The wind is blowing the other way, so I only heard the guitar, but what I heard was beautiful."

She shivered, and he immediately removed his jacket and draped it around her shoulders, pulling the sides together. She glanced up at him and smiled, whispering, "I've been waiting fifteen years for you to do that."

"And I've been waiting my whole life to find a woman who gets as wild as you did last night. What came over—"

"The pineapple wine," she said, cutting him off and pressing her hand to her forehead. "You can blame Joanna for that."

"I'll be thanking Joanna more like it and sending that woman some flowers."

She rolled her eyes. "I probably shouldn't have opened that second bottle."

"Oh, but it was the second bottle that brought out wild Jules, and wild Jules is fun. Wild Jules put my jacket on and rode me like a—"

"Yeah, my memory isn't fuzzy, just my tongue."

"I don't care. I love you, and I'm going to kiss you with your morning breath and fuzzy tongue anyway," he said with a chuckle, swooping in for a kiss.

Later that morning, after they collected Hope from Evan's moms' place, the three of them wandered into Brewed with a View. Juliet was still feeling a little queasy from over-imbibing in the pineapple wine, so she didn't bother to take off her sunglasses as they stepped inside.

She held the door open so Evan could push the stroller inside.

Normally, the smell of fresh baked goods and coffee made her stomach grumble and her brain do a little happy dance, but today, she couldn't imagine putting anything in her stomach besides some water or maybe a bit of Gatorade.

They joined the line and waved at a few people they knew.

Juliet's head pounded.

When she woke up to the gentle sound of Evan's music, she felt okay. She even felt all right when she joined him on the beach wearing nothing but one of his T-shirts that she found in his drawer, but as they drove over to Evan's moms' house, her stomach started to revolt, her liver was huddled in the corner crying, and her brain began to lecture her on responsible drinking.

The only part of her body that seemed to be happy and screaming for a repeat of last night was between her legs.

She hadn't been so drunk that she didn't remember what happened last night, and as each and every memory came back to her, she smiled through the headache and her lady parts tingled with the desire for more.

Yes, she had been a little wilder than normal, but it wasn't all fueled by alcohol. Some of her reckless abandon was simply because she was just incredibly happy. Evan Spencer was in love with her.

Evan Spencer wanted to make their relationship work and not just have this be a summer hookup.

He wanted her in his life for the long term, and together they were going to figure out how to make that happen.

What woman wouldn't celebrate with pineapple wine and then loosen the strings on her inhibitions after getting glorious news like that?

If she really thought about it—well, not too hard because her brain really hurt—she was showing Evan more and more of who she actually was. Because she was a fun person. Yes, she was cautious, but in the right moment, with the right people, she knew how to have fun. She knew how to pull the pencil from her hair and embrace adventure.

She'd come out of her shell a lot when she went to Virginia for art school. She partied—which was something she never did in high school. She drank. She dated. She had boyfriends. She even posed nude for a sculpting class that a friend was teaching after her model canceled at the last minute.

She'd been nervous as hell to sit there naked for hours as strangers' eyes raked her bare body and slowly sculpted clay into her likeness, but the longer she sat there, the more liberating it became.

The more beautiful and comfortable in her own skin she felt.

Her back became straighter, her chin higher, her shoulders drew farther back, and even though she'd been told not to move, the proud, confident smile that lifted on her lips was unavoidable.

By the end of the night, after twelve people had stared at her and molded clay into the shape of her breasts, her hips, her face, her ears, her belly, she was no longer afraid to be seen. She was no longer afraid to be her quirky self.

Because she felt seen, and those that had seen her had been inspired by her.

After the class had emptied and it was just her and her friend, she wandered around the room and took in each piece, brought to tears by the way she was depicted.

And they weren't tears of sadness.

They were tears of appreciation.

The emotions overwhelmed her. Every person saw her from a different angle, saw her in a different way, and yet, every single person saw her as beautiful.

It was the first time she was able to see herself through someone else's eyes and in turn, truly see herself.

She'd changed that night.

Changed the way she carried herself, the way she viewed herself and how she valued herself. She'd walked around for so long with crippling insecurities, feeling invisible and overlooked, but that night she realized that people actually did see her, and how they saw her was beautiful.

Only when she saw Evan at the concert and then again on the beach, the Juliet she used to be, the Juliet that *he* knew her as, started to creep back in.

She felt invisible again. Not memorable.

She began to revert to her old self because that was who Evan knew.

But she needed to let him see more of the real, new her. And last night, with practically an entire bottle of pineapple wine to herself, she finally started to do just that.

"Well, don't you three just look so happy together," came a voice behind them that Juliet didn't recognize. Holding her temple in an attempt to ward off the pounding, she turned halfway around to find Beatrice Brewster, a friend and old lady co-conspirator of the trio, standing behind them.

"Hello, Nana Bee," Evan said before Juliet could open her mouth. "And Tim, how are you both?"

Nana Bee, as she preferred to be called, was with a young boy probably around eleven or twelve who Juliet knew to be Tim Medina. Tim's mother, who had recently passed away, had been good friends with Joanna over at Bottles of Bliss. Now Tim was being raised by his aunt, Shiloh Salcido, who was a firefighter, with her boyfriend Marvin Brewster, Beatrice's grandson.

Tim smiled. "Just here for the sweet rolls. They're Marvin's—and my—favorites."

Evan's eyes widened. "Oooh, I haven't tried the orange sweet rolls. I'll have to get some."

"So long as you don't take the last one," Nana Bee said, touching a hand to her perfectly coiffed chestnut hair, which curled lightly behind her ears. She gazed down into the stroller. "She really is a beautiful little girl. And you two are taking such good care of her."

"What's her name?" Tim asked, bending down to pick up the rubber bunny that Hope had tossed to the ground and smiling as he handed it back to her.

149

"Hope," Evan said.

Tim's hazel eyes widened. "That was my mother's name."

Juliet nodded. She knew that Hope Medina's passing had been hard on the whole town. "It's a beautiful name reserved only for the most beautiful people."

Tim's watery gaze brightened, and his back straightened. "You're right." He bent down and peered into the stroller at a wide-eyed and smiling Hope. "And you definitely are a beautiful person. You suit the name ... Hope."

Tears burned the back of Juliet's eyes, and her throat became tight. She exchanged looks with Evan and Bee, but none of them said anything.

"You're her parents, then?" Tim asked.

Evan's lips twisted, and Juliet stepped forward in the line, all them moving like well-trained caffeine-addicted cattle.

"Her parents passed away last month," Evan said slowly, his eyes darting between Bee and Tim. "I'm her dad's best friend. Her parents didn't have any brothers or sisters so now I'm taking care of Hope."

"Like me," Tim said, looking back down at Hope. "She's like me. My aunt now takes care of me because my mom passed away. My aunt and Marvin." He glanced at Nana Bee. "And Nana Bee, of course."

"Kind of," Nana Bee said, rubbing Tim's back. "She has lots of people who love her and will take care of her. A huge family, a whole village. Just like you."

Tim's smile was radiant, and Juliet could feel exactly how he was feeling, could see it on his face when he looked down at Hope and the way his smile changed. He didn't feel as different anymore. He'd met someone else—albeit a baby—who was in a similar situation as him, and it was comforting.

"I'm part of Hope's village, right?" Tim said.

"Absolutely, buddy," Evan agreed, resting a hand on Tim's shoulder and squeezing. "We all are."

It was their turn up at the counter. Olga Lindstrom, a beautiful blonde from Switzerland, was the barista behind the counter today. She often worked weekends since she was attending classes during the week at the local community college.

150

Her smile was big and bright and only grew wider when she spied Hope in the stroller. "Good morning, everyone," she said with her slight German accent. "What can I get you today?"

"Not morning anymore," Evan said, glancing at the clock on the wall behind the counter.

"Ah, so you are here for lunch then?" Olga teased.

"Orange sweet rolls, at least two," Evan said. "As well as two coffees, and—" He turned to Juliet. "A hangover cure smoothie, darling?" His tone was mocking and his grin cheeky.

Juliet closed her eyes and nodded at Olga. "I think that's probably a good idea."

Olga chuckled. "You got it. And for the little one? Maybe a small bowl of Cheerios? Dry? Eva keeps a box behind the counter for babies. Grace loved them."

"Sounds perfect," Evan said, handing over his credit card. He turned around to Nana Bee and Tim. "I only bought two orange sweet rolls. The rest are all yours. And tell Marvin I said *hi*."

"Will do," Nana Bee said with a grin.

Once they had paid and collected their rolls, coffees and smoothies, they went and found a place to sit inside, opting to take advantage of the air-conditioning.

Juliet took a sip of her smoothie.

It did not taste good.

It tasted like grass, dirt, metal—probably from the tomato juice—with just the most subtle hint of pineapple.

Evan chuckled at the face she made after she dared to swallow the sip. "That bad, huh?"

She pushed it toward him. "See for yourself."

His face was almost a mirror image of hers. "That's nasty."

She accepted the cup back from him and took another sip. "Yeah, but everybody I know swears that it helps."

Hope was happily munching on her Cheerios in her stroller, garnering a lot of cheerful and adoring glances from customers. Several of them would also look up at Juliet and Evan, smile and then whisper to the person they were with.

What was all this about?

Juliet sipped her hangover cure sludge and closed her eyes.

"Such a cute little family."

Juliet opened her eyes to find a friend of her mother's—Gladys Sherbourne—standing there smiling at the three of them.

"Hi, Gladys," Juliet said, shoving down the blob that lifted in her stomach. "How are you?"

"Still full from that potluck last night, that's for sure. Your mother and that lasagna of hers."

Juliet nodded. "Any excuse to make it, she finds it. And the bigger she can make it and for more people, the better."

Gladys nodded. Her blonde hair with streaks of silver was tucked into a white visor. She looked like she'd just come from tennis in her pastel yellow skirt and matching tank top. "I just have to say that the three of you look so happy together. So at peace and comfortable with each other. And the two of you and the way you've stepped up for little Hope, well ..." Her gray eyes turned sad, and she frowned. "Such a shame what happened."

Juliet felt Evan stiffen beside her.

Her hand landed on his arm. "It truly is. We're just doing the best we can."

"And together. It's just so wonderful." Gladys waved goodbye and headed out the door with a box of pastries under her arm.

Juliet glanced at Evan and grimaced. "I know it's probably really hard when people bring up Tony and Jacqui. I'm sorry."

He gripped her thigh. "It is, but it's bound to happen." He looked at Hope, then Juliet. "But they're not wrong in that we all look good together. In that we've found a groove, found some peace." He wrapped his arm around her, and she snuggled into his shoulder. "I mean, I don't think I could have done this without you."

She snuggled deeper into him and brought the paper straw of her disgusting—but helpful—smoothie to her lips. "And you'll never have to."

Chapter Fifteen

July Fourth came before they knew it, and the whole Daigle, Clarkson, Spencer, Rodriguez bunch gathered down on the beach to not only celebrate Hope turning one, but to celebrate her parents' lives as well. Evan could feel Tony and Jacqui there with them, celebrating as their daughter took her first steps, digging her bare, chubby baby toes in the sand, determined to follow the older children down to the water.

Evan held her hands, and she walked between his legs, grunting and giggling as he helped her chase after Ruby, Dia, Ashton and Silas. But she didn't want to hold his fingers; she wanted to do it on her own. She could only make it a few steps before she'd wobble and topple, spitting sand out of her mouth, since it'd been open and laughing when she fell.

He could feel Tony walking right beside him. Practically heard his friend say, "That's my girl," as Hope continued to pick herself up and try again.

Eventually, she would get frustrated with her lack of progress and reach for Evan's fingers, only to get frustrated with her lack of independence and let go of his hands again, determined to do it on her own.

It took her a while, but eventually, she made it to the water, where, not giving two hoots about the fact that she was in a diaper or the birthday dress that Juliet had bought for her, she plopped down at the shoreline and played gleefully in the waves.

Evan laughed, and he could have sworn he heard Tony laugh, too.

His friend had had such a distinct laugh, a booming, carefree and infectious laugh.

Maybe it was just the breeze mixed with the seabirds, but at that moment, standing beside a giggling and soaking wet birthday girl, on the edge of the water, Evan had never felt Tony's presence so strongly.

A hand landed on his back, and he knew who it was before he turned around.

"You okay?" Juliet asked, sliding her fingers down his arm and linking them with his.

He nodded and swallowed past the hard lump in his throat. "Just wishing her parents were here."

"They are," she said softly. "They'll always be here. For every birthday, every milestone."

He nodded again.

Hope giggled again and splashed her hands in the water, sending it and sand to splatter all over her dress.

"Good thing we have backup clothes," she said.

"Wonder when the day of backup clothes will end."

"I still spill coffee and get donut jelly on my shirt sometimes, so ... never?"

That made him laugh, and he turned to face the dunes where people were beginning to gather for the celebration of life portion of the day.

It wasn't quite sunset, but it would be soon, and then they would scatter Tony and Jacqui's ashes into the water.

His parents and Juliet's parents had handled all the food. There was a popup tent with a table heaped with platters and bowls of delicious food cooked by his moms, his sister, Juliet's sister-in-law and Juliet's parents.

Juliet had taken care of all the decorations and ordered a beautiful cake from The Rolling Pin Bakery.

Evan actually felt kind of useless when he thought about it. He had no job, no responsibility, but everyone assured him that it was all taken care of and that he just needed to make sure Hope was rested and in a great mood for the party.

Not caring that it got his dress shirt all wet, he scooped up Hope and plopped her on his hip, gathering strength and courage from Juliet's hand on his back as they made their way back up toward the tent and growing group of people.

Anybody who didn't know Tony and Jacqui would say that to hold a baby's birthday on the same day as her parents' celebration of life would be weird. But Evan knew—as did everyone else—that Tony and Jacqui would have wanted it this way.

Juliet took a sopping wet Hope from his arms and went to go change her into dry clothes, while Evan made uncomfortable small talk and shook hands with various people.

They'd ordered chairs and had them set up in the sand, though some people seemed to prefer to just sit on a blanket on the sand.

Within fifteen minutes, everyone had settled into their seats, and Hope was once again in dry clothes.

Evan cleared his throat and stepped up onto a small sand dune so that everyone could see him. A vice began to crank and tighten around his heart, and tears stung his eyes as he let his blurry gaze coast across the faces of everyone.

The trio were near the front, all of them dressed in dark gray or black. He recognized Addison and Travis Ford, Brock Gibson and his wife, Rani, as well as Eva Hollaway, her husband, Mac, Craig and Kolbi and a lot more somber but familiar faces.

He cleared his throat again, went to speak, but nothing came out.

Within seconds he felt her warmth beside him and her hand in his. "You've got this," she whispered.

But he didn't have this.

How did you say goodbye to your best friend?

He found Eric at the front, and their gazes locked.

Evan didn't even have to say anything, and Eric understood what he needed. He was up out of his seat, but rather than go and stand up with Evan and Juliet, he stepped behind the tent and emerged a second later with Evan's guitar. "You always were better at putting your feelings into song than saying them out loud," Eric said, handing Evan the guitar.

Evan nodded. "Thank you." He pulled the strap over his shoulder, lifted his head and gazed back out at the crowd. "This isn't one of my songs, but I think that this song would have been what Tony wanted to hear today. If any of you remember the Drakes, you'll remember that they were all hardcore Queen fans."

A few chuckles, smiles and nods drifted around the group.

"Like I'm sure you all probably called in a complaint for how loud Mr. Drake blasted his music when he was working in the yard, only to remember that you were calling the police to complain about a cop."

More laughter echoed through the crowd.

"Tony said he would never be able to marry a woman who didn't recognize the true genius that was Freddy Mercury, and I think he actually may have found an even more hardcore fan than himself in Jacqui. An honest-to-goodness match made in heaven. So they wouldn't want a sad song today. No Sarah McLachlan or Linda Ronstadt." He started to strum and watched the recognition of "You're My Best Friend" dawn in each and every person's eyes. "But somehow, I just don't think 'We Will Rock You' is *entirely* appropriate."

The crowd laughed again.

"Feel free to disagree with me." He licked his lips, and started to sing.

Continuing on with the acoustic version of the song, he glanced beside him at a teary-eyed Juliet. She was staring at him in awe, and he had to avert his eyes. Otherwise her tears would encourage his tears.

He closed his eyes, hoping that by not looking at the crowd, he could finish the song without tearing up or breaking down. He could already feel his throat getting tight the longer he sang. More images of Tony smiling and laughing and just being his wonderful self flitted behind his closed lids.

He also knew that if he opened his eyes and found Hope, he wouldn't be able to finish the song at all.

He was at the final chorus now, and he was sure he sounded awful. That people were probably scratching their heads, wondering how this guy had scored a record deal and went on tour with some big-name indie bands.

He drew his thumb down over the strings one more time and sang, "You're my best friend" for the last time before finally opening his burning eyes. Clenching his teeth, he lifted his head to find a still, silent and sniffling crowd, all of them staring at him in what he could only describe as awe.

He cleared his throat for probably the millionth time and was about to say something when Juliet slid her hand back into his and spoke up. "At this time, we'd like to invite anyone who wishes to say something about the Drakes to stand up either where you are or you can come up here."

She took the guitar from Evan and gently led him off the dune as a few people made their way up to the front.

They ducked behind the tent, and she put his guitar back in its case. "You okay?" she asked, concern filling her gaze.

He nodded and swallowed, his hands finding her hips. "Yeah."

She took his hand, and together they went and found a seat with Evan's moms and Hope.

The rest of the celebration of life was beautiful. Although sad, it wasn't as depressing as some funerals could get. Yes, there were tears, but there were also a lot of laughs. And when Eric got up to speak, telling the story of the time Evan, Eric and Tony went on a road trip down to Florida the summer before their senior year and ended up getting robbed and forced to hitchhike home rather than face the shame of having to call their parents for help, the whole crowd was in stitches by the end.

When the stories finally finished and the tears had somewhat dried up, Evan and Juliet brought Hope up in front of everyone, and Evan's moms wheeled out a cake and a bunch of cupcakes from The Rolling Pin. The entire crowd sang "Happy Birthday" to Hope, which had the little girl giggling, and then Evan and Juliet helped her blow out the candles.

It was sunset, Hope's face was covered with frosting, and everyone seemed to be having a wonderful time.

Eric approached Evan, two wooden boxes in his hands.

Evan didn't have to ask what they were to know what his friend wanted him to do next.

Licking frosting off his thumb, he passed Hope to Juliet, ditched his socks and shoes and rolled up the cuffs of his pants to just below his knees like Eric already had. He accepted one of the boxes from Eric, and the two of them, along with Hope and Juliet, headed back down to the water.

He didn't have to look behind him to know that the gathering of people was watching them. The conversations had died down, and he could feel their eyes on the back of his head.

They waded into the water until the waves lapped at the bottom of their rolled cuffs.

"We'll see you when this life is over, my friend," Evan said, opening the box. "This time on Earth is but a blip in eternity, where we can be together again soon."

"It's not goodbye," Eric said, his words coming out in a croak.

"Only see you later," Evan added.

Then together, they gently turned the boxes upside down and allowed the ashes of Tony and Jacqui—Hope's parents—to spill into the sea.

Evan turned to Hope. "If you ever need to talk to them, you just come right down to the water, baby. They're right here."

Hope's legs and arms flapped, and she giggled, smiling her beautiful three-toothed smile.

Evan lifted his gaze to Juliet, and she wiped a tear from beneath her eye and smiled at him.

And it was like being hit over the head with a saxophone or having his head clanged between two cymbals.

Yes, he had been living his dream for the last fifteen years. But dreams could change, couldn't they? Surely, not everyone's dream had to remain the same for their entire life.

And the woman smiling at him right now holding Hope—and everything Juliet encompassed—was his dream.

His new dream.

He loved music and always would, and he didn't want to break up the band, but now more than ever, he needed to figure out a way to have it all. To have both dreams, the old and the new.

Because if losing Tony had taught him anything, it was that their time on this Earth was short and precious, and if you didn't seize the opportunity to live your dream now, you might never have the chance.

Once the box was empty, Eric took it from Evan.

Juliet's cool, delicate hand found his, and together with Hope, they turned back toward the crowd and went to go finish celebrating a little girl turning one.

Chapter Sixteen

T hey were only days away from the charity music festival Rock the Shores, and it seemed like the whole town was talking about it.

Juliet had offered to donate four of her mugs, as well as a twelve-by-twenty-four painting of The Boardwalk that she'd painted last summer when she was visiting her parents for a week. She'd taken a bunch of pictures of the lively, colorful strip, then spent nearly three weeks in the evenings toiling away on it until it was just right. She hadn't parted with it yet, since she'd hung it in her house back in New Mexico for a while as it reminded her of home.

But now that she was home for good, she didn't need the reminder anymore since she could see that scene every day in the flesh.

She also donated a beginning pottery class, which was worth several hundred dollars, and ten hours of wheel time.

Everything would be put on the auction table, and people could go and bid at their leisure as they bought all the donated food and listened to the music.

Last week, Evan had met with Addison Ford at The Factory, and together they figured out where the best place for the portable stage would be. She also introduced him to a few local bands and musicians who would be opening for him.

It was Wednesday night—the festival was Saturday—and Juliet was cleaning up in the studio alone after her pottery class had left for the night. She told Terry he could head home after he helped her move all the bowls and mugs that the students had made to the drying rack.

She brought out her phone and found her favorite playlist. Many songs in that list she knew by heart, and she also happened to know the lead singer quite intimately.

She bit her lip at that thought.

Yes, she knew Evan Spencer of the October Coyotes intimately.

She knew every inch of the man's body by heart, just like she did his songs.

Once she was finished cleaning up, she spotted the freshly wiped wheel in the corner, and like a siren on a jagged rock in the sea, it called to her.

It'd been nearly two weeks since she sat down and threw a bowl or a mug or a vase. She'd been so busy with her pottery classes and then helping Evan with Hope that she hadn't done anything for herself in a while. She'd even started canceling on Joanna, Craig and Isla and bailing on their Saturday morning yoga ritual at Zen Bodies. Which was something she loved.

And when was the last time she went for a run?

Sure, she was getting *other* forms of exercise, but it wasn't the same.

Cracking her neck side to side, she filled up a small bucket with water, grabbed a sponge, opened up a bucket with pre-wedged clay balls that she'd prepared for her students, and walked over to the wheel.

She turned it on, sat down and spread her legs so the wheel was settled between them.

With just a little bit of water in the center of the wheel, she slammed the clay down into the center, put her foot on the pedal, dribbled water over the ball, got her hands wet and gently let her foot drop so the wheel began to spin.

With her elbows securely on her thighs, she pressed down hard on the clay, and as if coming up for air after being under water for far too long, she exhaled deeply.

She hardly told anyone this—Stella might be the only person who knew—but when she was at the wheel, it was where Juliet felt closest to her mother.

Edith Clarkson had developed an inoperable brain tumor and was taken from Juliet and her father when Juliet was only six.

Her memories of her mother were fuzzy, but they were still there, and when she sat down at the wheel—any wheel—she felt her mother there with her. Felt her mother's hands guiding her, helping her center the clay, center herself and focus.

A tear slipped down Juliet's cheek as she reached for more water, the clay cool and slippery beneath her fingers.

She hadn't sat down to sculpt in weeks, and in doing so, she felt a distance between her and her mother that she hadn't felt in ages.

She had no idea what she was making. Sometimes her fingers did the talking and what she thought might be a bowl turned into a vase or a mug.

She brought the clay up into a cone-like shape, then smashed it back down, repeating this process over and over again until she could feel with her fingers that the clay was centered.

Closing her eyes, she double-checked. It was easier to tell if the clay was centered by feel rather than sight. Did it hit anywhere weird in her hands? Was there a *clunk* against a finger pad?

The song changed over the speakers in the studio, and another Evan Spencer and the October Coyotes song came on, a slower one. Evan's deep, smooth voice slid through her ears and into her veins, into her soul until she found herself swaying with her eyes closed.

He really did have the most beautiful voice.

Soothing.

Gentle.

Sensual.

"Have you always listened to my music when you work?"

She nearly jumped clear out of her skin.

How did he manage to get in?

How did he manage to get in without jingling the bell?

You gave him a key a couple of weeks ago, and he probably came in through the back staff door.

Right!

After the shock wore off and the electricity in her limbs started to settle, along with her rapidly beating heart, she lifted her head to find the rock star of her dreams standing there behind the counter with a very cocky grin on his face.

She rolled her eyes, but her heart rate only picked up again. "You're on my playlist."

"I feel like the innuendo is just *right* there, but I can't figure out how to spin it." He stepped closer, his eyes taking in every inch of her. Every clay-covered inch of her.

"I'm too tired to think of one." She already knew that her hair was coming out of the pencil she held it up with. She'd been tucking and blowing the strands off her face since they weren't quite long enough to stay tucked behind her ears.

She hadn't bothered with makeup besides a little mascara, and that was probably falling under her eyes by now since she'd been wearing it for nearly fourteen hours.

"I've never seen you in action," he said softly. "Never seen the artist at work."

She rolled her eyes. "Well, stand back because the clay tends to fly."

"Was there a scene about this in a movie?" he asked, not taking a step back but rather several steps forward.

She eased her foot on the pedal, and the wheel slowed down and eventually stopped.

"There is." She jerked her head toward the bathroom. "*Ghost* with Demi Moore, Patrick Swayze and Whoopi Goldberg." Her brows pinched. "How do you not—" But she stopped herself when his expression turned coy. "You knew. You were just teasing me."

His smile made her insides get all tingly. "I might be Oblivious Evan, but I'm not an idiot."

Her cheeks grew warm, but that didn't keep her from grinning at him. He was right behind her now. She had to tilt her head up to look at him. His gentle, sexy brown eyes bored right into her, turning her into a puddle.

"My mom came over to watch Hope for a bit," he said, grabbing a stool and setting it right behind her, sitting down and leaning against her back. The heat of him and the way his legs bracketed hers was enough to make every one of her synapses fire at the same time.

This was *literally* her ultimate fantasy.

Not only had she watched *Ghost* more times than any preteen ever should, but she had fantasized about Evan Swayzeing her also probably more than she ever should have. Probably more than was healthy.

Normally, she felt really close to her mom when she was working on the wheel, but she was really hoping her mom had decided to go for a walk along the beach or The Boardwalk right about now.

He was wearing a fitted black T-shirt with a slight V-neck that had made her jaw drop and her mouth pool with saliva when he put it on this morning.

His fingers started at her elbows and slowly moved along her arms until his big hands covered her clay-caked ones. "Show me how to do it," he said, his breath warm against her ear.

She smiled and pushed her foot down on the pedal just enough for the wheel to start spinning slowly.

Just like she'd imagined it, just like in the movie, his fingers slid through hers, both of them now covered in clay just like hers.

She'd centered the piece. Now it was time to start shaping it.

"What are you making?" he asked, kissing her neck.

"I didn't have a plan," she said. "Sometimes I just sit down at the wheel and let the muse find me."

"Mmmm," he hummed. "I'm the same way with the guitar."

"You were working on something when I left ..." She guided their hands up a little, then together they stuck two fingers each, his on top of hers, into the center of the clay and began to press out.

The eroticism, the symbolism of what they were doing with their fingers and how it all looked and felt was not lost on her in the least.

Pottery could be extremely erotic. Everything was done with the hands; everything was wet and smooth and involved pressing down with your fingers. She'd certainly found herself aroused on more than one occasion watching a pottery video, even when the view was of just the person's hands.

He started to hum the tune she recognized from that morning.

It was beautiful.

Then he started to put words to it. "Taken by surprise ... every day I see the love in your eyes. I was a fool not to see what was right in front of me. You're my new dream, the one I want forever ... the one I can't live

without. You are my sunrise, my last goodnight ... the love of my life."
He cleared his throat and chuckled awkwardly. "It's a work in progress.
Definitely won't be ready for Saturday. But hopefully for September
when we head back into the studio to start recording again."

Her throat hurt, and more tears burned the backs of her eyes. "It's
beautiful," she said, though it came out more as a croak.

He kissed her neck again.

With their fingers having made a decent-size hole in the center of the
clay, she used their other hands to help maintain the shape and push in
and pull up at the same time their fingers inside the clay did the same
thing. This made the hole become wider, the wall between their fingers
to become thinner but also taller.

Every movement, every slide of their fingers against each other, every
puff of his breath against her neck turned her on even more.

"Did you ever fantasize about us doing this when you were younger
and madly in love with me?" he asked, the humor in his voice sending
ripples of warmth through her and making her nipples pebble, despite
how hot she was getting.

"More times than I will ever admit to you," she said before swallowing.

"And how did those fantasies end?"

"When I was younger ... just with a kiss ..."

"And when you were older?"

"More than a kiss."

"Mmm," he hummed, his lips against her neck buzzing her skin and
sending a jolt of electricity through her. "So how long is the process from
start to finish?"

She glanced at him over her shoulder, which caused his lips to leave her
neck. "Another innuendo?"

"No. I'm serious. If we made something today, how long until it was
completely done and ready to sell?"

Her lips twisted. "A few weeks."

Evan's eyes went wide. "A few *weeks*?"

"The clay has to dry. I have to then carve away the excess, add my
stamp, add a bottom base, let it dry more, bisque-fire it, glaze it, let the
glaze dry, rub away the excess glaze, then wait for enough other pieces to
be made to make firing the kiln cost-effective. Then it's at least nine and

half hours in the kiln, followed by waiting for it to cool down, which can take a day to a day and a half. So, yeah, a few weeks. It's why I discourage tourists from throwing clay and encourage them to paint a bisque-fired piece like one of those pirate figurines the trio was painting. But those who *do* want to throw clay also pay for shipping and shipping insurance."

His eyes were still wide. "And yet many tourists still do throw clay?"

"A few. I have two kilns dedicated to the bisque-fired ones and one for the handmade pottery. So far, the system we have works." She lifted a shoulder and turned back to focus on the clay. She'd eased her foot on the pedal so they didn't ruin whatever it was they were creating. "I have space for one more kiln and would like to have two dedicated to each craft, since I can't mix as they fire at different temperatures. But the kiln fairy doesn't seem to hear my wishes. I'm going to have to get another one the old-fashioned way, by paying for it."

"And what about those ones up there?" he pointed to a bunch of large white vases with intricate floral patterns painted on them. Mostly pansies and irises, but a few had birds of paradise and poppies. There were also some that had gold leaf painted on them with the flowers.

"Those are mine," she said. "They're in their final stages of drying before I send them to a store up in Maryland for commission."

"You *made* those? Like painted them, too?"

Her lips twisted as she tried to hide her smile of pride but then finally gave up the fight and nodded. "Yeah. I throw the vase, fire it, then paint on it, give it a clear glaze and fire again. That's actually my speciality. What I'm known for. That and my petal-edged salad bowls."

"What you're *known* for." It was impossible not to detect the awe in his voice. "And what does one of those beauties sell for?"

She pointed to the largest one that was not quite two feet tall and was covered in purple and yellow pansies. It had taken her several hours on the wheel and even longer to paint the flowers. And her time was worth a lot. "That one is about four hundred," she said. "Keep in mind, I only make around forty-five percent on commission. The store takes the rest. So I need to price them high enough that my time spent making them is worth it."

"Right," he said softly. "That makes sense."

She pressed down on the pedal again, and the clay started to spin. Her fingers guided open the mouth of the piece while Evan's fingers traveled up her arms, sensually massaging her wrists and forearms. "Wasn't this what Patrick was doing?"

She giggled. "Did you watch a clip of the movie on YouTube before you came here?"

"I plead the fifth," he said, scraping his teeth up her neck, which caused her eyes to flutter closed.

"You won't hear me complaining. You've got sixteen-year-old Juliet nearly having a heart attack from happiness right now."

"Hmmm ... and what about thirty-one-year-old Juliet?" Not caring that he got clay all over her face, he reached up and cupped her jaw, angling her head backward. She released the pedal again.

"Thirty-one-year-old Juliet is pretty happy that you showed up and sat down behind her, not gonna lie."

"Your work is stunning," he said, his breath mingling with hers. "You're stunning." Then he took her mouth and swept his tongue inside.

She released the clay and spun around on the stool, only breaking their kiss for a moment. Neither of them cared about the mess. He wrapped his arms around her waist, and she wrapped hers around his neck as she climbed up onto his lap and they continued kissing.

As much as she knew that Demi and Patrick took things all the way past third base and home, not caring that their hands were covered in clay as they rounded the base, Juliet knew better than to indulge her fantasies too fully.

Kissing was as far as they would go here in the studio, but even this was enough.

He Patrick Swayzed her, and it had been wonderful. It was everything she'd ever dreamed of, and even though "Unchained Melody" wasn't playing in the background to complete the fantasy, the fact that it was another Evan Spencer and the October Coyotes song seemed to just make it all the better. This was their reality. It was no fantasy, no movie reenactment.

She felt his need for her against her inner thigh and rocked against it, drawing a groan out from the depths of his chest. She caught it in her mouth and bit his lip, making him smile against her mouth.

"We're going to need a shower," he said, breaking their kiss but only enough to drag his lips across her cheek.

"Your shower is bigger than mine. Big enough for two, I believe."

"It *is*," he said cheekily. Glancing behind her, he lifted his chin. "Not a bad bowl for a beginner and a very distracted professional."

She craned her neck around to look at what they'd created.

He wasn't wrong.

Sure, she could never sell it, but because they had made it together, that made it priceless.

Climbing off him, she went to go and get the wire she would use to cut the clay from the wheel. "Go over to the wall and pick a glaze color."

He did as he was told, only to return to her a moment later. "Green," he said matter-of-factly, watching her slide the wire beneath their bowl. "Just like your eyes."

She gently lifted the bowl and motioned for him to hold out his hands. He did, and she placed their masterpiece into his palms. "Over to the drying shelf, please." She pointed to where all her student's pieces sat on plywood. Again, he did as he was told, returning back to her, and just when she thought he was going to let her start cleaning up, he grabbed her hand and hauled her against his hard body, once again cupping her face.

"Addison told me everything that you've donated to the silent auction," he said, staring down into her face with those soulful brown orbs of his. "It's too much."

She shook her head and glanced away for a moment. "I had hoped we could say they were from an anonymous donor, but Addison said that wouldn't fool anyone."

"It wouldn't. You've become famous and fast."

She scoffed. "I wouldn't say *famous*. Even though there is a huge pottery community in North Carolina, the fact that I offer both paint-your-own and throw-your-own is unique, that's all."

"No, it's not, and don't sell yourself or your success and accomplishments short." His expression turned a little grim. "But you've donated a lot. More than anyone else."

"It's for a good cause. A cause close to my heart. I am happy to do it."

His thumb, now rough with dried clay, grazed her cheek. "God, I love you, Jules. I wouldn't have been able to do any of this without you. I don't *want* to do any of it without you."

She blinked up at him, determined not to let the tears of extreme joy break the dam. "And I love you, Evan. I always have."

Chapter Seventeen

I t was the day of Rock the Shores, and thankfully, Evan's moms had offered to take Hope for the day so that Juliet and Evan could help Addison and the rest of the crew set up for the music festival.

Evan was helping set up the sound stage and the speaker system now that the portable stage had been erected outside. It was the perfect day for a festival, if a little hot. But Addison had thought of everything and made sure there were plenty of shady pop-up tents and umbrellas scattered throughout the area so people could escape the heat.

Evan was taking a breather and drinking from a water bottle while chatting with Raleigh Carmichael and Travis Ford when a nervous-looking guy with copper-colored hair and blue eyes stepped forward. The kid couldn't have been more than twenty-two, but he hadn't put on any muscle since his puberty growth-spurt. He was tall and lanky, and his arms seemed to damn near reach his knees.

"M-Mr. Spencer?" the guy asked, clutching something in his large palms; his gaze shifted across the men's faces.

Evan nodded. "Call me Evan, please. I don't have a dad, so I can't say, 'Mr. Spencer is my father,' but I don't like being called Mr. Spencer either way." He chuckled, sipped his water and held out his hand. "What's your name?"

The guy swallowed, and his large Adam's apple jogged in his throat. "Um, Denver ... Denver Stratten."

"Nice to meet you, Denver. That's a great name. Great band name."
He turned to Travis. "Denver Stratten and the Brown Shoe Gang."

"I take it you didn't name *your* band," Raleigh teased. "Because that
was garbage."

Evan grinned. "I did not. And you're right." He and Denver released
hands. "What can I do for you, Denver?"

Again, Denver swallowed. "I, um ... I am in a band. N-not Denver
Stratten and the Brown Shoe Gang, b-but a band by a different name."

"What's the name?" Evan asked, glancing quickly at Travis and
Raleigh. All three of them knew exactly why Denver had approached
him. Twenty bucks said the kid had a flash drive in his hand and it was a
demo of his band's music.

"We're called Beach Glass, and I, um ... I was wondering if you might
be able to take a listen to my band or pass it on to your record label or
something. We're from Cinnamon Bay, just like you, and it's so hard to
get noticed. I mean, we're on YouTube and TikTok and stuff, but even
still ..." He held out the flash drive, which shook in his trembling hand.

Evan took it. "You playing today?"

Denver nodded. "Yeah, Mrs. Ford booked us in the second slot. We're
really excited. It's our first live gig." There was the kid's spark. Evan had
been worried he didn't have one. But the more he talked about his music
and playing, the more alive he became.

That was exactly how Evan felt.

He empathized with Denver. However, unlike this kid, Evan had
left Cinnamon Bay at eighteen, studied music for a couple of years in
Nashville, found his band while he was there, and the rest was kind of
history. Up until then, he'd only ever played on his own. He wasn't sure
he was even the band-playing kind of musician, but when he and the
other four guys in the band played together, it all just clicked.

He missed his band.

Missed them a lot.

The summer with Juliet and Hope was great, and despite the grief he
still felt in his heart over Tony and Jacqui, he was making the most of his
time off the concert circuit.

But he missed the guys. Missed people who understood what it was
like to *have* to play music. People who understood the demand and

the toll life on the road took on your mind and body. People who understood the adrenaline rush you experienced when you stepped on stage and thousands of people cheered and screamed because they loved your music.

"I'll tell you what," Evan started, giving Denver another once-over and seeing so much of himself in the young kid's eyes, "I'll listen to your set today, and if I like it, I'll give your demo a listen, since we all know live and recorded are different. Then I'll see about passing it on to my record label."

Denver's face lit up like the night's sky on the Fourth of July. "Really, Mr. Sp—I mean Evan. Really, Evan? That's so amazing. Thank you. Thank you so much."

Evan grinned. "Just play a great set, man. Make the crowd go wild."

Denver nodded. "I will—I mean, *we* will. I promise." With a skip in his step and excitement all over his face, Denver took off toward a minivan, where it looked like three other guys were waiting inside with terrified looks on their faces.

Evan, Raleigh and Travis remained silent as they watched Denver climb into the van. Seconds later, a roar of cheers echoed out of the Dodge Caravan.

"Well, you made somebody's day," Travis said with a deep chuckle. "How often does that happen?"

"Often enough that I knew it was happening before it happened. Everybody has big dreams. I'm not going to be the one to squash his. I'll do what I can if I like his music."

"That ever actually amount to anything?" Raleigh asked, reaching down into a cooler filled with ice, pulling out another water bottle and cracking open the lid. "Have you ever helped launch someone's career?"

Evan squinted and stared down at his feet for a moment. He'd certainly taken several demos over the years, listened to all of them, and those he liked he passed on to the manager at his record label. But he never followed up. He kind of just left it in Remy's hands. If Remy liked it, then he'd pursue the person. But he also couldn't recall Remy actually moving forward with anyone Evan had sent to him.

All those dreams that had been squashed.

All those aspiring singers and musicians that he had given false hope to.

Had he given them false hope?

Would it have been better to have not accepted their demos and let them leave without any hope that he could help springboard their music career? What would have been the lesser of the two evils? Immediate disappointment with no hope, or hope, then disappointment later?

"You okay?" Travis asked, putting a hand on Evan's shoulder and bringing him back to the now.

Evan grunted, nodded and sipped his water. "Just realizing that I don't think the record producer I've given demos to in the past has ever called or signed any of the people I sent his way." He shook his head. "I'm not even sure he listened to their music."

"Record producers probably get a hundred demos a week," Raleigh said. "Just be lucky you're one of the ones he *did* listen to."

"Yeah ..." Evan said, not really paying attention.

Addison appeared, sidling up next to Travis. They were whispering something. His brows pinched in concern before his hand subtly rested on her lower belly. She gazed up at him with love in her eyes but also slight irritation. He defused her ire with a swift kiss, leaving her rosy-cheeked and starry-eyed. "We're almost ready, gentlemen," she said with a smile as she leaned into Travis when he wrapped his arm around her possessively.

"Can't wait to hear all the other bands you have lined up," Evan said just as his phone in his pocket began to vibrate and ring.

He pulled it out.

Trey Garber.

His band manager.

He hadn't heard from Trey in a couple of months. Along with the band, Trey was taking some much-needed R&R.

He apologized to the people around him and stepped behind a box truck for privacy, connecting the call. "Trey, buddy, how goes it? Long time. How's your summer?"

"Been awesome, man. Mostly been at my brother's place in the Hamptons. I tell you, New Yorkers know how to vacation."

"Yeah? Nothing but beach, booze and Upper East Side beauties?"

"Spot on, brother. But listen, I have incredible news. Incredible. This is going to blow your freaking mind. This is what we've all been waiting for. This is it."

Unease fought excitement for top emotion inside of Evan.

Trey was prone to hyperbole, but at the same time, it could actually be something amazing.

"What is it?" Evan asked, finding the drawn-out lead-up to be more frustrating than anything.

"Have you heard of a little band called ... Janice's Homemade Casserole?"

Evan snorted.

He snorted every damn time he heard that stupid band name. They were huge in the indie rock band world, despite their awful name. They were who Evan Spencer and the October Coyotes dreamt of being—minus the dumb name.

"No," Evan said teasingly. "Haven't heard of them."

"You're a dick," Trey retorted. "But I love you anyway. Janice's Homemade Casserole, or JHC as they are now being called, since their band name is freaking awful—"

"Agreed."

"One of the bands set to headline for their nine-month European tour just broke up and pulled out. And guess who they asked to come in their place?"

Evan's bottom lip nearly hit the dirt.

"You, you dick! The whole band. Janice's Homemade Casserole—damn it, I hate that name—"

"Agreed," Evan said, but he still hadn't completely pulled his bottom lip up from the dirt.

"JHC have invited Evan Spencer and the October Coyotes to open for them for the next nine months IN EUROPE! Isn't this amazing? Didn't I tell you I had amazing news? Like the best news in the freaking world. Like tell me you don't love me and that you don't want to marry me right now. Tell me."

"I, uh ..."

Holy crap. This was *the* dream.

"Speechless. I get it. I was, too."

173

"This is amazing, Trey. Oh my God!" He pushed his fingers through his hair, his face now hurting he was smiling so hard. "This is incredible. I ... I can't believe it. We've always wanted to do a European tour. To hit that untapped market."

"Right! There's that Evan Spencer enthusiasm. This could catapult your career, man. Take you from sort of known to a freaking household name if things go well. I nearly crapped my pants when their manager called. I definitely spat out the scotch I was drinking. Pissed off my brother since it wasn't cheap scotch. But whatever, at least I managed to do it on the tile and not his Persian rug, am I right?"

"Janice's Homemade Casserole wants *us* to open for them?" He still couldn't believe what he was hearing. Despite their tragic choice of band names, he actually really loved JHC's music. He'd only met the band once or twice, but all the guys had been friendly, kind and encouraging. The music industry could be cutthroat, but over the years Evan and the Coyotes had made some solid friends and allies.

Shaking his head and still smiling, he turned around and lifted his gaze. Out of the corner of his eye, he spotted dark hair in a ponytail and black-framed glasses. He turned slightly, and there she was.

Juliet.

Smiling and chatting with Addison.

She wore a pair of denim cut-offs and a white T-shirt with a V-neck, and he honestly could not remember her ever looking so damn sexy. Yes, that dress at the pirate festival had been something else. So had her crop top at the concert. And he couldn't forget how she'd pulled off his leather jacket—and nothing else.

The woman looked amazing in everything, anything and nothing. But today, in jean shorts and a white tee with her hair up, her glasses on and that genuine Juliet smile, he honestly couldn't think of a more beautiful woman in the whole damn world.

An all-American, girl-next-door, natural beauty.

She spotted him watching her, and her face lit up. She waved at him, then winked.

He waved awkwardly like an idiot only to realize that Trey was still nattering away to him on the phone. "We need to commit by July twenty-seventh," Trey said.

"What day is it today?"

"The twenty-first. I mean, I was hoping that after talking to you today, I could just call their manager back as soon as we hang up and then confirm that we're doing it."

His excitement about the prospect of a European tour deflated like a popped balloon, and a sinking feeling formed deep in his belly the longer he looked at Juliet.

He'd been so pumped about living the dream, about going on tour and opening for a big band, that for a brief moment he forgot about the real world, about reality. About the dream of a woman standing just fifty feet away and the baby he'd been given the responsibility of caring for.

"Ev?" Trey said, drawing Evan out of his confusion. "So can I call their manager back and say *yes?*"

Evan shook his head. "Sorry. No ... I need to talk to the rest of the band."

Trey released a loud sigh. "That's what I figured. I was just hoping that you'd be able to speak for them, but I get it."

"A lot has happened over the summer. Like a lot. I ... I need time to think."

"Think about what, man? This is the opportunity of a lifetime. This is the dream."

"Yeah ... the dream." Evan lifted his head again to see Juliet laughing with Addison. Eva had also joined them, and all three women were standing under a white popup tent sipping from water bottles. "Don't you think dreams can change, though, Trey?"

"To what? You want to start singing country? Folk? You're indie alternative rock, man. And you sing it well. Don't switch genres now, not when you're on your way to the top." He chuckled. "Do you want me to call the rest of the band, or do you want to?"

"I'll do it," Evan said quickly. "I'll do it tomorrow. I'm getting ready to sing at a charity music festival."

"Oh, raising money for stray dogs or something?"

"Something like that." Evan didn't have it in him to go into detail with Trey. Not about Tony, Hope or even Juliet. The man was a good manager, had done well by the band over the last several years, but the guy could be shallow. There wasn't much deep down with Trey

Garber. He liked money, he liked women, and he liked them by the wheelbarrow-load. But he also ran his mouth a bit too much, which was why he hadn't been able to sign on to manage any bigger bands, because none of them could stand his nonstop flapping lips.

However, Evan and his band put up with Trey because for all his faults, they also weren't afraid to be honest with him, to tell him to stop talking and go sit in the corner and be quiet.

"Okay, well, let me know in the next day or so. Then we can get back into the studio and practice. I'm sure you're all a little rusty."

"Probably," Evan said blandly, his brain no longer on the conversation but rather the upcoming conversations he was going to have to have with certain people.

And one of those certain people was walking toward him, a vision in Daisy Dukes with a smile only for him.

"Listen, man, I'll talk to the band, then call you by Wednesday, okay?" He needed to end the call before Jules got there.

Trey made a strangled noise in his throat. "Wednesday?"

"Yep. Wednesday. Today's Saturday. That gives me until the twenty-fifth. You said we had until the twenty-seventh. Still lots of time. Okay, I gotta go. Nice hearing from you, Trey. Say hi to your brother. Okay, bye." He ended the call, shoved his phone in his pocket and lifted his head just as Juliet got there. "Hi."

"Hi," she replied, giving him a suspicious look. "Who was that?"

He shook his head. "My band's manager. Just checking in. Making sure I haven't given up music and decided to start a microgreens farm and wear socks with Birkenstocks."

Her laugh mellowed him. "Are those things mutually exclusive? Socks and Birkenstocks and growing microgreens?"

Forcing a chuckle, he faked a smile to go with it and wrapped his arms around her waist, rubbing her back. "I'm sure they must be."

She looped her arms around his upper torso, and tilting her head back, she hit his eyes with hers before lifting a brow. "You okay?"

He nodded. "Yep."

"Getting performance anxiety? Stage fright?" Her smile was wicked and sexy.

Now that actually made him laugh and eased the tension and dread that he could feel building inside him like a freak storm. "When have I *ever* had performance anxiety? Hold your tongue, woman. Musicians can be incredibly superstitious, and even mentioning such a thing could wreak havoc." He brought his voice down. "On stage *and* in the bedroom."

She chuckled and rested her cheek against his chest. "I can't wait to hear your new songs."

His fingers played invisible piano keys along her vertebra. "Songs inspired by you."

Tightening her grip around him, she inhaled deeply. "We're going to make this work, right? You being a big, famous rock star and me a—"

"Big, famous sculptor," he finished.

"Well, ceramic artist, but I appreciate the effort." She glanced up at him, the humor gone from her eyes, replaced now with worry. "We'll figure out how to have it all, right?"

His throat grew tight again, and he rested his chin on the top of her head after kissing it. "We will, Jules. With everything inside me, I know we will."

Chapter Eighteen

Rock the Shores went off without a hitch.

Evan, of course, was the final performer on stage, with all the other bands playing several songs, building up the crowd's anticipation for their headliner.

And even though he was without his band, Evan Spencer of the October Coyotes brought down the house. Or the outdoor festival area beside the factory.

Whatever. He was amazing, and that was what mattered.

Juliet sat on the blanket near the front of the stage, beside Evan's mom, his sister and her family, and Eric and his family. Hope was perched in Juliet's lap—well, for as long as a newly walking one-year-old would sit still. They'd gone and bought her some enormous baby headphones that looked hilarious on her. She could still hear the music, but they didn't want to damage those little eardrums of hers. The little girl seemed just as taken with Evan as Juliet was, watching in awe as he sang his heart out.

It felt as though he was singing each and every song right to Juliet.

She was sure he did take his eyes off her and look out to the crowd at some point, but it didn't feel like he did so for long.

His gaze remained glued to her, and she barely blinked as she watched him perform, listened to his voice and sang along with her favorite songs.

But it was when he broke out some of his new stuff—the songs he said had been inspired by her—that she was unable to hold back her tears and let them fall unchecked down her cheeks.

His "hidden soul mate," as he'd called her in one song, *off in the shadows, never far,* but *leaving him in the dark.* It was powerful, emotional but also uplifting, because even though now she knew more than ever that Evan Spencer finally saw her, hearing it in his song and having him sing those words right to her made it all just feel a million times more real.

When she went to him earlier and he quickly shoved his phone in his pocket, she'd been hit with an unnerving feeling that even now she couldn't quite shake. He seemed distant and distracted. There was definitely something bothering him, and it was more than just a bit of cold feet to step back on stage after a few months' hiatus.

There was passion and love in his eyes as he sang and looked at her, and maybe she was manifesting something that wasn't there, but she also thought she saw pain, confusion and this weird hesitation as he looked at her.

She did like to consider herself an Evan Spencer expert and that she knew all of his expressions and what each one of his looks and smiles meant, considering she'd basically worshipped the man her entire teenage life.

But this was a look she didn't know.

A look she didn't understand and that worried her.

Halfway through his set, Stella joined their blanket, since her shift at the studio was over. She and Juliet had, of course, made up after what Stella said about Evan being a flight risk, but even so, the way Stella regarded Evan was with quiet caution and more reserve than she had before.

Juliet hoped that when Stella finally saw that she and Evan were rock-solid and going to make it work, she would thaw the last of her frosty exterior.

"I can't go on living in this big blue world without you!" Evan finished, ending the song with a final chord before placing his hand over the guitar strings and lifting his face out to the crowd, a big smile on his face.

Everyone cheered, hooted, hollered and whistled.

Juliet and all the people at her blanket stood up and clapped, along with several others at surrounding blankets, too.

Soon the entire fenced-off area for the festival—which was really full—resounded with a thunderous roar of applause as everyone stood up and clapped and cheered.

Evan's eyes found hers, and his smile grew wider.

Tears stung her eyes, and she wiped them away, clapping her hands harder as he bowed and waved to the crowd before walking offstage.

Addison Ford made her way past him, thanked him, then stepped in front of the microphone.

"Thank you so much, Evan!" she said, turning to face Evan, who was now standing at the corner of stage left and taking a quick sip of water. "Come on, everyone. Let's hear it one more time for Evan Spencer of the October Coyotes."

Just like they had a moment ago, the crowd went nuts, clapping and cheering, so much so that Hope became scared and Juliet felt pudgy little hands grip her shins.

She looked down to find a wide-eyed, crying Hope, her three little teeth exposed as she wobbled on her legs and looked up at Juliet.

Juliet picked up the baby and planted a kiss on her cheek. "That's noisy, huh?"

Hope calmed right down once she was no longer on the ground and forced to stare at hundreds of sets of knees. She smiled and giggled in Juliet's arms, clapping with everyone else until the ruckus began to calm down.

"I just want to thank all of you for coming out today, for your donations, for your support. To all the businesses who donated food, drinks, items for the silent auction and to those who just donated their time. We couldn't have done this without you."

The clapping started up again, but it wasn't as insane as when Evan finished his song.

Speaking of Evan, the main attraction himself wandered back out on stage, this time without his guitar.

He stood next to Addison and spoke softly to her. She nodded and stepped aside so he could speak into the mic.

Everyone found their seat on their blankets again, and the crowd settled down until it was almost eerily quiet.

He cleared his throat. "I just want to say my own thank-you to all of you. To Addison and Travis Ford, to the Carmichaels for the use of Aggie Hall, to Eva and Mac at Brewed with a View, to Top This, The Rolling Pin, Brock Gibson at Tradewinds, to everyone who donated items for the silent auction. Your generosity, your selflessness have not gone unnoticed." He swallowed, and Juliet could see him fighting back the tears. "Tony Drake was one of my best friends. He was ... Mr. Silverlining. Even though he'd been dealt a pretty crappy hand in life, what with his parents dying when he was seventeen, the man remained one of the most positive people I have ever met. He never stopped volunteering, never stopped giving, never stopped helping. And Jacqui was the same way. They would both give you the shirts off their backs and walk home in the snow naked if it meant you were warm.

"Tony meant a lot to Cinnamon Bay. Both he and Jacqui did, and now that Hope is back in The Bay, I hope you will help me keep the memory of her parents—and her grandparents—alive by telling her just how amazing they were every chance you get. Because they were incredible people, and Hope deserves to know that we all thought so."

He cleared his throat again and wiped his knuckle beneath his eye.

"I don't know what Tony and Jacqui were thinking naming me Hope's guardian, but I'm going to need everyone's help raising her. Don't they say that it takes a village? Maybe that's why they did it, because they knew I'd need a village to raise her and that the perfect village to do so was right where I left it."

A few chuckles echoed around the still mostly quiet festival grounds.

"Every one of you here tonight is part of that village, and I hope you know just how much I appreciate you. Just how much Tony and Jacqui appreciate you. Hope is one amazing little girl, and I can't wait for us to all share our stories of how amazing her parents were with her, too." He glanced at Addison for a moment, then turned back out to the crowd. "So thank you, everyone. All the proceeds tonight will be going into a trust for Hope Drake so that she may have the absolute best life possible. Good night, and thank you."

He waved, then started to clap, which instigated the crowd to begin clapping again.

Hope started clapping and smiling, and when Juliet caught Evan's eyes, he was encouraging her to stand up and lift Hope up so that she could see all the people who had come out to support her.

Juliet did so, even though she felt like it was her who was on display more than anything.

Hope's enormous blue eyes scanned the festival space, and her smile grew wider.

"You going to wave?" Juliet asked her. Hope had only recently learned to wave and was having a ball busting out her new skill to anyone she could. She also knew the word *wave,* and upon hearing Juliet say it, she started to wiggle her hand in the air.

Juliet turned back to Evan.

He was looking right at her.

She gave him the biggest smile she could muster, but that look from earlier was back in his eyes, and her smile suddenly felt forced and the corners of her mouth became heavy.

The crowd's clapping began to die down, so she pulled Hope down and put her back on her hip, then the two of them sank back down to the blanket.

Now Juliet was doing everything she could *not* to look at Evan. She focused all her attention on Hope, handing her a rice cracker and going on the hunt for her water bottle.

The man was wreaking havoc on her emotions right now.

She couldn't figure him out.

Or it's all in your head and he's completely fine.

Yeah, that was a possibility, too.

She'd worried herself sick with other boyfriends before, thinking they were quiet and slightly withdrawn because they were planning to break up with her, only to find out that something was wrong with the motorcycle and they were just mentally trying to figure it out. And it had absolutely nothing to do with her.

Maybe that was the case here.

Maybe Evan was just working through a song he was struggling with, or his manager had said something to him that upset him or made him need to think extra hard. Was he being called back into the recording studio before the summer was over?

Was there a problem with his record label?

A problem with his band?

It could have nothing to do with her, and here she was nauseous with worry because she didn't recognize the look in his eyes.

But when he worried, she worried.

She loved him, and to not see joy in his eyes but rather confusion hurt her heart. He'd already been through so much this summer with the loss of Tony and Jacqui and trying to figure out how to be a parent to Hope, he didn't need more stress in his life.

"Great set, bro," Eric said, standing up, clasping hands and then hugging Evan as he made his way toward them on their blanket nest. "If I wore panties, they would have melted right off."

Evan joined the laughter, all smiles—except for his eyes. "Thanks, man. That *is* the goal. Get those panties melting right off. You saying you're going commando?"

Eric snorted and did no more than lift his brows, flashing that token bright white Eric smile. "Only Isla gets to know for sure."

A loud crash somewhere in the distance echoed through the fenced-off area, making them all jump and turn to see where the noise came from.

Hope startled in Juliet's arms and started to cry.

Someone had dropped their cymbals as they were unloading from a van.

"Shh, it's okay," she said, trying to comfort Hope, but Hope's arms were stretched out, reaching for Evan, and she was kicking Juliet in the thighs to propel herself forward.

Evan's gaze widened, and when he realized that Hope wanted him for comfort over Juliet, over everyone else there, something in his expression changed.

A realization of sorts. Maybe an epiphany?

His gaze softened, and he stepped forward and reached for Hope, only giving Juliet a half glance before focusing all of his attention on the little girl. "It's okay, peanut. That was a big noise, wasn't it?"

Hope calmed right down as soon as she was in Evan's arms.

Juliet exchanged looks with the people around her. Everyone was thinking the same thing.

Not quite like a duckling fresh from the egg, but Hope had finally imprinted on Evan and now, he was her everything.

As it should be.

Knowing smiles coasted across faces before Juliet turned back to Evan and Hope.

"And did you have fun, peanut? Did you dance and sing?" he asked her, running his palm over her short blonde peach-fuzz hair and kissing the side of her head. She was holding on to his pinky finger on the other hand like it was a joystick for a video game, jerking it around aggressively. He didn't seem to mind.

"She was certainly trying to dance," Evan's mother Glenda said. "She was bouncing to the beat, those little knees just a-bending."

Juliet looked up at Evan and tried to snag his gaze, but just like she'd been trying to avoid his gaze on stage, he seemed to be avoiding hers now.

Why?

They were so out of sync, and it was giving her serious anxiety.

"We should probably think about getting this little love bug home," he said, finally focusing on Juliet. "I'm happy to do it by myself if you'd rather stay with everyone else here for a bit longer."

Why was he offering that?

He'd never offered her that before. He always asked her or just insinuated she join him.

Did he not want her to stay the night?

Did he not want her to come back to his place at all?

She couldn't get a read on him, and it was bugging the crap out of her.

Just an hour before the show, they were in each other's arms and he was saying that they would do whatever it took to make this work while not giving up their dreams. Then he sang to her, sang songs inspired by her, and now he didn't want to be around her, could barely look at her? What was up?

"I—I can come with you," she said, standing up while also avoiding the curious glance from Stella. She didn't have time to try to decode her boyfriend's weird looks and her best friend's twitchy eyes.

Evan nodded and thanked his mom for Hope's diaper bag.

It struck Juliet as odd that Evan didn't want to stay and hang out with everyone else on the blankets. It wasn't *that* late, and there was music playing from the speakers now and still plenty of food. Yes, it was getting dark, but it was also the summer, and Hope had had a great nap earlier that day.

She slid her hand into his only to have him pull it free and adjust Hope on his hip and hold her with both hands.

Juliet couldn't stop herself, and she looked down at Stella.

Stella was staring at her unblinkingly.

Dammit. Why'd she look at her friend?

"What was that?" Stella mouthed, her eyes darting back and forth between Evan and Juliet like she was watching the U.S. Open.

Juliet pressed her lips into a thin line and shook her head.

"All right, we'll see you all later," Evan said, stifling a big yawn. "Thank you so much for coming out."

"You played beautifully, honey," Evan's mother Joan said. "Always do."

"Thanks, Mom," Evan said, his cheeks taking on a boyish pink color.

"I always said you'd make it big, baby," his other mom Glenda added.

Evan and Juliet wished everyone a good night before heading across the fenced-in grounds toward the parking lot and her Jeep.

They didn't say anything the whole walk.

Evan secured Hope into her car seat, then hopped into the passenger seat.

Juliet swung behind the wheel, glanced into the back, then whipped her head around to face him. "Where's your guitar?"

He closed his eyes and his head dropped. "Shit. It's back behind the stage."

He forgot his guitar?

Now something was really up.

That instrument was like a fifth—or *sixth*—appendage.

"I'll drive through the service gate and behind the stage," she said, turning over the ignition. "I'm sure it's open and shouldn't be a problem."

He nodded and released a heavy breath. "Thanks. I guess I was just itching to get back out to you guys and I forgot it."

She nodded and gnawed pensively on the inside of her bottom lip as she maneuvered her way through the parking lot and inside the service gate.

There were lots of bright spotlights and at least six vans being loaded up with supplies.

She pulled right up beside a minivan where a bunch of guys in their early twenties were busy loading up instruments. She recognized them as a band that had played earlier. Beach Glass or something. They were good. Really good.

The lanky lead singer had a surprisingly deep, soulful voice, despite his barely-legal appearance.

Evan jumped out, nodded at the guys loading up the minivan and ducked behind a white tent. He emerged a moment later with his guitar case and put it in the back seat beside Hope.

Sliding back into the passenger seat, he barely looked at her and merely muttered a thanks.

With a glance at Evan and a pained sigh, she put the Jeep in reverse and slowly backed out of the loading zone.

A quick look in the rearview mirror and the mirror that faced a rear-facing Hope showed that the little one was already asleep.

Sunshine, fresh air and a lot of dancing would wipe out anyone.

Not ten minutes later, Juliet pulled down the grassy single lane that led to Evan's cottage.

He still had a rental—a coupe—which was why they used her Jeep more often since it had four doors and was easier to get Hope in and out.

Why hadn't he bought a vehicle? One that could better accommodate a car seat and all the things that came with a small child?

Was he still just thinking this life was temporary?

As temporary as the Honda Civic he was paying to use each week?

She turned off the ignition and the headlights and opened her door. Evan grabbed the guitar from the back after climbing out his side, so Juliet went about getting a snoring Hope and her diaper bag.

Again, in more excruciating silence, they walked to the front door.

It was agony waiting for him to fish his keys from his pocket and open the door. And Hope's car seat was freaking heavy.

Eventually, they got inside, and thankfully, Hope was an easy baby to transfer from car seat to bed. Her diaper was also fresh, and she slept through having her face wiped.

In no time, Hope was in the crib Evan had bought her. The light in her room was out and the door closed.

She already knew he'd have turned on the baby monitor, since he rarely stepped foot out of the house for even a second without it if her bedroom door was closed. Not even to sit on the deck with the sliding door open.

Evan might not think it, but he had some real parental instincts when it came to Hope, and each new one Juliet witnessed warmed her heart to him all the more.

She wandered down the hallway and into the living room, not knowing if she was welcome to stay or where he would be.

She found him outside on the deck chair with a beer in his hand and the gentle lap of the waves the only indication they were on the beach, it was so dark out now.

Swallowing, she stepped over the threshold from the dining area to the deck, preparing her heart for the worst.

He lifted his gaze to her when he saw her, and to her relief, he reached for her.

With a tremble to her fingers, she took his hand and let him pull her down to the foot of the lounger, facing him.

This was where *they* started. Where he'd first kissed her.

Where he'd finally fulfilled her most longed-for, most coveted fantasy of all time—a kiss from Evan Spencer.

Was this where it ended?

Was it coming full circle?

They started here so they were going to end here?

He took a sip from his beer bottle, then set it on the ground beside him, avoiding her gaze.

"You're killing me," she said softly. "I know something is up. I've known since you quickly put your phone away today. Why won't you talk to me?" She had to blink back the burn of threatening tears and tell her throat that it didn't dare close up.

She'd come too far in life to break down and let rejection by Evan Spencer tear her to shreds. She'd been rejected by him her whole life, and she lived to tell the tale. If she was rejected by him again, she would still live to tell the tale. She wouldn't crack like a broken clay pot; she wouldn't shatter like a mug dropped on the floor. She would keep moving forward, keep moving like the clay on the wheel, adapting and molding to the pressures of life, emerging as something beautiful and unique.

He was still holding her hand, and his calloused thumb strummed across her knuckles. "You're right," he said, still not looking at her. "That was my manager on the phone, and he had the most incredible news."

And this made him shut down?

"What's the news?" she asked, shaking his hand to get him to snap out of his weird funk and look at her.

He did look at her, but it instantly made her wish he hadn't. Pain swirled in the mottled brown of his irises. Pain and uncertainty.

"We've been offered a spot as the opening act for a huge indie rock band. A band way bigger than us."

"That's great," she said. But there was going to be a *but*. There had to be.

"But it's in Europe ... for nine months."

Chapter Nineteen

Evan gauged Juliet carefully.

He knew this was going to be an atomic bomb, which was why he'd been so weird all night. He couldn't keep this news from her, but he had no idea how to tell her without devastating her. Without devastating both of them.

This European tour was his band's dream.

They'd toured all over the U.S. and always talked about taking their music abroad, and now that opportunity was being handed to them on a silver platter. A silver platter with Janice's Homemade Casserole on it.

He twisted his lips and squeezed her hand.

She'd been staring blankly at where his hand joined hers, her bottom lip open.

Had she blinked?

He wasn't sure she'd blinked.

"Nine months goes by really fast," he said gently. "And I've been thinking that maybe you and Hope could come with me. Or you could bring her and meet me for half the leg of the tour. It would be fun. A mini-European vacation."

Slowly, her head lifted, her eyes wide. She'd pressed her lips together, but the look was no less disconcerting as the one she'd held a moment ago.

"You're expecting me to keep Hope while you go to Europe?" Her words were slow, calm and articulate, and they sent a frisson of unease down his spine, making his entire body break out in itchy gooseflesh like someone had just dropped an ice cube down the back of his shirt.

"Well ... I can't exactly take a one-year-old on tour with me," he said with a small scoff and a shoulder lift. "I mean, I *guess* I could hire a nanny, but don't you think it'd be better if she was being raised by—"

"You," she said with a firm, quick nod and fire in her eyes. "You were named her guardian, Evan. Not me. If this"—she pointed back and forth between them—"works out and we take the next logical steps, then yeah, I'll be more than just your sleepover buddy to Hope. And I always will be there for her, but you're talking about me taking care of her *full time* while you go off gallivanting around Europe for nine months."

"I can't let down my band," he said. "It's not gallivanting   . It's my career."

"And yet you're expecting me to put *my* career on hold and either join you in Europe with Hope so that you have not only a full-time nanny to ease your guilt but also a warm body in your bed. Or you want me to rearrange my entire life so that I can be Hope's sole provider and guardian while you go off to the salt mines in Europe for nine months."

"I—"

She stood up from the lounge chair and held out her hand for a moment. "Really think about what you're asking of me here, Evan. We've been together for two months."

Well, *technically* it was two months. But she'd been in love with him for years, so didn't that count for something?

"Two months," she went on. "And you're asking me to give up my life in one way or another. Sacrifice *my* dreams so that you can fulfill yours."

He took a deep breath. Did she not understand that this was bigger than him? That he had a band he had to think about? That it wasn't just his livelihood or his dream. It was the livelihood and dreams of four other men. Four other men who were his best friends. Who were his brothers.

"It's not just me I'm thinking about," he said. "I have to think of the band."

She planted her hands on her hips. "You have to think about Hope. Yeah, unfortunately, you got saddled with your dead best friend's baby, and now your life is forever changed. It happens. Which means you need to adjust your expectations of not only yourself but others as well, and they need to adjust their expectations of you. Have you even told any of your bandmates that you inherited a baby?"

No. He hadn't told any of them.

And he had no idea why.

"I can tell by your silence that that is a no." She snorted in derision, glanced away and shook her head. "Did you think that Hope would just disappear? Or that someone else would step in and take over, leaving you to go back to your nomadic rock-star life, popping into Cinnamon Bay with a stuffed animal for her every few months? Playing the hero but ultimately a very absent one?"

"No ..."

"But you didn't think to let your bandmates or your manager, obviously, know that you are now the legal guardian of a one-year-old and your life and their expectations of you have to change."

His shoulders slumped. "No."

"You've never been one hundred percent committed to this, have you?"

Now it was his turn to surge to his feet. Heat percolated along his arms. "I have, too. My best friend died. He DIED. His wife DIED. And they left me their daughter. Eric told me why they did it, but I still can't wrap my head around the notion. Why me? Why me and not Eric? Why me and not ... *anybody* else. Kate and Rick? My moms? Your parents? Why me? So, yeah, I'm struggling to come to terms with the giant shift my life has unexpectedly taken—without my say, I might add. I never knew they named me as her guardian."

"And if you had, would you have turned it down?"

Well, that right there was the million-dollar question.

Would he have turned it down?

If Tony and Jacqui had come to him and said that they would like to name Evan as Hope's legal guardian should anything happen to them, would he have said, "No, thank you, but thanks for the offer?"

Probably not.

191

He would have probably nervously laughed, said *okay*, then made them both promise to go through life wearing duct tape and bubble wrap so nothing fatal befell them and he wasn't saddled with the guardian gig.

"No, I wouldn't have said *no*," he replied quietly.

Her gaze softened but not by much. "We've only been together two months, Evan. You're asking a lot from me."

"But it hasn't been two months, Jules," he said, reaching for her but recoiling his arms when she stepped back. He shoved down the instant hurt he felt at her dismissing his touch and mustered the courage to press on. To beseech to her nostalgic side with the hope she could understand where he was coming from. "You've loved me for years. This isn't just a two-month relationship, not really."

The flames were back in the green of her eyes. "The difference between the girl back then and the woman now is that *that* girl only had one dream. And it was you. You loving me back was my only dream. You kissing me was my only dream. You asking me to prom or finding me on the dance floor and asking me to dance was my ONLY dream. It was all I lived for."

She laughed sarcastically but more to herself than out loud. As if she couldn't believe the things she'd felt and done all those years ago.

"Loving you was an exquisite form of self-destruction. I couldn't stop even if I tried. And I did try. No matter how much my love went unrequited, I just kept loving you. Dreaming of you. But it took that self-destruction, that one-sided love, for me to be brokenhearted and broken down time and time again for me to realize just how strong of a person I am."

A tear slid down her cheek. He reached for her again, but she held her palms up and stepped back again.

"I know that no matter what, I will never stop loving you, Evan. But now, I have another dream. The woman now is not the same person as the girl back then. The woman now is living her dream of running her own studio, selling her art and starting a life in her hometown. This relationship, because a relationship is *mutual* affection, is only two months old. You cannot use my past love for you as a tool of manipulation to get me to do something for you."

"Jules, I'm not—"

She shook her head, sniffed and wiped away another tear. "Your continued dismissal of me, not noticing me for all those years, only made me stronger. And I know that even now, as my heart shatters into a million pieces, that I will regroup and be stronger because of it. I'm not going to give you an ultimatum, Evan. I'm going to make it easy for you. It's not me or the band. Because there is no me. My dream of a life in Cinnamon Bay and running my business is what I love, and I love it more than the dream I once had of you finally loving me back. So choose the band. Choose your dream. Live your dream. Because that's what I'm doing."

"Jules," he said, though it came out as more of a croak from his painfully tight throat. He reached for her, but again, she stepped back, shook her head, and this time retreated through the sliding-glass door.

He went after her as she headed toward the front door, grabbing her purse from the couch as she went.

"I'll always love you, Evan, always be there for Hope, but I'm not a nanny, I'm not a fling, and I'm not someone whose love for you can be manipulated. You've got a lot of thinking to do. A lot of sorting out of priorities, so I'm just making it easier on you and taking myself out of that priority equation." Her hand found the knob, and she turned it, opening the door and letting the balmy evening breeze waft in.

"Juliet," he said, his hand falling to hers on the knob, his gut reeling, head spinning. "Don't go. Stay, please. Help me figure this out."

Her head shook, and tears streamed down her beautiful face. "You need to figure this out on your own, Evan. Stop relying on others to solve your problems for you and solve them yourself." With agony in her eyes, she slid her hand out from beneath his on the knob and stepped out onto the porch. "I'll remove Hope's car seat base now and put it on the steps for you." Her throat moved on a swallow. She gave him one final tearful look, then turned to go.

He stood in the doorway the entire time watching her. It only took her seconds to remove the car seat base from her Jeep, and without looking at him, keeping her eyes on the ground, she walked it back up to the porch and set it on the stairs like she said she would.

He wanted to run to her. To take her in his arms and carry her back inside, kiss her until the tears dried up and they could sit and figure it all out together. But he knew that she wouldn't let him do that. And if she did, she'd be angry with herself in the morning for allowing him to overpower her like that.

This was not the mousy, quiet Juliet Clarkson he remembered growing up. Yes, she was still just as sweet as an orange sweet roll from Brewed with a View, but now she was more like one of those spice cookies. She had some heat to her. Some zing and zest. She'd grown up a lot—probably more than he had—in the last fifteen years, and although he still saw the love in her eyes, he also saw a lot more confidence. A lot more self-love.

He didn't go back inside the house until her taillights had disappeared completely.

The house felt empty and cold without her in it. Lifeless and dull.

Juliet made the entire world more vibrant, more alive. She added color to what he now realized had been a very monochromatic, gray-hued world.

If he didn't have Hope sleeping in the spare room, he would have jumped in his rental car and raced after her. Followed her home and refused to leave until they sorted it all out.

But he couldn't leave Hope.

He couldn't leave Hope.

With a growl, he shoved his fingers into his hair and stalked back through the house to the porch.

But he didn't stop on the deck. He made his way down to the sand, in his bare feet, and began to pace.

He had the baby monitor with its volume turned to *high* in his pocket, and it had a wide enough range he didn't have to worry about not hearing Hope if she woke up.

He couldn't leave Hope.

What in the hell had he been thinking?

He was all Hope had in this world.

Yes, she had her village. But Tony and Jacqui had entrusted her to Evan for a reason, and that reason had not been because he was a successful musician with money and a record deal. It was because they trusted him to step up when things got dicey. When life handed them a shit biscuit on a garbage platter. Because up until this moment, a moment where Evan was only thinking about himself, he had been the kind of person who stepped up when he was asked to.

Just like he'd stepped up and taken Hope, and now he was thinking about leaving her. Or about dragging her across Europe with him.

And he was also thinking about leaving Juliet.

He growled again and quickened his pace in the sand, this time pulling on the ends of his hair.

He'd royally messed up.

He knew that.

The look on Juliet's face said it all.

He'd taken for granted her lifetime of love for him, that she'd be willing to put her life on hold for him and just do as he asked.

How low could he get?

But he also couldn't *not* think about his band.

Just because he was the lead singer and his name was in the title didn't mean they were a one-man show.

They always made the big decisions together.

He didn't want to leave Evan Spencer and the October Coyotes, would be devastated if they replaced him with someone else, but the reality of it was that he couldn't have it all.

Not anymore.

Six months ago, he could have had it all.

Because six months ago he'd only had to take care of himself. Think about himself.

Now he had a baby to think of, a woman he loved and a different future to plan for.

It wasn't necessarily a future he'd ever envisioned himself having, but the more he thought about a life with Juliet in The Bay, a life with Hope *and* Juliet, the slower his steps became and the less his heart felt like it was going to burst clean out of his chest.

He needed to talk to the band.

Yanking his phone out of his pocket, he fired off a text to all of them, not caring that it was ten o'clock. They needed to meet via video chat tomorrow morning. He couldn't keep this information close to his chest any longer than necessary; otherwise, it would burn a brand that would surely scar. He needed to tell The Coyotes what Trey had told him and then see what they wanted to do.

After he got a response from every band member that ten in the morning worked for them, he fired off another text this time to Juliet.

I'm sorry. Please let me figure out how to make this right.

He wasn't expecting her to respond but was no less disappointed when she didn't.

If he knew her as well as he hoped he did, Juliet would have run over to Stella's for commiseration and comfort.

She didn't deserve to be alone when she was as upset as he knew her to be.

It made a knot form in his throat and his gut spin at the thought of not being able to go to her now, to reassure her that they weren't over, that she and Hope meant more to him than anything else and that they would figure it all out.

But when he had no idea what "figuring it all out" meant, he knew going to her would only further upset her.

He needed to have a plan next time he went to Juliet. A solid, concrete, make-no-demands-of-her plan.

Having carved a decent trench in the sand with his pacing, he headed back into the house and opened Hope's bedroom door.

She was on her belly with her bum in the air. Her little lips were barely parted, and her lashes fell across her round and rosy cheeks.

He never asked for this.

Never asked for her.

Never wanted her, if he was being honest.

But now that he had her, now that this perfect, beautiful little soul was in his life, in his heart the thought of leaving her behind made his chest ache.

He would miss her.

Hell, he missed her when she was just asleep in the other room and he was sitting alone in the living room or on the deck.

He longed for her laugh.

For her smile.

For the way she looked at him.

Yes, he loved Juliet with all his heart and soul, but the love he had for Hope was different. It was instinctive. It was deeply rooted in his chest, in the fibers of his body.

Was this the love that parents felt for their children?

He had a difficult time describing it, but the best he could do was call it almost primal. Like a father wolf protecting his pup, willing to snarl and take out the jugular of anything that threatened his child. Because he would. Evan would snap at and lunge out teeth bared at anything he perceived as a threat to Hope.

The impact of such an epiphany made his head spin, and he pressed three fingers to his temple and closed his eyes.

She was his daughter. His responsibility. His child. He couldn't uproot her life. A life she was finally beginning to recognize as normal. That would be beyond selfish of him. She was what mattered. He needed to put her first, even if it meant sacrificing his own dreams with his band.

Hope was the priority now, and he needed to show her, Juliet and the rest of the world that Tony and Jacqui hadn't been wrong naming him Hope's guardian. That he did step up when the chips were down and that those who he loved the most could always depend on him.

Chapter Twenty

It was nine o'clock on Sunday morning.

Evan had barely slept, but when he did, all he saw when his lids closed was Juliet.

He woke with the sun, made himself a coffee, then took his guitar down to the beach, along with the baby monitor.

It made sense that Hope was sleeping in. She'd had a busy day and had gone to bed late. He did hope that she would be awake when he had to video-chat with his band, though. He was looking forward to introducing her to everyone.

With his guitar on his thigh and his notebook beside him, he let his emotions flow from his heart, through his fingers.

A ballad to Juliet was what came to him. It wasn't fully formed, but the feelings were all there, the rhythm and the notes. He just had to organize the words so they made sense.

Humming with the second verse, he leaned over and scribbled down a few words in his notebook.

"You're that guy from the music festival yesterday," came a young voice behind him.

Evan turned to find a kid, maybe eleven or so—he was crap at estimating ages—making his way through the grassy dunes toward Evan.

"I am," Evan said. "You were there?"

The boy nodded. "Yeah, ate way too much pizza."

Evan grinned. "That's the only way to do it. And I also don't blame you. The pizza from Top This is amazing. What's your name?"

The boy came to sit beside Evan, leaving about six feet between them. "Ryker. My family just moved here a couple of weeks ago."

"Well, nice to meet you, Ryker. I'm Evan."

"Who taught you how to play the guitar?" Ryker asked, his gray gaze fixed on Evan's fingers as they gently slid across the strings.

Evan shrugged. "I mostly taught myself. I watched videos online and borrowed a couple of books from the library. Then I joined the school band for a few years, but the music we had to play wasn't for me, so I just practiced and figured it out myself." With his head down, he glanced at Ryker. "Do you play any instruments?"

Ryker shook his head. "No, but I want to. My parents want me to play football, though, like my older brothers."

Ah.

"But you're more interested in music?"

The kid nodded. "Yeah. I bought a keyboard at a garage sale when I was visiting my nana last summer, but it didn't make it in the move here."

Evan's back straightened, and resentment toward Ryker's parents simmered in his gut. He was so grateful to his moms for allowing Evan and his sister the freedom to try and experience anything they wanted. Sports, music, art. There were no limits to what was offered to them.

But he knew not all parents were as receptive or open-minded as his. Some parents only valued athleticism and viewed the arts as weak.

Removing the strap from his back, he held the guitar out to Ryker. "Try it on."

With wide eyes and a smile, Ryker slid the strap over his back and rested the guitar on his thighs like Evan had.

Evan positioned Ryker's fingers on the frets. "Now put your index finger here, your middle finger right there, and your ring finger here." It was a little awkward, but Ryker did as he was told. "Now strum gently down the strings."

Ryker again did as he was told, and when he played the chord his face lit up and his mile-wide smile competed with the sun for brightness.

"That there is a C chord," Evan said.

He went through a few more chord positions with Ryker, and within about five minutes, the kid was able to move between the four chords pretty easily. Evan said each one slowly and gave Ryker time to move his fingers, then he'd mix it up, and before too long Ryker was playing a tune that Evan had just made up.

Evan could feel Ryker's pride. It radiated off him in strong waves that warmed Evan's heart and eased all the things that had been plaguing him.

"Wow," Ryker said, taking the strap off his back and handing the guitar back to Evan. "That was really cool. Thank you."

Evan nodded. "Anytime." He pointed to his cottage. "You tell your parents that you ran into the guy from the music festival on the beach and that I think they're wrong for not encouraging you to pursue music. Anytime you want to learn more, just knock on my door." He paused. "And I mean knock. Don't ring the bell. I have a one-year-old, and if you ring the bell and wake her up from a nap, then nobody is going to learn any music and I'll make you babysit her instead."

Ryker laughed and nodded. "I'd like that."

"Also, bring your parents over so they can meet me before you come over again. I don't want them thinking you're running off to hang out with some thirty-four-year-old man you met on the beach."

Ryker snorted. "Yeah, I know all about stranger danger." He glanced back toward the cottages that lined the beach. "I should probably get home though. I said I was just going to go for a walk before breakfast."

Evan nodded. "It was nice chatting with you, Ryker, and promise me you won't give up on your dream of music, if that is your dream."

Ryker brushed the sand off his legs and headed back up the dunes. "I won't, Evan. I promise."

They said goodbye, and just as Evan was pulling out his phone to check the time, the baby monitor and Hope's cooing echoed from his other pocket.

He brought up the video baby monitor, and she was wide awake, sitting up in her crib, happily talking to her bare feet.

"I'm on my way, baby," he said, though not into the monitor, because last time he did that, it freaked the bejesus out of her and she started crying. Then he jogged back down the sand toward his house, feeling even lighter, even more at peace than he had when he woke up. He just couldn't put his finger on why.

❧❧❧❧❧❧ ❧❧❧❧❧❧

"Guys, I would like to introduce you to Miss Hope Layla Drake," Evan said, sitting on the couch with Hope on his knee, both of them staring at his laptop while four other men looked back at them.

Hope was gnawing happily on a waffle he'd pulled from the freezer and toasted. She even liked them frozen when she was teething.

"Hello, Hope," Omar, Jackson, Simon and Luca all said one at a time.

"A niece?" Omar asked, his deep voice booming over the speakers.

"Sort of," Evan said. The knot in his throat was threatening to pull tighter, but he took a deep breath, kissed the side of Hope's head and pressed on. "My best friend Tony and his wife died a couple of months ago. Hope is their daughter."

All his bandmates' faces fell, and each one offered their condolences.

"They named me as her legal guardian. So now, Hope is my ... well, daughter."

Four sets of eyes went wide.

"Whoa, bro," Jackson said. "That's a big life change."

Evan nodded. "Not exactly the carefree summer I had been expecting, but we're making the best out of it." He turned to look at Hope. "Right, peanut?"

Hope grinned around the waffle.

"Well, as long as we're in the announcement portion of this meeting, I might as well let you all know that Tasha is pregnant," Luca said, his blue eyes conveying what was obviously still shock. "Found out last week."

"Congratulations, man," Evan said, the rest of the band echoing his sentiments.

"Desiree is on me about starting a family, that's for sure," Jackson said. "Jumping my bones the whole week she's ovulating or whatever. Had to push her off me last week as I had nothing but dust left." He made crazy eyes. "Woman is baby-bonkers."

Simon had remained quiet, and his eyes stayed focused on Evan. He'd always been the gentle giant of the group. Their unflappable bass player. "Not that I haven't missed you, bro, but what's the reason for the group call?"

Evan closed his eyes for a moment, took a deep breath, then opened them and looked one by one at each of his bandmates. "Trey called me yesterday. Janice's Homemade Casserole—"

"Godawful name," Omar muttered.

"Agreed," they all echoed.

"Anyway," Evan continued, "their opening band bailed on them last minute, and they asked if we wanted to step in."

Excitement crackled on his laptop as the men all nodded and pumped their fists in the air.

"It's for a nine-month European tour," he finished. "We'd leave the week before Labor Day."

Faces sobered, and the enthusiasm came to a screeching halt until you could damn near hear a pin drop.

"Nine months?" Luca said. "I ... I can't be gone for nine months. Tash is already two months along. She'd have the baby before I even got back. I don't want to miss the pregnancy or the birth of my kid."

"And as much as I complain about Desiree humping me even while I'm trying to do my online banking, I'm a willing participant in this baby-making thing. I'm not getting any younger," Jackson added. "Don't wanna be like Rod Stewart, in my sixties or whatever with toddlers. No, thanks."

Evan looked at Simon. "Si?"

Simon shrugged. "How would you make the tour happen with the little one there?"

"I don't know," he said plainly, honestly.

"As much as this has been our dream and we talked for years about doing a tour in Europe, I'm kind of over that dream," Omar said. "I mean, that's a long time to be away from home. To be on the road, living in hotels. I don't want the band to break up, but ..."

"I'm kind of content with the level of fame we have now," Luca said. "I want to get back into the recording studio, put out a new album, promote that, but keep our gigs local, you know. Maybe eight or ten across the states per year, but keep on the Eastern seaboard for the most part."

"Yeah, Philly, New York, Charleston, Nashville, Miami," Jackson said. "All the greatest venues are quick flights, put us home just in time to tuck the kids in bed."

A few of them snorted.

It wouldn't quite be like that, but they understood his sentiment.

Being relatively close to home meant that they could do away gigs for one or two nights but then be home in a reasonable amount of time.

"Hey," Evan started, bouncing Hope on his knee gently, "whenever you guys have given a demo to Remy, you know, from an aspiring band, do you know if he's actually listened to any of them?"

All of their heads shook.

"Not that I'm aware of, man," Omar said. "And there have been some really good bands that I liked and thought had promise. Why? You think Remy just garbages them?"

Evan lifted both shoulders. "I don't know. But I'm going to call him and ask. I'd love to actually help more bands get eyes and ears on them. Open the doors for some new blood."

"So then we all agree?" Simon said, interrupting Evan's train of thought, though it'd barely left the station. "We're going to turn down the offer from Janice's Homemade Casserole?"

"Awful name," Luca murmured.

"Agreed," the rest of them said.

"And yeah," Jackson added. "I don't think Europe is in the cards for us right now."

All their faces turned to look at Evan—their lead singer, their leader.

A wave of relief swept over him, and his shoulders left his ears. "I knew there was a reason you guys were the best damn band in the world."

Simon's smile was knowing. "You'd already made up your mind, but you didn't want to crush our dreams. Needed to make sure we were all on the same page."

"Gotta do right by that little girl, bro," Jackson said. "She's going to need you present, not off in Europe playing gigs every night while she's learning to talk and high-five and fist-bump and shit. You gotta be around for all that."

He really did.

"Trey's not going to be happy," Luca said, making a face that Evan felt deep down in the small lump of dread still swirling around in his gut.

"Then he jumps on with a band that's headed for Europe. He can stay with us if he wants, but we don't squash his dreams just because ours have changed," Omar said. "Dreams change."

Dreams change.

"The R&R help at all with that songwriter's block you were having?" Simon asked, addressing Evan.

Evan nodded. "Yeah. Big-time. I've written like seven new songs, got eight and nine nearly done."

"Whoa!" several of them said.

"Look who's got his groove back," Luca teased. "Inspiration?"

Evan simply smiled.

"She got a name?" Jackson probed.

"She does ... and it's Juliet."

Chapter Twenty-One

With the weight of letting his band down and crushing the dreams of four men he considered brothers now off his chest, Evan made the next difficult call—to Trey.

Needless to say, their manager took it better than Evan had been expecting but not as well as he could have.

There had been a long litany of expletives, followed by some whining, some bargaining, some bribery, then came the guilt-tripping and finally, at long last, acceptance. It was like the band manager's five stages of grief.

For the time being, Trey was going to stay on as manager for Evan Spencer and the October Coyotes, but he did *warn* Evan that if a big-name band came knocking that he might just have to take them up on their offer.

Evan, of course, said he wouldn't expect Trey to stay if a big band did come knocking.

They ended their phone conversation on good terms, with Trey saying he would book the band some practice time at the usual place in Nashville. Evan encouraged him to look for somewhere closer to Cinnamon Bay or Summerfield, and Trey replied with a reluctant, "I'll see what I can do."

The band members themselves were only within four to five driving hours from each other, and Evan knew for a fact that none of them besides maybe Luca and Jackson were opposed to moving closer to each other.

Could he convince them all to move to Cinnamon Bay?

He'd leapt over the biggest hurdle with them. He could approach the shorter ones in the coming weeks.

His next big call, and the one he was dreading almost as much as he had been dreading calling the band, was to Remy Izard.

"Go for Izard," Remy said, answering his phone on the sixth ring.

Evan's eye twitched at the arrogant greeting, but he tossed on a smile and made sure to be calm and pleasant when he spoke. "Remy, it's Evan Spencer. How are things?"

"Evan! I heard the news about Janice's Homemade Casserole—god awful name—"

"Agreed."

"Congratulations. Any chance we can squeeze you guys into the recording studio before you go? We're ready to sign you with another deal. I'd love to have a new album out to promote while you're on tour." The constant, rhythmic *click, click* of Remy's pen in the background grated on Evan's nerves. The man was very fidgety and always had something to twiddle or fiddle with in his hands. He usually had six or seven fidget spinners in his office, but if he didn't have a spinner, he was clicking his pen.

"You haven't talked to Trey then?" Evan asked slowly. He thought for sure that Trey would have called Remy as soon as he got off the phone with Evan to relay the bad news. He'd obviously called Trey to relay the good news last week—quite possibly before he even told Evan.

"Not since last week when he told me the awesome news. Why?"

Evan took another deep breath and welcomed Hope onto his lap as she toddled over to where he sat on the couch. "The guys and I—I mean, the band and I—have decided to decline the offer to open for JHC."

"What?" Evan could just picture Remy surging to his feet, possibly sending his big, high-back leather office chair scooting across the floor. "What the hell?"

"Our lives are in different places right now. I just became legal guardian to my best friend's daughter after he and his wife passed away a couple of months ago. Luca is expecting a baby. Jackson and Desiree are trying.

Simon and Omar say they're still tired from the last tour and want to lead more normal lives, maybe settle down."

Remy's loud scoff made Hope startle on his lap and turn toward the phone with big blue eyes. "That's bullshit. You can rest when you're dead. You have an obligation to this record label."

Counting back from ten, Evan hugged Hope tighter to him. Pressing his nose to her head, he inhaled her sweet, calming scent, then put his mouth back to the phone and addressed Remy. "If you read our contract, we have fulfilled our obligations as a band with RJB Records fully. Yes, we signed a three-sixty contract for three albums with you, but that obligation has been fulfilled. We toured after we released the last two albums. And you haven't signed us for another album yet."

"And I freaking won't if you guys don't agree to tour with JHC. You guys are not at the top yet, but you have the potential to be there. But you need to keep putting out new content, new music to bring in new fans. Get big with the untapped European market. You're a fool to give this up now, and RJB Records does not sign with fools."

"Can I ask you a question, Remy?" Evan wasn't going to bite and let Remy's insults derail him. The band had made a decision, and Evan wasn't going to let their record producer bully him into changing his mind—the band's mind.

Remy grunted.

"All those demos that I gave you from other aspiring singers and songwriters, did you ever listen to any of them? Ever call any of them back, bring them into the studio, sign any of them?"

Another derisive snort from Remy. "I decide what's good, not you. You're lucky I even signed your ass."

"So the answer is *no*."

"Of course not. I don't have time to listen to every demo that crosses my desk. I'm in the studio seven days a week, haven't seen my kids in like two months, and they and their mother only live forty-five minutes from my house."

"And your life makes you happy?"

"Listen here, jackass, if you don't agree to tour with Janice's Casserole or whatever then RJB Records isn't signing you again. You can go throw your demo across someone else's desk and pray they give it a listen. I'm in the business of making money, but if you're not willing to help me do that, then you can go bark up someone else's tree."

Hope's little hand cupped Evan's jaw, and she ran her pudgy fingers over his short whiskers, giggling when he wiggled his mouth and chin beneath her touch.

Her smile lit a light inside of him. Made his heart beat with purpose and intention, filled him with a sense of joy he hadn't ever felt before. A sense of peace that not even the man yelling into his right ear could tamper with.

"Plenty of people with kids go on tour," Remy said, his voice just a touch less venomous than before. "It can be done."

"But only if it wants to be done," Evan said. "And I don't want to shake up Hope's world after everything she's lost. I'm her person now, and her person can't be her everything when he's bouncing from city to city, show to show, rehearsal to rehearsal."

"You know my conditions," Remy said. "I'm in the business of making money."

"Understood." Evan wiggled his jaw and reveled in Hope's beautiful smile. "It has been a true pleasure working with you, Remy. Thank you for everything you have done for Evan Spencer and the October Coyotes. I don't want us to part ways on bad terms. Just creative differences."

Remy snorted, which made Hope giggle. "Irreconcilable differences. Same as my divorce."

"Go see your kids, Remy. I guarantee they miss you."

Remy muttered something that Evan couldn't quite hear, then the two said goodbye. Evan tossed his phone to the other side of the couch and lifted Hope into the air above him like an airplane as he fell onto his back. "Up for a little drive, peanut? I have a Carmichael I need to go talk to."

Hope grinned wide at him, showing off her three teeth.

"I'm going to take that as a *yes*."

With tired eyes and concrete in every one of her steps, Juliet wandered listlessly around the studio, cleaning up after the last of the customers for the day had left. She'd flipped the lock, put on a melancholy playlist to reflect her melancholy, brokenhearted mood, and went about the daily grind of preparing the studio for the next day.

She sent Terry home, telling him that she didn't need his help cleaning up and he could go.

She preferred to be alone.

A studio full of people all day had done very little to distract her from her feelings and the hollow, debilitating ache she felt in her chest.

But Stella helped.

She didn't do the whole "I told you so" dance but merely comforted Juliet because she knew how much this breakup, this heartache hurt.

"I'm not *really* considering this a breakup," Stella had said early that morning before they opened for the day. "You're taking *a break*. Like Ross and Rachel—but an actual break, without the cheating." Her big, brown eyes went wide. "He knows that, right? That he can't be Ross and go jump into bed with some girl from the copy center with a crop top and belly ring?"

"I think it was an actual breakup," Juliet said. "He's got *so* much on his plate. So much upheaval in his world. I don't want to be another thing he needs to consider."

"But that's *all* you've ever wanted," Stella said. "Was for him to see you. To consider you. To love you. And now you're throwing it all away?"

"I don't know if he wants me for me or if he wants me because I'm somebody to help with Hope. Am I Juliet the girlfriend or Juliet the nanny with benefits? Because honestly, the way he was talking, it sounded a lot like he just wanted me to be Juliet the nanny with benefits. Like he couldn't do this without me ... because he needed me to help with Hope. Not because he needed me because he couldn't go on breathing without me."

"When was the last time you talked to him?"

"Not since I left the other night."

"Three nights ago?"

She nodded.

"Has he texted?"

She shook her head.

That was probably what stung the most. That he hadn't reached out. He'd sent that one text shortly after she left but nothing since. He hadn't called, come by the studio or her house. It was like he'd already taken off to Europe and completely forgotten about her.

Maybe he had?

She glanced at Stella, a rock the size of a small apple in her throat. Her facial muscles were getting tight, and she could feel the tears beginning to build. "Is it too much to ask to just be *that* person for someone? The person who is more important than oxygen? The person who keeps the other person's heart beating?"

Stella's frown and sad eyes only made Juliet feel all the sadder. "No, honey. It's not. We all deserve that. Deserve to be that person to someone and feel that way about someone else."

She wiped away a tear. "I just don't know if I will ever be able to stop loving him. Or if I'll ever find anybody else who I crave more than oxygen. I've loved him for over half my life."

"But you have a long life ahead of you. If he's not the one, then the *one* is out there and he will find you."

And he will find you.

"Don't chase," Stella added. "Attract."

Don't chase. Attract.

Stella's words came back to Juliet as she sullenly wiped down tables and put the paint bottles back in their respective places.

At Stella's suggestion, she'd bought three dozen large ceramic butterflies, then painted them all monochrome to show the customers what each paint color looked like when done. On one wing she did one coat, in the center of the body two coats, and on the right wing she did three coats.

Then for three nights, she and Stella painted a beautiful black tree on the wall, reaching all the way up and onto the ceiling. And it was on the branches of those trees that they hung the butterflies. Customers, on more than one occasion, had commented on the tree and the butterflies and how helpful they were in showing them the final outcomes of each paint color and number of coats.

Continuing to putter, she took in the space that she had created from scratch.

Yes, she still owed the bank a hefty amount of money from the small-business loan they gave her, but Marvin Brewster had helped her out and got her the lowest interest rate he could.

And besides, what new small business owner paid themselves in the first year anyway?

That was why she needed to keep up with her commissions. That was how she paid the rent on her apartment and kept her fridge full.

But this studio was her baby. Her dream. Her magnum opus.

Art had saved her as a kid, when she was up to her eyeballs in grief over her mother's death. And it was also the way she felt closest to her mother.

She couldn't give up her dream, give up the studio or pottery to follow Evan around Europe. And she certainly didn't have the ability to be a full-time mom or guardian or whatever to Hope while Evan was off in Europe and she tried to run a business.

She knew that relationships and love were about compromise and sacrifice, but what Evan suggested didn't involve any compromise or sacrifice on his part, only hers. And although she hadn't had too many relationships in her life, and none of them had been overly successful, she'd seen enough good ones—her parents, Evan's parents, and all the happy couples in Cinnamon Bay—to know that a relationship where only *one* person sacrificed something was a recipe for disaster, resentment and ultimately failure.

She snorted a laugh to herself and filled an old pickle jar with water, then tossed in all the dirty paint brushes. "He really is Oblivious Evan. Hot Oblivious Evan."

Shaking her head and turning off the tap for the sink, she nearly jumped clear out of her skin when there was a knock on the studio door.

It was Stella.

She had a large, green cardboard box in her hand and was miming for Juliet to open the door.

Drying her hands on her apron, Juliet hustled to the door and unlocked it. "Did you forget something?"

211

Stella was smiling as she shook her head, making her black and purple hair shimmy against her jaw. "No, this is for you. I've been given very explicit instructions to deliver this to you."

"By who?" Juliet's brows bunched.

Stella shrugged. "I've been given very explicit instructions to only give this to you and not say anything else."

"And since when do you follow the rules or instructions?"

"When it involves my best friend's happiness, I'll follow the instructions to the letter," Stella said softly, a twinkle in her eyes. She handed Juliet the box. "I have to run. But do what the letter says. Trust me." Then before Juliet could grab her friend, haul her inside, tie her up and interrogate her properly, Stella took off down the sidewalk.

Juliet relocked the door and walked back into the studio, holding the box carefully.

She reached the main counter, set the box down and gently lifted the lid.

Beneath a sheer white piece of tissue paper was the most beautiful silver slip dress.

It was like something an A-lister would wear to the Oscars.

She couldn't think of a place in Cinnamon Bay that would sell something like this, let alone anywhere she would need to wear it in The Bay either.

Pulling the dress out, she held it in front of her.

It was stunning.

Thin-strapped with a gathered neckline and virtually no back at all.

She'd never worn anything like this in her life.

There were thin, silver strappy heels beneath the dress, too. And of course, exactly her size.

She'd probably break her neck walking in them, since she lived life in flats, but she'd take that risk.

Wait, didn't Stella say something about a note?

She glanced into the box, where sure enough, there was a handwritten note on a piece of yellow lined paper.

Juliet,

Would you go to prom with me, please?

If your answer is yes, please meet me at The Factory, third floor, second door on the left, at 9:00 p.m.

Love,

Your Romeo

aka Oblivious Evan.

A sob mixed with a laugh bubbled up from her chest as she re-read the note.

He was asking her to prom.

Prom.

Had he created a prom just for her?

Was there a big formal gala or ball somewhere in Cinnamon Bay that she didn't know about?

She clutched the dress to her chest, only to immediately pull it away. More often than not, she had wet paint or clay on her apron, and to get that on such a beautiful dress would be sacrilege.

Phew.

Nothing.

Checking her phone for the time, she realized that it was eight thirty.

She didn't have time to run home and shower. She'd have to make do with what she could at the studio. She rarely wore makeup except for some mascara and maybe a little bronzer on days she thought she looked a little pale. But she did have a small travel bag of makeup in the cabinet under the sink in the bathroom for emergencies.

Taking the dress and shoes with her, she rushed off to the bathroom to get ready.

Not exactly the white stretch Escalade that Eric, Tony and Evan had rented with their dates for their prom night, but it was all she had. Rolling up to the factory in her white Jeep at eight fifty-five, Juliet checked her makeup in her rearview mirror one more time, wiped a little bit of lipstick from the corner of her mouth, took a deep breath and turned off the ignition.

There were no other vehicles in the parking area, but there were lights on inside The Factory.

With her keys, phone and wallet in her hand, she toddled and stumbled across the gravel to the door propped open.

"Hello?" she called inside.

No answer.

But she did hear music.

A step inside revealed a pathway lit with LED votive candles. It guided her through the maze-like hallways and closer to the music.

She climbed the stairs, holding onto the railing for dear life.

Butterflies swarmed and crashed into each other in her belly, and her palms became sweaty on the railing.

She held on tighter and slowed her steps.

Her hands were full of her keys, wallet and phone so she couldn't lift up the hem of her dress and also hang onto the railing.

She would be late for *prom,* but at least she would show up alive.

Eventually, with slightly ragged breath, she reached the third floor, and as the note said and the votive candles continued, she turned left.

The music was much louder now, and light shone from the open doorway of the second door.

Her body trembled in anticipation, so much so that she had to reach out to the wall for support.

When she reached the door where the music was coming from, she stopped and gasped.

More LED candles lined the windowsills and were gathered in clusters on the floor and a couple of small tables. Twinkling fairy lights hung from the ceiling, and there were turquoise, silver and white balloons fastened together into an arch.

And there he stood.

Looking handsome as ever in a dark gray tuxedo and holding a plastic container with a corsage in it.

Another sob-laugh tickled in her chest, and her hand flew to her mouth.

He stepped forward. "You look amazing."

Her smile was small, and her chest lurched as the crying threatened to commence.

Opening the box, which had a Petal Pushers sticker on it, he pulled out the corsage of beautiful turquoise and white flowers and offered it to her. She held out her hand, and he gently slid it onto her wrist.

"Now we're a little older than eighteen, but that also means we're legal drinking age." His eyebrows bounced. "Can I offer you some champagne?"

That's when she noticed the pewter ice bucket and bubbly nested inside.

Nodding, she followed him the couple of steps over to what looked like a very high reception counter. He poured the pre-popped bottle into two flutes and handed her one.

"What is this place?" she asked. It looked to be an office waiting room of some sort. There was a door to the right leading deeper into The Factory.

"This is the new location for Bay Town Records."

She wrinkled her nose in confusion. "Huh?"

"The guys and I—I mean, the October Coyotes and I—are starting our own record label. Right here in Cinnamon Bay. Luca and Jackson are going to start looking for places to buy in The Bay, and Omar and Simon want to live in Summerfield since it's a little bigger and more their style."

Her head shook. "I still don't understand."

"We're not going to Europe. None of us want to." He reached for her champagne and put it back down on the counter, taking her hands in his. "And by none of us, I mean, *none of us*. I don't want to leave you. And I don't want you to ever give up your dream."

She swallowed hard. "But touring Europe was your dream."

"It *was*, but dreams change. Priorities change. People change. Music is in my veins, and it always will be, but being a big, famous rock star is not what I need to breathe anymore. I want to help other aspiring singers and songwriters fulfill their dreams."

It's not what I need to breathe anymore.

"The guys and I are still going to record our own stuff—but this time under our own label—and we'll still do shows, but we're going to stick to the East Coast mainly. Maybe half a dozen shows a year elsewhere.

Nothing too demanding or dragging us too far away from what matters most."

From what matters most.

"I was ready to leave the band, but the fact that all of them want the same things that I do meant we could stay together, do what we love but not leave the people that we love." His fingers intertwined with hers, and he led her under the balloon arch. "I realized that if you love someone, it's better to bend a little than break, and you've been bending for me so much, it's time that I got a little kinky, too."

She giggled at his choice of words, which only made his smile grow warmer and wider. "You know what I mean. But I'm not against the innuendo either."

"I didn't want to be a factor in your decision-making," she said quietly, getting all swoony from just how dashing he looked in that tux.

"But you were because I wanted you to be. I want *you*, Juliet. Not as my nanny, my babysitter or my friend with benefits. I want you as my partner. My person, my ..." He sucked in a deep breath. "My oxygen."

Now it was her turn to suck in a breath.

The music changed over to something that had been very popular top forty around the time he would have gone to prom.

"Would you do me the honor of dancing with me at prom?" He took her left hand in his right hand and his left found her hip.

The man could dance.

Blinking back tears of pure joy, she took in her prom-like surroundings. He'd gone to a lot of work, but she knew he hadn't done it alone. Stella and possibly Eric and Isla probably helped, maybe even a Cinnamon Bay townsperson or two. The Carmichaels owned The Factory, so she was sure one or two of those happily married siblings had a hand in the execution of it all, too.

He spun her out, then back in again. This time, his hand moved down her butt, and he gave it a little squeeze, which caused her to toss her head back and laugh.

They moved around the room, and he pulled her closer. She felt so safe, so loved in his arms. When he looked back at her, she knew he finally saw her, and finally wanted her just as badly as she'd wanted him.

He was fulfilling her fantasies, one by one.

First by just asking her out.

Then kissing her and taking her to bed.

And how could she forget either of those nights in her studio? The *Ghost* one or the one after the Pirate Festival, where she drank a little too much pineapple wine. And now tonight. He literally asked her to prom. He gave her a prom.

A prom just for her.

Just for them.

And then he asked her to dance.

When the song ended, he held her there and she wrapped her arms around his neck. His kiss was sweet but also possessive, sending a warm zap of longing through her body and straight down to her toes.

It was like a fairy tale.

The nerd and the rock star.

The introvert and the bad boy.

"I'm looking at buying a place," he said. "Something big enough for you, me, Hope and ..." His grin turned boyish and hopeful. "Maybe one day, more kids, if you want."

He was planning for the future.

For their future.

For their family.

"I'm going to buy a car, something a lot more practical than the coupe I'm renting now, and I'm having a moving company empty my storage locker in Nashville and drive everything here."

"You're moving back to The Bay." Tears burned the backs of her eyes.

His forehead pressed against hers. "I'm moving home."

She sob-laughed for what felt like the millionth time that day. "You're moving home."

Releasing her hips and pulling his head away from hers, he gently tugged her with him as he walked over to a table covered in delicious treats. All of which she recognized as pastries from Brewed with a View. There were also two to-go mugs. He handed her one.

"I haven't even had a chance to sip my champagne," she chided.

"You will."

He picked up the other mug, then grabbed a cookie, took a bite and offered her a bite as well. She did as she was supposed to.

It was a spice cookie.

Chewing, she sipped the to-go cup to wash it all down, only to realize that the drink was a café amour. Her eyes went wide.

"Just making sure," he said, moving the to-go cup away from his mouth, a little speck of white milk froth on his upper lip. "Between the matchmakers and you feeding me this spice for over a month—"

"You brought me several at the studio, too," she added. She wasn't going to let him pin it *all* on her and the trio.

"True. But I didn't know about the legend until Eric told me."

"How do you not—"

"Oblivious Evan, remember?" His smile was cheeky. "And even though we've both consumed enough spice blend to fill a wheelbarrow, now I'm giving you the spice. Because I want this, too. I want you."

Juliet's bottom lip quivered.

"Jules, will you drink the love blend with me at prom and let it work its magic on us?"

With a million happy butterflies dancing in perfect formation in her abdomen, she clinked her to-go cup against his and took another sip of her drink. But then she set it down on the table, looped her arms back around his neck and let her lips hover over his. "I don't think we need magic anymore." She licked the milk froth off his lips just as they turned up into a wicked smile.

"I think you're right." His gaze turned molten hot, and his touch burned a brand against her skin even through her dress. His brand. "Because you'd have to be pretty oblivious not to know that we're meant to be."

"Pretty oblivious, indeed."

Then he crashed his mouth to hers, held her tight and gave her the prom night and the promise of a future she'd always dreamed of.

Epilogue

Labor Day, two years later ...

"Happy birthday, Garrett and Gavin. Happy birthday to you!" Everyone at the beach birthday party sang for the twins as they stared blankly at the cupcakes in front of them.

Garrett moved his foot, and icing got stuck on his big toe, diverting his attention from the confection to his now mint-green toe.

Gavin was mesmerized by a dancing and jumping Hope, who was trying to keep her brothers' attention in one direction so Evan could take a video.

Juliet gathered her flowing yellow sundress and bent down, picking up each cupcake, holding it in front of the little boys and "helping" them blow it out.

Everyone around them clapped, which of course prompted the twins to clap as well. Their mouths split into big grins, showing off their two bottom teeth.

Evan thought back to Hope's first birthday and how many emotions had packed that day.

It had been a day of not only celebration but sorrow.

Did he regret holding Hope's first birthday on the same day as her parents' celebration of life? No. Tony and Jacqui would have liked that.

They wouldn't have wanted people to cry over them. They would have wanted people to celebrate them, celebrate their daughter.

Hope's last two birthdays, however, had been nothing but joy, laughter and celebration.

Yes, each time Evan wished Hope Happy Birthday, he thought about his best friend and all that he was missing, but then he remembered that Tony hadn't really gone anywhere.

He and Jacqui were watching over Hope, watching over all of them. They were with her on her birthday, celebrating beside her. Just like they were there now, celebrating Evan's sons' birthdays. As friends should.

Since the boys were September babies, they decided to hold the celebration on the beach. All the grandparents were there, as well as family friends, playgroup friends, and of course, Evan's bandmates with their kids and Juliet's staff from the studio.

Had they planned on getting pregnant only a few months into dating? Of course not, but life had a way of throwing curveballs at you that you had to dodge, get hit in the face with, or catch.

And in this case, they caught that curveball, called it a blessing and embraced the chaos of three under three. Well, now that Hope was three, it was more like three under four. But it was still insane.

However, he knew that if he asked Juliet, she wouldn't have it any other way.

The record label was thriving. The first band they signed—Beach Glass—had just gone platinum for the second time and was nominated for a Billboard Music Award. Not only was Beach Glass killing it, but Evan and the rest of the recording studio team were gearing up for another busy year with the bands they'd signed, as well as their own band endeavors.

The new album with all the songs that Evan wrote about Juliet was Evan Spencer and the October Coyotes' most successful record yet, with three songs from the album reaching number one on the *Billboard* Hot 100 music chart and the album itself reaching platinum.

They were turning down concert requests from all over the country daily.

They liked making music; they liked making money, but not at the cost of not being with their families.

They needed to keep their priorities in check.

A couple of shows on the West Coast were planned for the fall, but that was only if every band member was able to bring their spouse and kids.

Once the twins were happily smashing and making fantastic messes of their cupcakes, Evan stowed his phone in his pocket and made his way over to a smiling Juliet. She had the pack of baby wipes in her hand, ready to clean up the cake-smash disaster when the twins suddenly decided they'd had enough.

He wrapped his arm around her waist and kissed the side of her head. "Amazing party, babe."

She sighed. He knew she was tired. She'd been up until after midnight finishing all the decorations for the party. "Thanks. I'm kind of glad that even though we have three kids, we only have to throw two birthday parties. This was a lot of work."

"Which they really won't come to appreciate until they have children of their own. Or so my moms have told me."

She chuckled softly and leaned into him. "I'm not sure you've ever said anything more accurate than that."

"Oh, I have," he whispered, pressing his mouth against the side of her head again, close to her ear. "Every time I say I love you."

He didn't have to see her face to know she was smiling. "Okay, well, that's true. But you're not wrong about the lack of appreciation until they're in the thick of it as parents themselves."

"I figured we'd just strip them down and take them into the ocean to wash them off. Feed the fish in the process," he said, turned back to watch as Garrett and Gavin looked at each other and simultaneously stuck a frosting-covered finger in the other one's mouth.

She laughed again. "A dip in the sea will save wasting baby wipes. And those two boys *do* love to be naked and in the water, and eat sand."

"It's what being a carefree kid is all about."

Eric, the hobby shutterbug, was ducking around with his camera. "Grab Hope, and the three of you sneak in behind the little guys. We'll get a family picture."

Making her squeal and giggle in delight when he flipped her upside down, Evan scooped up Hope. He and Juliet made their way around the blanket where Garrett and Gavin were sitting. Both of their naked torsos—they were in matching jean shorts but no shirts—were covered in frosting and cake.

Positioning Hope between them, Evan and Juliet slid down to sit and leaned in, careful to avoid getting hit with a flailing hand of cake.

"Beautiful family," several party guests said.

Evan looked at Juliet. "Beautiful life."

She grinned at him, her green eyes glittering with so much love. "Living the dream."

Click went the camera.

———

"Look at that happy family," Trixie said, pulling the brim of her sun hat down a little farther over her eyes to block out the sun. "I still say that was one of our easier matches."

"It helps when fifty percent of the couple is already madly in love with the other half," Hattie said with a chuckle, fanning herself in her lounge chair. "They do make cute babies, though. And little Hope is just an adorable pistol."

"She's a really good big sister to the twins," Birdie added.

Hattie took a sip of her icy beverage. "Hard to believe they're a year old already."

Her friends glanced at her and snorted.

"Okay, well, it's not *that* hard to believe, I suppose."

"Took the boy long enough to see her, though. Thought we were going to have to club him upside the head, strap him to a chair and force-feed him more of the love spice just to get him to notice her." Trixie shook her head. "It might have been an easy match, but that boy can be oblivious."

"Speaking of oblivious." Trixie pointed to the gentle giant the town had come to know as Simon Jade, the quiet bass player of Evan Spencer and the October Coyotes. Even though the man lived in Summerfield, he worked in Cinnamon Bay and spent a lot of time here. He was a regular at Brewed with a View and had become friends with Travis Ford over at Top This.

Over the last year or so, the trio had heard a lot of murmurings from local single women about how hot and mysterious Simon was. His gray eyes were dark and flecked with silver, and he had a faint pink scar running up the left side of his jaw to his ear.

Nobody knew what the scar was from, but over the last two years, the trio had certainly heard a number of different theories.

Some thought he was ex-military or had once been part of a street gang. Others said it was a fight with a bear, while some said that he'd narrowly escaped getting eaten by a shark.

"Miss Yang has been absolutely smitten with Mr. Jade for a while now," Birdie said, digging her toes into the sand from where she sat in her matching lounge chair next to the other two. "I think since Evan and Juliet's wedding last fall. Do you think there's something going on between them?"

"Hard to say," Trixie said. "They're on opposite sides of the birthday party, and yet ..."

Hattie nodded. "The way she's looking at him says something is up. At least with her. She's feeling something for him for sure. He seems a little oblivious."

"Given the company he keeps with his lead singer, some of that is bound to rub off," Birdie said with a snort.

Hattie scrunched her nose in frustration. "I say we offer them both a cookie and see what happens."

"Do you have any?" Birdie asked.

Hattie reached into her big cooler bag that housed all their beach beverages and pulled out a plastic container. "Never leave home without a bit of the spice."

"Well then," Trixie said with a smile, heaving her Mrs. Claus frame out of her seat, then giving Birdie a hand out of hers. "Let's go join the birthday party and see if Mr. Jade and Miss Yang would like a cookie."

Birdie and Hattie grinned at her. "Lead the way," they both said.

If you enjoyed this book

If you've enjoyed this book, please consider leaving a review. It really does make a difference.

Thank you again.

Xoxo

Whitley Cox

Don't forget to subscribe to my newsletter to stay up to date on all my releases, sales, promotions, giveaways, and more.

Go here to subscribe —>
http://eepurl.com/ckh5yT

Grab the next book in the Cinnamon Bay World

Get it here —>
https://books2read.com/FFU-CinnamonBayRomance

A CINNAMON BAY ROMANCE
COLLECTION FOUR

Everyone's a Critic by Nikki Lynn Barrett

https://books2read.com/EAC-CinnamonBayRomance
Fight the Burn by Brea Viragh

http://books2read.com/FighttheBurn
Unexpected Tides by Crystal St. Clair

https://books2read.com/UT-CinnamonBayRomance
Care Package by Lexi Miles

https://books2read.com/CarePackage-CinnamonBayRomance
Rock the Shores by Whitley Cox

https://books2read.com/RTS-CinnamonBayRomance
Falling for You by Ja'Nese Dixon

https://books2read.com/FFU-CinnamonBayRomance
Portrait of Regret by Connie Dave

https://books2read.com/POR-CinnamonBayRomance
Discovering Love by Chloe Quinn

https://books2read.com/DiscoveringLove-CinnamonBayRomance
Blurring the Lines by Erin Cristofoli

https://books2read.com/BTL-CinnamonBayRomance
Love Untangled by Alexa Padgett

https://books2read.com/LU-CinnamonBayRomance

Wood You Knot by J.C. Hannigan

https://books2read.com/WYK-CinnamonBayRomance
Her Wild Ride by Shannyn Leah

https://books2read.com/HWR-CinnamonBayRomance

Entire Collection

https://acinnamonbayromance.com/collection-four/

SIGN UP FOR THE CINNAMON BAY NEWSLETTER

https://landing.mailerlite.com/webforms/landing/p2z6v1

ACKNOWLEDGMENTS

There are so many people to thank who help along the way. Publishing a book is definitely not a solo mission, that's for sure. First and foremost, my friend and editor Chris Kridler, you are a blessing, a gem and an all-around terrific person. Thank you for your honesty and hard work.

Thank you, to my critique groups gals, Danielle, Felicia and Jillian. I love our meetups where we give honest feedback. You are my bitch-sisters and I wouldn't give you up for anything. Kathleen Lawless, for just being you and wonderful and always there for me. Author Jeanne St. James, my sister from another mister, what would I do without you?

Authors Brooke Burton and Brea Viragh for beta-reading this for me.

Sarah Paige, thank you for making such a beautiful cover.

BBB publishing for their proofreading, thank you.

My assistant, Meghan MacPhail, thank you for all your help.

My reader group, Whitley Cox's Fabulously Filthy Reviewers, you are all awesome and I feel so blessed to have found such wonderful fans.

Author Ember Leigh, my newest author bestie, I love our bitch fests—they keep me sane. My parents, in-laws and brother, thank you for your unwavering support. The Small Human and the Tiny Human, you are the beats and beasts of my heart, the reason I breathe and the reason I drink. I love you both to infinity and beyond. And lastly, of course, the husband. You are my forever, my other half, the one who keeps me grounded and the only person I have honestly never grown sick of even when we did that six-month backpacking trip and spent every single day together. I never tired of you. Never needed a break. You are my person. I love you.

OTHER BOOKS BY WHITLEY COX

Love, Passion and Power: Part 1
The Dark and Damaged Hearts Series: Book 1
https://books2read.com/LPP1-DDH
Kendra and Justin

Love, Passion and Power: Part 2
The Dark and Damaged Hearts: Book 2
https://books2read.com/LPP2-DDH
Kendra and Justin

Sex, Heat and Hunger: Part 1
The Dark and Damaged Hearts Book 3
https://books2read.com/SHH1-DDH
Emma and James

Sex, Heat and Hunger: Part 2
The Dark and Damaged Hearts Book 4
https://books2read.com/SHH2-DDH
Emma and James

Hot & Filthy: The Honeymoon
The Dark and Damaged Hearts Book 4.5
https://books2read.com/HF-DDH
Emma and James

True, Deep and Forever: Part 1
The Dark and Damaged Hearts Book 5
https://books2read.com/TDF1-DDH
Amy and Garrett

True, Deep and Forever: Part 2
The Dark and Damaged Hearts
Book 6
https://books2read.com/TDF2-DDH
Amy and Garrett

Hard, Fast and Madly: Part 1
The Dark and Damaged Hearts
Series Book 7
https://books2read.com/HFM1-
DDH
Freya and Jacob

Hard, Fast and Madly: Part 2
The Dark and Damaged Hearts
Series Book 8
https://books2read.com/HFM2-
DDH
Freya and Jacob

Quick & Dirty
Book 1, A Quick Billionaires Novel
https://books2read.com/QDirty-
QBS
Parker and Tate

Quick & Easy
Book 2, A Quick Billionaires Novella
https://books2read.com/QEasy-
QBS
Heather and Gavin

Quick & Reckless
Book 3, A Quick Billionaires Novel
https://books2read.com/QReckless-QBS
Silver and Warren

Quick & Dangerous
Book 4, A Quick Billionaires Novel
https://books2read.com/QDangerous-QBS
Skyler and Roberto

Quick & Snowy
The Quick Billionaires, Book 5
https://books2read.com/QSnowy-QBS
Brier and Barnes

Hot Dad
https://books2read.com/Hot-Dad
Harper and Sam

Lust Abroad
https://books2read.com/Lust-Abroad
Piper and Derrick

Snowed In & Set Up
https://books2read.com/SISU
Amber, Will, Juniper, Hunter, Rowen, Austin

Love to Hate You
https://books2read.com/Love2HateYou
Alex and Eli

Hired by the Single Dad
https://books2read.com/HBTSD-SDS
The Single Dads of Seattle, Book 1
Tori and Mark

Dancing with the Single Dad
https://books2read.com/DWTSD-SDS
The Single Dads of Seattle, Book 2
Violet and Adam

Saved by the Single Dad
https://books2read.com/SBTSD-SDS
The Single Dads of Seattle, Book 3
Paige and Mitch

Living with the Single Dad
https://books2read.com/LWTSD-SDS
The Single Dads of Seattle, Book 4
Isobel and Aaron

Christmas with the Single Dad
https://books2read.com/CWTSD-SDS
The Single Dads of Seattle, Book 5
Aurora and Zak

New Years with the Single Dad
https://books2read.com/NYWTSD-SDS
The Single Dads of Seattle, Book 6
Zara and Emmett

Valentine's with the Single Dad
https://books2read.com/VWTSD-SDS
The Single Dads of Seattle, Book 7
Lowenna and Mason

Neighbors with the Single Dad
https://books2read.com/NWTSD-SDS
The Single Dads of Seattle, Book 8
Eva and Scott

Flirting with the Single Dad
https://books2read.com/FWTSD-SDS
The Single Dads of Seattle, Book 9
Tessa and Atlas

Falling for the Single Dad
https://books2read.com/FFTSD-SDS
The Single Dads of Seattle, Book 10
Liam and Richelle

Hot for Teacher
https://books2read.com/HFT-SMS
The Single Moms of Seattle, Book1
Celeste and Max

Hot for a Cop
https://books2read.com/HFAC-SMS
The Single Moms of Seattle, Book 2
Lauren and Isaac

Hot for the Handyman
https://books2read.com/HTHM-SMS
The Single Moms of Seattle, Book 3
Bianca and Jack

Doctor Smug
https://books2read.com/DoctorSmug
Daisy and Riley

Hard Hart
https://books2read.com/HH-HB
The Harty Boys, Book 1
Krista and Brock

Lost Hart
The Harty Boys, Book 2
https://books2read.com/LH-HB
Stacey and Chase

Torn Hart
The Harty Boys, Book 3
https://books2read.com/THART-HB
Lydia and Rex

Dark Hart
The Harty Boys, Book 4
https://books2read.com/DH-HB
Pasha and Heath

Coming Soon

The Asshole Heir
Winter Harbor Heroes, Book 2
https://books2read.com/the-asshole-heir
Amaya and Carson
August 16, 2022

Mr. Gray Sweatpants
A Single Moms of Seattle spin-off book
https://books2read.com/MrGraySweatpants
Casey and Leo
September 10, 2022

Not Over You
https://books2read.com/not-over-you
Rayma and Jordan
October 1, 2022

Raw, Fierce and Awakened: Part 1
The Dark and Damaged Hearts Series, Book 9
Jessica and Lewis

Raw, Fierce and Awakened: Part 2
The Dark and Damaged Hearts Series, Book 10
Jessica and Lewis

Website: WhitleyCox.com
Email: readers4wcox@gmail.com
Twitter: @WhitleyCoxBooks
Instagram: @CoxWhitley
TikTok: @AuthorWhitleyCox
Facebook : https://www.facebook.com/CoxWhitley/
Blog: https://whitleycox.com/fabulously-filthy-blog-page/

Exclusive Facebook Reader Group:
https://www.facebook.com/groups/234716323653592/
Booksprout: https://booksprout.co/author/994/whitley-cox
Bookbub: https://www.bookbub.com/authors/whitley-cox
Goodreads:
https://www.goodreads.com/author/show/16344419.Whitley_Cox
Subscribe to my newsletter here:
http://eepurl.com/ckh5yT

ABOUT THE AUTHOR

A Canadian West Coast baby born and raised, Whitley is married to her high school sweetheart, and together they have two beautiful daughters and a fluffy dog. She spends her days making food that gets thrown on the floor, vacuuming Cheerios out from under the couch and making sure that the dog food doesn't end up in the air conditioner. But when nap time comes, and it's not quite wine o'clock, Whitley sits down, avoids the pile of laundry on the couch, and writes.

A lover of all things decadent; wine, cheese, chocolate and spicy erotic romance, Whitley brings the humorous side of sex, the ridiculous side of relationships and the suspense of everyday life into her stories. With single dads, firefighters, Navy SEALs, mommy wars, body issues, threesomes, bondage and role-playing, Whitley's books have all the funny and fabulously filthy words you could hope for.

Made in the USA
Las Vegas, NV
02 May 2022